ALSO BY GILES TIPPETTE . . .

Unforgettable novels of the Williams clan and the Old West:

JAILBREAK . . . When a man's got his back against the wall, there's only one thing to do. Break it down.

HARD ROCK . . . Rough country breeds a rougher breed of man . . .

SIXKILLER . . . No one fights harder than the man who fights for his kin.

GUNPOINT . . . There are two things more important than money: honor and survival . . .

DEAD MAN'S POKER . . . Outlaw life is a deadly game. But going straight is the biggest gamble of all.

AVAILABLE FROM JOVE BOOKS

Praise for Giles Tippette's novels:

"TIPPETTE CAN WRITE ROUGH AND TUMBLE ACTION SUPERBLY."
—*Chattanooga Times*

"TOUGH, GUTSY, AND FASCINATING."
—*New York Newsday*

"TIPPETTE CAN PLOT AWAY WITH THE BEST OF THEM!"
—*Dallas Morning News*

CHEROKEE

GILES TIPPETTE

JOVE BOOKS, NEW YORK

To my daughter Shanna, and Jamie, and my grandchildren.

CHEROKEE

A Jove Book / published by arrangement with
the author

PRINTING HISTORY
Jove edition / June 1993

ISBN: 0-515-11118-X

Jove Books are published by The Berkley Publishing Group,
200 Madison Avenue, New York, New York 10016.
The name "JOVE" and the "J" logo
are trademarks belonging to Jove Publications, Inc.

PRINTED IN THE UNITED STATES OF AMERICA

10 9 8 7 6 5 4 3 2 1

CHAPTER 1

Howard said, "Son, I want you to get twenty-five thousand dollars in gold, get on your horse, and carry it up to a man in Oklahoma. I want you to give it to him and tell him who it's from, and tell him it's in repayment of the long-time debt I've had of him."

I didn't say anything for a moment. Instead I got up from the big double desk we were sitting at facing each other, and walked over to a little side table and poured us both out a little whiskey. I put water in Howard's. Out of the corner of my eye I could see him wince when I did it, but that was doctor's orders. I took the whiskey back over to the desk and handed Howard his tumbler. It was a little early in the afternoon for the drink but there wasn't much work to be done, it being the fall of the year.

Howard was father to me and my two brothers. Sometimes we called him Dad and sometimes Howard, and in years past quite a few other things. He liked for us to call him Howard because I think it made him feel younger and still a part of matters as pertained to our ranch and other businesses. Howard was in his mid-sixties, but it was a poor mid-sixties on account of a rifle bullet that had nicked his lungs some few years back and caused him breathing difficulties as well as some heart trouble. But even before that, some fifteen years previous, he had begun to go down after the death of our mother. It was not long after that

1

that he'd begun to train me to take his place and to run the ranch.

I was Justa Williams and, at the age of thirty-two, I was the boss of the Half-Moon ranch, the biggest along the Gulf Coast of Texas, and all its possessions. For all practical purposes I had been boss when Howard called me in one day and told me that he was turning the reins over to me, and that though he'd be on hand for advice should I want it, I was then and there the boss.

And now here he was asking me to take a large sum of money, company money, up to some party in Oklahoma. He could no more ask that of me than any of my two brothers or anybody else for that matter. Oh, he could ask, but he couldn't order. I held my whiskey glass out to his and we clinked rims, said "Luck," and then knocked them back as befits the toast. I wiped off my mouth and said, "Howard, I think you better tell me a little more about this. Twenty-five thousand dollars is a lot of money."

He looked down at his old gnarled hands for a moment and didn't say anything. I could tell it was one of his bad days and he was having trouble breathing. The whiskey helped a little, but he still looked like he ought to be in bed. He had a little bedroom right off the big office and sitting room we were in. There were plenty of big bedrooms in the big old rambling house that was the headquarters for the ranch, but he liked the little day room next to the office. He could lie in there when he didn't feel well enough to sit up and listen to me and my brothers talking about the ranch and such other business as came under discussion.

It hurt me to see him slumped down in his chair looking so old and frail and sunk into himself. I could remember him clearly when he was strong and hard-muscled and tall and straight. At six foot I was a little taller than he'd been, but my 190 pounds were about the equal of his size when he'd been in health. It was from him that I'd inherited my big hands and arms and shoulders. My younger brother Ben, who was twenty-eight, was just about a copy of me except that he was a size smaller. Our middle brother, Norris, was the odd man out in the family. He was two years younger than me, but he was years and miles different from me and Ben and Howard in looks and build and general disposition toward life. Where we were dark he was fair; where we were hard he had a kind of soft look about him. Not that he was; to the contrary. Wasn't anything weak about Norris. He'd fight you at the tick of a clock. But he just didn't look that way. We all figured he'd taken after our mother, who was fair and yellow-haired and sort of delicate. And Norris was bookish like she had been. He'd gone through all the school that was available in our neck of the woods, and then he'd been sent up to the University at Austin. He handled all of our affairs outside of the ranch itself—but with my okay.

I said, "Dad, you are going to have to tell me what this money is to be used for. I've been running this ranch for a good many years and this is the first I've heard about any such debt. It seems to me you'd of mentioned a sum of that size before today."

He straightened up in his chair, and then heaved himself to his feet and walked the few steps to where his rocking chair was set near to the door of his bedroom. When he was settled he breathed heavy for a moment or two and then said, "Son, ain't there some way you can do this without me explaining? Just take my word for it that it needs doing and get it tended to?"

I got out a cigarillo, lit it, and studied Howard for a moment. He was dressed in an old shirt and a vest and a pair of jeans, but he had on his house slippers. That he'd gotten dressed up to talk to me was a sign that what he was talking about was important. When he was feeling fairly good he put on his boots, even though he wasn't going to take a step outside. Besides, he'd called me in in the middle of a workday, sent one of the hired hands out to fetch me in off the range. Usually, if he had something he wanted to talk about, he brought it up at the nightly meetings we always had after supper. I said, "Yes, Dad, if you want me to handle this matter without asking you any questions I can do that. But Ben and Norris are going to want to know why, especially Norris."

He put up a quick hand. "Oh, no, no. No. You can't tell them a thing about this. Don't even mention it to either one of them! God forbid."

I had to give a little laugh at that. Dad knew how our operation was run. I said, "Well, that might not be so easy, seeing as how Norris keeps the books. He might notice a sum like twenty-five thousand dollars just gone without any explanation."

He looked uncomfortable and fidgeted around in his rocking chair for a moment. "Son, you'll have to make up some story. I don't care what you do, but I don't want Ben or Norris knowing aught about this matter."

Well, he was starting to get my curiosity up. "Hell, Howard, what are you trying to hide? What's the big mystery here? How come *I* can know about the money but not my brothers?"

He looked down at his hands again, and I could see he felt miserable. "If I was up to it, *you* wouldn't even know." He kind of swept a hand over himself. "But you can see the shape I've come to. Pretty soon won't be enough left to bury the way I'm wasting away." He hesitated and looked away. It was clear he didn't want to talk about it. But finally he said, "Son, this is just something I got to get off my conscience before it comes my time. And I been feeling here lately that that time ain't far off. I done something pretty awful back a good number of years ago, and I just got to set it straight while I still got the time." He looked at me. "And you're my oldest son. You're the strong one in the family, the best of the litter. I ain't got nobody else I can trust to do this for me."

Well, there wasn't an awful lot I could say to that. Hell, if you came right down to it, it was still all Howard's money. Some years back he'd willed the three of us the ranch and all the Half-Moon holdings in a life will that gave us the property and its income even while he was still alive. But it was Howard who, forty years before, had come to the country as a young man and fought weather and bad luck and *banditos* and Comanches and scalawags and carpetbaggers, and built this cattle and business empire that me and my brothers had been the beneficiaries of. True, we had each contributed our part to making the business better, but it had been Howard who had made it possible. So, it was still his money and he could do anything he wanted to with it. I told him as much.

He nodded. "I'm grateful to you, Justa. I know I'm asking considerable of you to ask you to undertake this errand for me without telling you the why and the whereofs of the matter, but it just ain't something I want you or yore brothers to know about."

I shrugged. I got a pencil and a piece of paper off my desk. "Who is this party you want the money to go to? And what's his address?"

"Stevens. Charlie Stevens. And Justa, it ain't money, it's got to be gold."

I put down my pencil and stared at him. "What's the difference? Money is gold, gold is money. What the hell does it matter?"

"It matters," he said. He looked at the empty glass in his hand and then across at the whiskey. But he knew it was wishful thinking. Medically speaking, he wasn't supposed to have but one watered whiskey a day. Of course we all knew he snuck more than that when there was nobody around, but drinking alone gave him no pleasure. He said, "This is a matter that's got to be done a certain way. It's just the way and the rightness of the matter in my mind. I got to give the man back the money the same way I took it."

"But hell, Howard, gold is heavy. I bet twenty-five thousand dollars worth would weigh over fifty pounds. We'll have to ship it on the railroad, have it insured. Hell, we can just wire a bank draft."

He shook his head slowly. "Justa, you still don't understand the bones of the matter. You got to take the gold to Charlie on horseback. Just like I would if I could. You understand? I'm askin' you to stand in for me on this matter."

I threw my pencil down and stared at him. I nodded at the empty glass in his hand. "How many of them you snuck before you sent for me? You expect me to get on a horse and ride clear to Oklahoma carrying twenty-five thousand dollars in gold? And that without telling Norris or Ben a thing about it? Howard, are you getting senile? It's either that or you're drunk, and I'd rather you was drunk."

He nodded. "I don't blame you. It's just you don't understand the bones of this business. Justa, this is a weight I been carrying a good many years. I done the man wrong some time back, but it took a while for me to realize just how wrong I done him. When I could of set matters straight I was too young and too smug to think they needed setting a-right. Now that I can look back and be properly ashamed of what I done, it's too late for all of it. But I got to make what amends I can. If you knew the total of the whole business you'd agree with me that the matter has to be handled in just such a way."

I got up, got the whiskey bottle, and went over and poured him out about a half a tumblerful. It was dead against doctor's orders, but I could see he was in such misery, both in his heart and his body, that I figured the hell with what the doctor had to say. I went back over to my desk, poured myself out a pretty good slug, and then said, "All right, Howard, you want me to do something I find unreasonable. I think the least you can do is tell me something about what you call the 'bones' of the business."

"Justa, you done said you'd do it without asking me no questions."

"Well, goddam, Howard, that was when I thought you were just talking about the money. Now you're talking about me riding all the way clear up to goddam Oklahoma hauling a tow sack full of gold. Hell, Oklahoma is a pretty good little piece from here. Where in Oklahoma, by the way? What town?"

CHEROKEE

He shook his head. "I don't know," he said. "I've lost track of Charlie Stevens for better than twenty years."

"Aw, hell!" I said in disgust. I took a sip of my whiskey and got out another cigarillo and lit it, having let the first one go out unsmoked in the ashtray on my desk. We sat there in silence looking at each other. It was quiet in the house. The room we were sitting in had once been practically the whole house. It had been built out of big sawn timbers that Howard had had hauled in by ox teams after he'd started making some money. The rest of the house had just kind of grown as the need arose. Far off in the kitchen I could hear the sound of the two Mexican women going about the business of starting supper for the fourteen or fifteen hired hands and cowhands we kept about the place. A man named Tom Butterfield cooked for the family. Us boys had always called him Buttercup just to get him riled up. As near as I could figure he was as old as Howard and should have been in worse shape, judging by the amount of whiskey he could put away on a daily basis. Outside, in that year of 1896, it was a mild October and the rolling prairies of two-foot-high grass were curing off and turning a yellowish brown. We'd hay some of it, but the biggest part of it would be left standing to be grazed down by our cattle and horses. The Half-Moon was right on the Gulf Coast of Texas about ninety miles south of Houston. Our easternmost pastures led right up to the bay, where soft little waves came lapping in to water the salt grass and lay up a little beach of sand. All told we held better than sixty thousand deeded acres, but we grazed well over a quarter of a million. At any one time we ran from five thousand to ten thousand cattle, depending on the marketing season. A more gentle, healthy, temperate place to raise cattle could not be imagined. There was plenty of grass, plenty of water, and except for the heat of the summers, a climate that was kind to the development of beef.

The nearest town to us was Blessing. It was nearly seven miles away and we owned about half of it, including the bank, the hotel, the auction barn, and any number of town lots. Blessing had once been a railhead for the MKT railroad, but now it was a switching point between Laredo and San Antonio. It would have been no trouble at all to have shipped $25,000 to a bank or a business or some party in Oklahoma. But it sure as hell was a different proposition to ride a horse all that way and try to protect such a sum in gold. Hell, you'd need a packhorse just for the gold, let alone your own supplies. And such a ride would take at least three weeks, going hard, to get there, not counting coming back. And even if it was all right with Howard to come back on the train, that was another three days.

Of course that didn't count the time that would have to be spent looking for this Charlie Stevens. That is, if he wasn't dead. Hell, the whole idea was plain outlandish. But I didn't want to tell Howard that, not as serious as he seemed about it. But I said, "Howard, you know this is a busy time for us. We got to get the cattle in shape for winter, and then there's the haying. And there's also this business with the Jordans."

The Jordans were our nearest neighbors to the southwest. They were new to the country. They'd bought out the heirs of one of the earliest settlers in our part of the country. And now they were disputing our boundary line that was common with theirs. They'd brought in a surveyor who'd sent in a report that supported the Jordans' claim, so Norris had hired us a surveyor and he'd sent in a report that backed up *our* position. So now it looked like it was going to be work for the lawyers. And it was no small dispute. The Jordans were claiming almost nine thousand acres of our deeded land, and that was a considerable amount of grazing. But what was more worrisome, once that sort of action got started in an area it could spread like wildfire, and we'd spend half our time in court and hell only knows how much on lawyers just trying to hold on to what was ours. And the fact was that there was plenty of room for argument. Most land holdings in Matagorda County and other parts of the old Nueces Strip went back to Spanish land grants and grants from the Republic of Texas, and even some from when it first became a state. Such disputes were becoming common, and I wanted to put out our own little prairie fire before it got a good start and spread. Norris was mainly handling the matter, but it was important that I be on hand if some necessary decisions had to be made.

I finished my whiskey and got up. "Howard, I don't want to talk about this no more right now. You think on it overnight and we'll have a talk again tomorrow."

He said in a strong voice, "Justa, I know you think this is just the whim of a sick ol' man. That ain't the case. This is something that is mighty important to me. It's important to you and your brothers too. Ain't nobody in this family ever failed to pay off a debt. I ain't going to be the first one."

"Something I don't quite understand, Howard. You appear to be talking about some money you borrowed some twenty-five or thirty years ago. Is that right?"

"Maybe even a little longer than that."

"Howard, who the hell did you know had that kind of money that many years ago? Hell, you could have bought nearly all of Texas for that sum in them days."

He fiddled with his glass and then drank the last of his whiskey. He said, clearing his throat first, "Wasn't exactly twenty-five thousand. Was less. I'm kind of roughing in the interest."

"How much less was it? Still must have been a power of money. Interest is four percent right now, and I don't reckon it was anywhere near that high back then."

He looked uncomfortable. "Damnit, Justa, if I'd been lookin' for an argument I'd of sent for Norris! Now why don't you go on and do like I tell you and not jaw me to death about it!"

I gave him a long look. "Who you trying to bully, old man? Now exactly how much was this original loan that you've 'roughed' in interest to bring it up to twenty-five thousand dollars?"

He looked at me defiantly for a moment, and then he said, "Five hunnert dollars."

I laughed a little. "Now that *is* roughing in a little interest," I said. "Five hundred to twenty-five *thousand*. How come you didn't pay this back twenty years ago when five hundred dollars wasn't more than a night of poker to you? And you and I both know you can't turn five hundred into twenty-five thousand in thirty years no matter how hard you try. Just exactly what kind of loan was this?"

He got slowly up out of his rocking chair, and then started shuffling the few steps toward his bedroom. At his door he turned and give me a hard look. "Wasn't no loan a'tall. I stole the money from the man. Now put an interest figure on that!"

I just stood there in amazement. Before I could speak he'd shut his door and disappeared from my view. "Hell!" I said. The idea of our daddy, Howard, stealing anything was just not a possibility I could reckon with. As far as I knew Howard had never owed anybody anything for any longer than it took to pay them back, and as for stealing, I'd known him to spend two days of his own time returning strayed cattle to his bitterest enemy. I could not conjure up a situation in which Howard would steal, and not only steal but let the crime go unredeemed for so long. Obviously he'd been a young man at the time, and he might have committed a breach of honesty as a callow youth, but there'd been plenty of years in between for him to have put the matter right rather than waiting until such a late date.

The truth be told, I didn't know whether to believe him or not. Howard's body might be failing him, but I'd never found cause to fault his mind. And yet they did say that when a man reached a certain age, his faculties seemed to go haywire and he got confused and went to making stuff up and forgetting everyday matters. But for the life of me, I just couldn't see that happening to Howard. And yet I couldn't believe he'd actually stolen $500 from a man and let it slide over all these years either.

I was about to leave the office when the bedroom door opened and Howard stood there. He said, "I charge you on your honor not to mention this to either of your brothers."

CHEROKEE

"Hell, Howard, I ain't going to mention it to nobody as far as that goes. But look here, let me ask you—"

I got no further. He had closed the door. I had seen the hurt and the helplessness in his face just before the door had closed. It did not make me feel very good. Now I was sorry I had questioned him so closely. But never in my wildest dreams would I have figured to stir up such a hornet's nest.

I left the house with a good deal of trouble on my mind. The big clock in the hall said the time was just a little after four. I didn't much feel like riding the four miles back out to where we'd been inspecting our herd of purebred Herefords when the summons from Howard had come, so I stepped out the front door and took a seat in one of the wicker chairs on the large roofed porch that ran around two sides of the house. I got out a cigarillo, lit it, and looked out over the land and the buildings, just kind of idling over in my mind what Howard had just said. Most of the outbuildings of the ranch were in front of me, headed west. We had two big barns, both made out of sawn lumber. They were out toward the edge of the headquarters area. In between was a bunch of corrals and holding pens, and then closer to the house was the bunkhouse where our regular hands slept and lived, and then another shack where we put up hired hands who we used seasonally. In between was a neat little frame house where our foreman, Tom Harley, lived with his wife. He'd been in Howard's employ for as long as I could remember, and the foreman for at least twelve years. It had been me that had fired his predecessor and put him in the job. Harley was a good steady hand who did what you told him and never tried to use too much imagination. I'd explained all that to him when I'd put him in the job, saying that if any imagination was called for I'd handle it. And now I sat there envying him the luxury of not having to do too much thinking. I was doing way more than I wanted to and it was not a pleasure.

Finally, I decided the hell with it and descended the steps of the porch, untied the big sorrel gelding I was riding that day, mounted up, and headed for my own house.

I had been married for a little more than two years, and I'd had a house built for my bride and myself about a half mile away from the big house where Howard and Ben and Norris lived.

Her name was Nora and she was six years younger than me. We now had a one-year-old son, but she'd led me on one hell of a merry chase before I'd ever got her roped and thrown. She had been a town girl, of religious parents, and she was some little concerned with the violence and the danger that simply living my kind of life involved. The country, even in that late year toward the turn of the century, was far from civilized, and she worried and fretted herself every time I had to tend to some ranch matter. She'd told me many times before we were married that she just wouldn't consider me a serious suitor until I'd done what she considered "settling down." Of course I'd many times tried to explain to her that it was rough country and that a man had to stick up for himself and his and protect what he owned or he'd get plowed under. But none of that had made any sense to her. Her daddy ran the general mercantile store in Blessing, and came home every noon for lunch and every evening for supper, and she'd wanted the same from me. To make it all worse she'd taught the little school in Blessing, and hadn't thought so much of the way I spoke. She'd gotten so fed up with me and my ways that she'd once gone through the motions of running off with a Kansas City drummer who traveled in yard goods. But it had been a bluff. She'd gotten off the train in Texarkana and come home, and we'd taken right back up where we'd left off.

But then, hell, I'd been a week late for my own wedding on account of me and Ben having to be down in Monterrey in Mexico getting Norris out of jail.

But she'd married me anyway, week late or not. What that had mainly meant was that I'd had to learn to lie to her in a different way when I was about to go off and do something she considered dangerous or uncivilized. You have to lie to a woman you live with in a different way than one you don't. Lying to your wife is a hell of a lot harder than lying to the girl you're courting. Wives get to know you a whole lot better, and they get that way of looking at you that lets you know you ain't fooling them for a second.

My house was a low, rambling *hacienda* of eight rooms with thick concrete and adobe brick walls and a roof of red Mexican tiles. Out back was a barn and a small corral where I generally kept anywhere from two to three horses. Ben ran the remuda, the horse herd, with the help of Ray Hays and three Mexican *vaqueros,* and he instinctively knew more about horseflesh than any man I'd ever met, but I kind of liked to keep a few ponies around to get them used to me and my ways. I generally kept a young horse around getting him finished off to my way of thinking. Of course he was a broke horse, tame and ready for cattle work by the time I got him from Ben, but I liked to keep him working his way up to my standards. And then I'd keep a quick horse around, a horse that had a lot of early speed and could get you out of a tight place in a hurry. And also, I liked to have a horse around like the big sorrel, who was part quarterhorse, but had a lot of American Standardbred in him. He was a stayer, a horse with good speed, but with legs enough to take you there and bring you back.

I turned the sorrel into the corral, unsaddled and unbridled him, and then turned him loose with the two other horses already there. Later I'd come out and give them some grain, but for the time being I just made sure they had plenty of hay and water.

I went in the house through the kitchen. Nora's maid, Juanita, was at the sink washing up some potatoes and onions and other truck. I just managed to squeeze by between her and the kitchen table. We might not have had the best maid around, but we damn sure had the fattest. She said that "Señora Viyliams" was in the parlor. I set my hat on the kitchen table, and walked on down the short hall and turned

13

into the sitting room. Nora was on the divan doing some kind of needlepoint. She was wearing a little light blue gingham frock, and she looked up when I came in the room. She said, "Well, mister, what are you doing home so early?"

Nora was just the exact amount of pretty. If she'd been any less pretty I wouldn't have been the envy of every man in the county. If she'd been any prettier I'd of never got any work done. She had hair that was a little more yellow than the curing prairie grass and soft blue eyes and delicate features. She was prim and proper and faithful in her churchgoing, but I knew what was beneath that innocent-looking blue frock, and just the thought of it made my throat close up and my jeans get too tight.

I didn't answer her right away. Instead I stepped into my office, which was a little room just off the parlor, and poured myself out a good drink of whiskey. When I came back in I sat across from her in a big overstuffed morris chair. I said, "Where's J.D.?"

J.D. was our year-old son. He was a junior, named after me: Justa Danford Williams. I had not wanted to hang that unhandy moniker on him, but Nora had insisted. We called him J.D. to cut down on the confusion—though I complained to Nora that it made him sound like a banker and that was an awful load to put on one so young.

My name had always given me trouble. My mother had named me, but she would never tell me where she'd come up with the Justa. The Danford was easy; that had been her maiden name, and it was the custom then to name the oldest son with his mother's family name as his middle name. Sort of a way of honoring both families. But she'd never told me or anyone else that I could find why the Justa. My brothers used to kid me that I'd been named from the words in a hymn, my mother being a powerful churchgoing woman. They'd said it had come from the hymn "Just a closer walk with thee . . ." Justa.

It had been a chore to carry around when I was growing up and every other boy had been named Joe or Bill or Tommy, and it had caused me a fair number of schoolyard fights, but then I'd gotten old enough and I hadn't cared and folks had quit taking notice.

Nora said, "He's having his nap. And you had better not wake him up. I'll be ever so glad when he quits teething. He's been crankier than you all day long."

I took a sip of my drink and didn't rise to the bait. My mind was on Howard and his startling statements. He had put me on my honor to not mention them to another soul, but I wasn't sure that included Nora. I always told Nora nearly everything—at least I did sooner or later, even the truth behind the lies I'd told her before. A man had to have someone he could talk everything out with, and for me that person was Nora. You can be close to a friend or a parent or a brother, but I didn't reckon there was any kind of bond to match that between a husband and wife who had made a truly good match.

She could tell my mood. She said, "What's the matter, honey?"

I shook my head. "Aw, nothing. I guess."

"Are you not supposed to talk about it?"

"Probably not," I said. "I think it'd be for the best if I waited and let it round itself off."

"You'll talk about it sooner or later. Why take it all on yourself right now?"

I looked across at her. "Now damnit, Nora, don't go to telling me my own mind."

"Don't swear in the house, Justa. And I'm not telling you your own mind. I can see you want to discuss something that's bothering you, and I wish you'd go ahead and do it without going clean to Houston and back before you get around to it."

"What's the difference between swearing in the house and cussing outside? You are always telling me not to swear in the house, but you never say a word when I cuss outside. Is that because you don't want to get a bunch of swear words trapped here in the house in case God opens the front door and they all come flooding out? You don't reckon He hears the ones I say outside?"

"Don't be taking the Lord's name in vain."

"I was not taking the Lord's name in vain! I merely asked you a question, damnit!"

Nora ignored it. "Are you in for the day or have you just stopped by to let me know something was worrying you so I could worry too?"

"Aw, hell, Nora." I got up and went in the office and picked up the bottle.

She called after me. "Why don't you have another drink? That will certainly help."

"Damnit!" I said, loud enough to be sure she heard me. I went clumping out through the hall and out the kitchen door. Behind me I heard a squall from J.D. Well, that was going to certainly make me popular around suppertime. I went in the barn and sat down on a barrel of salt blocks. I got out a cigarillo and lit it and sat there thinking. But after an hour I still didn't have any more idea about what Howard was up to than I had before.

Nora didn't make me pay at supper. We had a nice quiet meal of steak and potatoes and gravy with a garden salad of tomatoes and lettuce and onions. Our climate was so mild you could grow garden truck nearly the whole year round. And Nora took advantage of that fact. I had never been much of a hand for vegetables, but Nora put them on your plate and you'd better damn well eat them all or you'd hear what for. For somebody who didn't weigh much more than a hundred and ten pounds, she had a hell of a nice way of throwing her weight around.

J.D. was back in what they chose to call the nursery getting his bottle from Juanita. Nora had weaned him about a month before and, as far as I was concerned, it was that and not cutting teeth that was making him cranky. Looking across at Nora's breasts testing the thin fabric of the gingham frock, I couldn't say that I much blamed him.

I said, "Good steak. Juanita's getting better."

"She's coming along."

"I'd of given up on her a year ago."

Nora put her fork down. "Justa, what is bothering you."

"Howard wants me to take twenty-five thousand dollars in gold to a man up in Oklahoma. Says it's in payment of an old debt."

"What's so worrisome about that?"

I looked down at my plate. "He says he stole the money. Thirty years ago or sometime. Says he wants to pay it back before he dies. Make it right."

She laughed, putting her hand over her mouth.

That made me a little hot. "What the hell's so damn funny?"

"The idea of Howard stealing anything. If everybody was like Howard there wouldn't be a lock in the world."

"Well, that's what he said."

"What do Norris and Ben say about it?"

I finished up my salad before I answered her. "I haven't told them. I ain't supposed to mention it to nobody, including you. But I especially ain't supposed to tell Ben or Norris. Though how I'm going to explain taking twenty-five thousand dollars out of company funds without making up an awful good story for Norris is beyond me."

"Justa, you are saying 'ain't' more and more. Your grammar is something awful. I do wish you'd be more careful, especially with J.D. growing up."

I glared at her. "You really figure this is the right time to correct my grammar? *Ain't* I just told you Howard wants me to return some money he says he stole? Wasn't you listening when I was telling you something I wasn't supposed to mention to nobody else?"

"Honey, don't be silly. Howard is getting old. Sometimes he gets confused in his mind."

I said grimly, "He wouldn't be so confused he wouldn't know whether he stole some money or not. Man don't ever get that confused."

"You'll see, it'll all come to nothing. A misunderstanding."

"Howard don't make those kind of misunderstandings."

"Why don't you talk to your brothers about it?"

"I told you. He don't want me to even hint at it to Ben or Norris. He got all upset at the very idea."

"You told *me*."

"Yes, and I shouldn't have. But I had to talk to somebody about it, and you've generally been pretty good at helping me in the past. And keeping your mouth shut."

"It's a whim of his," she said. "Now finish your supper and go on over to the big house and get your business done and don't be so late getting back. I'll let J.D. stay up a little past eight if you get back in time."

I got up from the table. "I'll still bet you that kid ain't never going to forgive you for hanging my name on him. Wasn't enough I had to wear it. Now he's got it as a hand-me-down."

"Stop saying 'ain't.' It's not a word."

I went on out the kitchen door and walked afoot the half mile over to the big house. It was a nice night. We were finally getting just a little nip of fall in the air. Made the walking pleasant. With it quiet as it was, I could hear the far-off sounds of the ocean. It took me back to when I was a kid and would lay awake nights thinking I could hear the sound of the surf booming up on the beach. Sometimes, when the wind blew hard in from the east, you could actually hear it. We used to go swimming down at a little beach about three miles away, but it had been a long time since I'd done that. I looked forward to J.D. getting up to an age when him and me could do such things together.

I went in through the back door of the big house. Just off the long hall that ran from front door to back was the large dining room with the huge round table in it. I passed by its open doors. It was still lighted with kerosene lamps, and the two Mexican women were clearing dishes away from supper. I reckoned my brothers and Howard had gotten lucky and Buttercup had been too drunk to cook, and the Mexican women had fixed their supper.

The big old dining table had been in our family since I could remember. It was an immense, heavy round thing. In my mother's day it had been polished and clean and unmarked. But since her passing, I was sorry to say, we had reverted to the manners of ruffians and the table reflected that. It bore spur marks where we'd propped our boots up on its surface, cigarillo burns, scuffs of all kinds, scars, and even a little carving with a pocketknife.

I turned to the left at the next door into the big office. It was funny, but we all sat the same way and in the same place for our evening meetings. We'd been doing it for as long as we'd been having them, and that was going on for five or six years. Ben always sat in a straight-backed chair against the wall facing the door. He always had it tipped back so its front legs were off the floor. Beside him was the sideboard table where the whiskey and tumblers were kept. If he was up, Howard always sat in his rocking chair just a yard from the door to his bedroom. Norris always sat on his side of the two desks we had pushed up against each other to make one big double desk, the desk Howard had been sitting at in the afternoon when he'd laid the light-running surprise on me. Norris had an office in town, in the building of the bank we owned, but he kept some work at home or brought some home that he had to check with me about or get my okay for. Besides the ranch and the real estate in town, we also put money in different municipal bonds and other such ventures as Norris thought profitable. He couldn't stand to see money just laying around and not working. He was harder on it than Howard had been on us, in turn, as boys. Howard had always figured if a boy had his eyes open he ought to be doing something with his hands. He didn't expect you to work when you were asleep, and our mother wouldn't let him work us on Sunday, but those were about the only exceptions.

I didn't sit at my desk in the evenings. I keep my herd books and my breeding records there, documentation that I used in the upgrading of our cattle. In the evenings I sat in a big overstuffed chair by the wall.

When I came into the room everybody already had a drink in their hands, so I walked on over to the sideboard table and poured myself out a tumbler of whiskey. I made as if to kick the legs of Ben's chair out from under him, and then looked over at the glass in Howard's hand. I said, "How many that make today, Dad?"

He give me a sheepish look, but he said, "Been waitin' and savorin' it all day."

Ben said, "Oh, yeah. We *all* believe that. Justa, I want to talk to you about gettin' some new breeding stock in here. You keep saying wait, wait, but we wait much longer we're going to be breeding back brother to sister."

I sat down in the big chair and took a sip of my drink. "I somehow doubt that. How many horses you got in the remuda, six hundred? Seven?"

He shrugged. "Round figures? About seven-fifty."

"That's a lot of brothers and sisters."

"I need some Thoroughbred stock, damnit."

"Don't swear in the house. Makes holes in the roof."

Howard said, "Dadgumit, Nora hasn't been over to see me in a coon's age. She forget me? And when is she gonna bring my grandbaby by to see me?"

I said, "Howard, he's cutting teeth right now and I guarantee you can consider yourself lucky to have him at least a half a mile away."

"Pshaw," he said. "Couldn't be no worse'n what you was. I swear your mother . . ." He stopped all of a sudden and looked away. It got kind of uncomfortably quiet. The death of our mother, Alice, had hit Howard uncommonly hard. I'd been about sixteen at the time, old enough to see and to understand what was happening. She'd died and, overnight, Howard had gone from a strong, full-of-life man to someone who seemed to be shrinking right in front of our eyes. It was about that time that I'd started having a hand in running the ranch matters. Howard seemed to have lost all interest in anything, including living. And then, just as he was starting to come out of it, he'd taken the bullet through the chest and that had completed the decline.

Into the silence Norris said, "Shay Jordan paid me a visit at the office today."

CHEROKEE

That was Norris for you. He'd been busy at some papers when I'd come in so he'd made no motion to signify he knew I was in the room. So now, without so much as a howdy, he was straight into business.

I said, "Yeah?" Shay was the oldest son of Rex Jordan, the man who was disputing our property line. Shay was twenty-four or twenty-five and he had a kind of swaggering way about him, just enough of the bullyboy that I hadn't cared for him even on short acquaintance. Besides him there was the younger brother, Roy, who was about nineteen or twenty and showed every sign of wanting to grow up just like his big brother. The father, Rex, was a man I figured to be in his late forties or early fifties. I'd never met the missus, but I understood that Rex's brother lived with them. They had moved out from somewhere in far west Texas, and did not appear to be interested in being sociable. They had bought Old Man Fletcher's place when he'd moved back to Tennessee to live with his married daughter. They hadn't much more than settled in when they'd started a squabble with us about our boundary line.

The trouble had come up over a drift fence we'd built to keep our cattle from straying too far to the southwest. It wasn't much of a fence, just three strands of smooth wire strung on cedar posts, and wasn't much more than a mile long. It wasn't intended to keep anyone out of our property or limit anyone's right-of-way. Its only purpose had been to throw our cattle back toward the east to keep them from mixing with the numerous brands on the smaller ranches that lay to the south and west of us. But the Jordans had taken it as an attempt to fence them in. They'd declared that where they came from was open range country and a man didn't go to fencing his neighbors out. They'd said the grass was there for all, that no man owned it, and that by gawd, they weren't going to stand for it. We'd agreed with them, and had said we weren't trying to fence anybody in or out, that we'd just put up a drift fence because our cattle tended to drift to the southwest on account of the eastern wind off the gulf and we were just trying to make for less work when it came time to gather.

But unfortunately, it was at the time that the troublesome barbed wire was just being introduced into the Southwest, and squabbles were breaking out all over the country about it. We'd tried to explain to the Jordans that we believed in open range also, and that the drift fence wasn't intended to do more than turn back a few wandering cows, that it wasn't strong enough to stop a herd of prairie jackrabbits. But that hadn't been good enough for them. They'd been convinced that the drift fence was the first step in a planned campaign on our part to fence off the whole range and shut out the small rancher. Nothing we had been able to say had seemed to convince them otherwise. The discussion had taken place on our front porch, the Jordans declining to enter the house or to accept any form of hospitality. Norris had dismissed them as trash, but even trash can be trouble if it keeps showing up on your doorstep.

After that was when they'd trotted out a surveyor and claimed the fence was on their property. They'd advised us of their intentions to tear it down, but a visit from the Matagorda County sheriff, Lew Vara, had convinced them it would be wiser to wait until the issue was finally settled. That Lew was our friend, and perhaps my best friend outside of my brothers, had had nothing to do with the matter. The fence hadn't been proven to be on their property. Then, of course, had come our surveyor, and after that a lawsuit on their part, except the lawsuit sought a little more than just the little strip of land the fence was on. It claimed a much larger chunk of our deeded land than had originally been in question.

But it made no difference about the lawsuit. They couldn't win it whether they were right or wrong, and there really was no telling about right or wrong with some of the rusty old land grants most titles were founded on. We'd win for two reasons. First, and most rightfully, we'd occupied the contested land for forty years. But more importantly, we had a hell of a lot more money than they did and we could keep dragging them through court until they either quit or went broke.

Norris said, "Yes, and young Mister Jordan was not particularly polite. He inferred that there was all sorts of ways to settle disputes and going to law—his phrase—was just one of them. I believe he was implying mischief."

Ben said, "I believe I might have to give that smart-alecky little bastard a school lesson. Teach him some manners."

I looked over at him and said sharply, "Ben! You stay the hell away from Shay. And the rest of the Jordans too. You understand me?" Outside of a man named Wilson Young, Ben was as good with a gun as any man I'd ever seen. He was good with horseflesh and handguns. But that's where it stopped. He was hot-tempered, had no judgment, and even at twenty-eight had a hell of a lot of growing up to do. Sometimes it was all I could do to manage him. I said, "The last thing this county needs is for you to start a blood feud."

He said, "Well, I ain't answering for my actions if he comes talking like that around me."

I said, "He was talking to Norris."

The words were no more than out of my mouth when I realized the mistake I'd made. Norris was overly sensitive about his toughness. It wasn't enough for him to be ten times smarter than the rest of us bookwise; he had to be just as tough with his fists or a gun. The minute I said it he straightened up in his chair and looked at me like I'd just slapped him in the face. I said, as quick as I could, "He went to Norris because he is in town and can be got to. And he knows can't no trouble break out in town. To see me or you he'd have to come on our property, and he ain't going to do that."

I could see it had mollified Norris a bit. I said, "What exactly did he say, Norris?"

My brother shrugged and leaned back in the chair. "Wasn't much that he said. It was more the way he was swelling around and making sure I could see how big the revolver was he was wearing. I told him I thought our lawyers might be close to some sort of an agreement, and he said close didn't count with him except in horseshoes and handguns."

Ben said, "Shit!"

I smiled. "Why Ben, that sounds exactly like something you'd say."

He give me a hard look. "You watch your mouth, big brother."

I said, "Just so long as you remember who the big brother is. And also who the boss is. I'd hate to have to fire you again."

He colored slightly and took a quick drink of his whiskey. It was true that I had indeed fired my own brother for directly disobeying an order. Of course I couldn't run him off the ranch; that was his home. But I'd taken away his job as boss of the horse herd, along with his salary, and told him if he wanted to work on the ranch he could apply to Harley for a job as a common cowhand and draw a cowhand's wages, sleep in the bunkhouse, and eat with the hired hands.

He'd done it, stiffly and angrily, until it had finally penetrated his thick skull that an outfit can't have but one boss and that that boss ain't got time to explain every order he gave. After that he'd come and apologized and said he'd gotten exactly what he had coming. I'd offered to reinstate him to his position with the herd and the salary that went along with it, but he'd insisted he deserved at least a month of punishment, and he'd stuck it out. There wasn't anything halfway about Ben.

Howard said, "Now don't be bringin' that up again."

Norris said, "Ben, I wouldn't think you'd want trouble with the Jordans. I saw the daughter on the street the other day. A mighty comely piece of yard goods. How old is she, twenty?"

"Nineteen," Ben said. Then he blushed again.

I said, "You better stay away from her until this matter is settled."

He said, "Goddamit, Justa, you want to write out for me in the morning what I can do during the day? Save me a awful lot of thinking."

I said drily, "You don't sound much like a man who is trying to get on my good side so's I might consider letting you buy some high-priced Thoroughbred breeding stock."

Norris laughed.

I finished my drink, got up, and set the empty tumbler on the sideboard table. "I got to get home. I can't sit here talking to such as you the balance of the evening." I glanced over at Howard, but he wasn't looking at me. He was staring off into space thoughtfully.

Norris said, "You've got to tell me soon how many steers you intend to sell off. The market is showing signs of dropping, and unless you want to winter the whole bunch you've got to make a decision fairly soon. There's a new issue of Treasury bills coming out that will pay four and a half percent. You sell a thousand head, that would give me some important capital to work with. It would certainly beat feeding that many cows all winter."

I said, still thinking about Howard, "I'll tell you tomorrow."

Before I could get out the door Ben said, "Do I get a yes on those Thoroughbred studs? Five or six would make a big difference in the quality of the horse herd in two or three years."

"Get me some prices," I said.

Howard said, a sort of plaintive note in his voice, "You be by tomorrow, son?"

"Yeah," I said. "I'll stop in."

I left then, walking home in the soft night. I decided, at least for a while, to forget about Howard and his revelation of being a youthful bandit. Like Nora had said, the old man was getting along. He wasn't just getting hard of hearing; he was getting hard of remembering too. I walked along, looking forward to playing with my son. But I was looking forward even more to playing with his mama a little later on.

I was a simple man; it didn't take much to make me happy, especially if it came in a package of goods like Nora.

CHAPTER 2

I didn't wait until the afternoon to go by and see Howard. Instead I dropped in mid-morning when I knew there was no one else around. I knew Ben was out with the horse herd and of course Norris had gone to his office in town. I wanted to get the business with Howard over with so I could spend the balance of the day surveying the herds with Harley. I had decided to sell all the crossbred steers over the age of four. I knew we'd have plenty of fives, and there ought to be a goodly number of sixes according to my books, and a couple of hundred sevens and some scattered eights. I figured the numbers would run to somewhere around eleven hundred head, and at an average price of ninety dollars a cow, that ought to give Norris some healthy money to buy Treasury bonds with. I had debated about marketing the fours also, which would have been about another thousand head, but I'd decided to hold them back for the spring market in anticipation of a better price. Of course the price could go down just as easily as it could go up. But that was ranching; there wasn't that much difference between it and rolling the dice for a living, except ranching wasn't against the law. That is, so long as you were ranching your own cattle.

I found Howard out on the big front porch taking the sun and having a cup of coffee. Somebody had brought him out his rocking chair and he was sitting there, looking content, looking out over the vast cattle business he'd started and mostly built.

I rode up, dismounted, and dropped my reins on the ground. All our horses ground-reined. If they didn't think they were as securely tied when those reins were hanging on the ground as if they were snubbed to a tree then they were on their way to the auction block. A rider in a hurry didn't have time to hunt up a hitching post when he was working cattle or some such. Ben had strict requirements for a Half-Moon horse, and they either made the grade or got sold to somebody that didn't expect as much out of an animal he might spend most of his day with.

I made my way up on the porch and sat down in a wicker chair next to Howard. I took note that he was wearing his boots, which I took as a good sign that he was not only feeling better, but might be thinking better about his request of the day before. I said, "Well, Howard, it appears you've looked the place over. You going to buy it?"

He was chewing tobacco. He made a futile effort to spit off the porch, and only managed to put a brown splotch on the white railing. He said, "Place looks run-down. Don't know who's been bossing it but it appears they ain't been steady on the job."

"That the way you see it, huh? Think you could do better?"

"Son, I learnt a long time ago they wasn't nothin' educational about getting kicked twice by the same mule. First time this particular mule kicked me, I found me the first fool I could to go back in the barn and get him harnessed up."

I lit a cigarillo. "Well, I always wondered what I was. Now I know. Just something for a mule to kick."

He looked over at me. "You thought anymore on what we talked about?"

I took a moment answering, drawing in a lungful of smoke and then slowly blowing it out. "I've thought enough to know you are going to have to tell me considerable more about this matter before I agree to do anything. I do, however, give you full permission to talk to Norris or

Ben. I'll agree to the money. It's the rest of it I've got to know about. They may not be so picky."

"Justa, I done told you I don't want Ben nor Norris to know about this."

"Why not?"

He looked kind of pained. Then he said softly, "Because . . . well, because there's some parts to the business that might shame me in their eyes. And it could hurt them."

"But not me, huh?"

He said slowly, "Yes, the same for you. But you're different, Justa. You're tougher, stronger." He looked over at me. "Understand, I ain't anxious for you to know this neither. But I'm betwixt the devil and the deep blue sea. This matter has got to be handled an' there ain't no one else. I'd do it if I was able. Comes to it, I might try. Me an' Tom Butterfield."

"Well, if you want to try it that way it's fine with me."

He looked over at me.

I said, "But if you want me to do it, especially under them damn silly conditions you set out yesterday, then you are going to have to tell me a hell of a lot more. Last thing I heard out of you was that you stole the money. That has been pretty steady on my mind, as it would yours if I'd told you such a thing. I have one hell of a hard time seeing Howard Williams stealing the sweat off a maverick calf, much less another man's money. You are going to have to tell me the straight of that, Howard. If it shames you, well, then so be it."

He looked out across the pasturage for a long time, no doubt seeing the herds of cattle in the distance, the herds that had slowly been upgraded from the native, all-bone, horse-killing, man-killing, wild-as-hell Longhorns to the manageable beef cattle we'd crossbred from whiteface and Hereford strains. He must have been looking back a lot of years to how it was when he'd come to this very range some forty years ago. Finally he turned and looked at me. "Is that the way of it?"

I nodded. "Yes. Unless you want to forget the whole matter. I'm sure as hell willing."

But he shook his head. "No, no, I can't do that. I was pretty down yesterday and I will be again. And one of these days I ain't going to come back up like I done today. I'm just gonna keep on going down until I'm six foot under. And I don't want that dirt to hit me in the face with this misdeed on my conscience."

"All right. I'm listening."

He squinted his eyes and looked far off again, like he was still going back, and not just in his mind. "Ya'll never heard me speak much about Charlie Stevens, did you? About the early days, I mean."

"Never heard you speak about him at all. Mainly just about Buttercup. May have been one or two others you mentioned, but it seemed like it was just you and Buttercup got the start on the place."

"Well it was Tom Butterfield and me on the one start. But what I never told you boys was there was two starts made on this ranch. Tom helped me on the second one, but as a hired hand. Of course you know that's why I keep him on around here as our cook. Even if he can't cook. But he's a proud man. Won't take wages without doing a day's work."

"We ain't talking about Buttercup, we're talking about this here Charlie Stevens." I could see he was reluctant to come to his subject and had gone off on a false lead. "You said something about there was two starts on this place."

He cleared his throat, looking uncomfortable. "Me an' Charlie grew up together in Georgia. Course I guess you knew our family started out in Georgia."

"I knew *you* did, but this is the first time I've heard you mention it with this Charlie Stevens."

"Well we did, him and me." He said it kind of defiantly. "Was good friends, damn good friends. That's how come it was us come West together looking for a new range, new opportunities. We'd heard all the stories about Texas and about the Oklahoma Territory and we figured that was the place to head for. I reckon that was in about 1851, '52. We was both just young bucks, barely reached our majority. Couldn't been more than twenty-one. I think Charlie might have been a year older'n me though not quite. Big good-lookin' fella. Good in a fight, good with horses. Good man to partner up with. Had an even temper, laughed a lot. I remember him bein' mighty popular with the young ladies back in Georgia. Easygoing feller. Didn't care much for arguing, though he'd back his partner in a fight."

He spit tobacco juice again and this time cleared the rail. He wiped his mouth with the back of his hand. "Anyways, we set out and ended up in the Indian Territory to start with. That's what they called Oklahoma then. Set out to catch on with some cattle outfit and learn the business and then set up on our own. Was plenty of land, though it wasn't shucks to what we got around here. There was plenty of water, but the dirt was poor, wouldn't grow grass like it did here. But anyways, we got in with some small outfit, can't remember the brand. Mostly what they was doin' was mavericking, and it didn't take no scholar to see wasn't much point on puttin' another man's brand on an ownerless calf when you could just as easy put your own on it. But we was drawin' wages and the outfit was providing the horses, so we played it straight. Was a good bit of Injuns around. Cherokees. Hell, they'd been moved from Georgia their own self. Army moved 'em an' put 'em on a reservation. They didn't much care for it, but they was a good people, nothin' like them murderin' goddam Comanches we had down here. And they was a handsome people. Some of the women . . ."

He stopped and didn't say anything for a moment.

I said, "What was you saying?"

He cleared his throat. "This talkin' is mighty hard work."

"And you figure a little drink would make it go easier?"

"Well, it is going on for noon."

I got up. "Hell, Howard, it ain't even eleven o'clock. But if it'll speed you up I'll bring you a short one. But it'll be watered."

"Now, Justa," he said, but I was already going in the house.

I brought him back his drink. I'd been a little more generous with the whiskey than I'd meant to be, forgetting for a second who it was for, and he smiled his appreciation as he took a sip. I said, "You was talking about the Cherokee women."

I thought I saw a little flinch come over his face. But he said, "Just in passin'. They was a handsome people, and as civilized as some white folks and more so than others. But that ain't got nothin' to do with what I was talkin' about. Where was I?"

"You and Charlie Stevens was branding mavericks for some small outfit."

"Yeah. Well, we done that about a year and right quick seen we wasn't getting nowhere. And I could see the country wasn't going to amount to much neither. Like I said, there was plenty of free land, but it was poor. You couldn't run one cow over at least twenty acres. 'Bout that time we'd commenced to hear about this country in the Gulf Coast. This here country we're settin' in right now. We heard it was belly-deep to a tall cow in grass, and plenty of water and mustangs and wild Longhorns and land for the asking. So we drawed what wages we had coming, throwed in together, and bought us an outfit, then headed this way with four good horses and plenty of powder and shot and damn little money left over. But we figured we'd eat. We'd heard there was plenty of game and anything you stuck in the ground would grow. Heard there was miles and miles of open country with nary a soul to bother you. Well, we was damn fool kids or that would have told us something right there. If the country was so wonderful, how come it wasn't full of people? We'd heard about the Comanches and that they was supposed to be powerful bad, but we'd been around the Cherokees and we didn't figure the Comanches could be that much worse. We'd also heard a little about Mexican *banditos,* but we wasn't scared of the devil himself, so what was a few outlaws?

"So on we come. Full of piss and vinegar and already figuring out how we was going to spend all the money we was gonna make. Took us about a week to figure out we'd cut ourselves out a job of work. Took about a month to come to the conclusion we might have made a mistake. And that month was mostly spent building a dugout cabin. I can damn near see the little knoll we cut it into from here. Yonder, just beyond that far windmill. Course there wasn't no windmills in them days. But if you'd of seen that dugout—wasn't no more than eight feet across in any direction—you'd of asked what we was doing the rest of the time because we couldn't have spent no more than a day and a half building such a shelter. But a month was what it took. Nearest timber of any size was four miles away on Caney Creek, and that was just willow and cottonwood. Reason we couldn't make it no bigger'n eight feet in any direction was we couldn't get no saplings or small logs that was longer than that in a straight line. And of course, we'd dug it into the side of that hump so we could use the earth for most of the walls. Except the earth was so damn wet it just oozed. So after that we had to go six miles to find clay on upper Caney Creek, and haul that back and stick the clay to the walls over a patchwork of branches. Then we had to build a damn fire in the damn dugout and harden the clay. Well, anytime it takes you a month just to build a temporary camp, you can bet you ain't getting no work done that would put a dime in your pocket."

"What about the cattle?"

He cut his eyes around at me. "Cattle? More like wild animals you be talkin' about. You remember—ten years ago, I guess, maybe more—when you started talking to me about bringing in some of them little gentle northern cattle to try and calm these Longhorns down and fatten 'em up? I remember you saying killing two horses to bring in one cow wasn't good business. Well, *them* Longhorns you was talking about was as tame as kittens next to them brutes me and Charlie was tryin' to gather. An' we didn't have but two horses apiece, an' them worn to a frazzle a week after we started trying to gather cattle."

I was getting a little impatient. "All right, I'm real interested in this pioneer business, not like I ain't heard it a dozen times before. But what has it got to do with what you want me to do and why?"

"Wa'l, damnit, just have a little patience, can't you? I'm tryin' to make the point that Charlie had damn good reason to pull out. I didn't think it at the time. I thought he was runnin' out on me. An' it was that attitude that caused me to think it was all right what I did. Of course lookin' back, I can see that Charlie done the right thing, an' that if I'd of had a lick of sense an' hadn't been as stubborn as a mule I'd a gone with him."

"But—"

He waved his hand at me. "Damnit, you asked to hear it, now shut up your mouth an listen. A damn fool could see it wasn't gonna work. Even if we could have gathered them cattle by the thousands, there wasn't no market for 'em. They was payin' four dollars a head delivered in Galveston, an' there wasn't no two men could have driven ten of them cattle, let alone fifty or a hundred, all the way to Galveston. Would of taken a drover for every head. Only thing left was the hide-and-tallow business, and I'll give you some advice right now, son. Don't ever go to work in the hide-and-tallow business. Prison is better wages, I hear, and the work ain't as hard."

"You gonna tell me about Charlie Stevens or am I gonna get up and go on about my own work? I have heard this story before, only it was Buttercup in it. You still ain't explained how that worked out."

He looked away. "One night Charlie told me right after evening grub that he was pulling out. He said he'd just take one horse, leave his other one, and leave me most of the powder and shot. He said he didn't mind the work, said he didn't mind living burrowed up in the mud like some animal, said he didn't mind the good chance of getting killed by the Mexican *banditos* or the Comanches. Said he didn't mind having to haul water and wood four miles.

Said he didn't even really much mind starving to death as we surely were. But he said what he couldn't take no more was the loneliness."

Howard stopped talking and looked off in the distance again.

I let him think on it a moment, and then I said, "Bad?"

He just shook his head. "Sometimes we'd go weeks without seeing another human face. An' then most likely it would be some Mexican with a herd of stolen horses heading for the border. Nearest neighbors was about a four-day ride away, and they was just a couple of ol' sourdoughs like me an' Charlie. Only time we ever saw anything in a skirt was when we took a load of hides and tallow into Galveston, an' them was the ugliest, filthiest women you ever wanted to get away from. Whores they was. An' they done a lively trade, which will tell you how bad things was. Course me an' Charlie never had more than five cents left by the time we got through buying supplies. So even if we'd of *wanted* to associate with such, we didn't have the coin for it." He stopped and thought, seeming to be looking for a way to explain how it was. He said finally, "Son, it was just lonely. You and your partner have both told each other every story you know and then told them again and again. And ain't nothin' happening that's current that's worth talkin' about. Finally you just ain't got nothing left to say. You're just by yourself without kith or kin for comfort. Stuck it out damn near nine years, Charlie and me."

"Pa, I never understood how come sodbusters didn't settle the country? Land was clear, good soil. I'd of thought there'd have been a farmer every half mile."

He shook his head. "Land wouldn't grow nothing on account of the soil was brackish. From the saltwater." He waved his hand in the general direction of the gulf. "That old saltwater has been soaking its way into this soil for millions of years. It'll grow grass and trash trees like mesquite and willow and huisache, but you couldn't make a crop of potatoes or corn or wheat or such. An' there ain't no running water. Think how many creeks and rivers there are within fifty miles of here. Ain't that many. We got windmills now, but there wasn't no windmills then. Nobody had ever heard of boring for water. And no timber to build a proper cabin. Just wild animals and *banditos* an' Comanches. Them kind of conditions don't draw many settlers, 'specially the kind with womenfolk. Too hard a life. This country killed women and horses. Course it's civilized now."

That wasn't what Nora thought, but I didn't want to get into that. "So Charlie Stevens pulled out on you."

"Yes. And I was plenty bitter about it. He tried to get me to come with him, but I wouldn't have none of it. Said when I set in to do a thing I got it done. But Charlie went on back to the Indian Territory. Said at least there was people there. Said if he was gonna starve to death he was at least going to do it with a woman in bed next to him."

"Did you think hard of him?"

"I did. Mighty hard. And I let him know it."

"Is that when you robbed him of the money?"

"Five *hundred* dollars? We didn't have five hundred anything between us. No, no, that come later. At least a year later, maybe more."

"Then tell me. And pretty soon too."

He looked off. "Let me see . . . Been so long. I remember sticking it out by myself for six months. Seven months, eight. Almost the best part of a year. Gawd, it was hard goin'. Before, it was just a miserable life. But without a partner, somebody to help you pull on the rope, well, it was near impossible."

"Wasn't anyone else around to help?"

He shook his head. "Months went by and I didn't see a soul. Once got trapped by a Comanche hunting party near Caney Creek. Hid out in the weeds for three days. Didn't have nary a bite to eat, and the only water I got was what dew I could lick off the morning grass. Them Injuns was camped right on top of me. Fortunately I'd left my horse well upstream and had been working my way down the creek looking for freshwater mussels when I run slam-dab into them Injuns. Wasn't nothin' to do but hop in the weeds and hide. I thought they was never gonna leave. At least they didn't find my horse. He'd done a sight better'n me. I'd left him tethered so he could get to fresh water and grass."

"You going to get to Stevens pretty soon?"

He spit again and looked at his empty tumbler and then at me. I just shook my head. He looked disappointed, but he said, "Wa'l, after that hard year things suddenly kind of took an upswing. There had come a pretty good influx of people into Texas and Tennessee and Arkansas and such places, and all of a sudden there was a demand for beef. Them ornery Longhorns went to six dollars and then eight and then ten, and I could see a man could make a pretty good piece of change if he had some help. So I saddled my horse an' set out for the Indian Territory. Didn't have no real sure idea where Charlie would be, but we'd originally been set up near a little settlement called Anadarko. So I headed that way and damned if I didn't find him! He'd gone into the sawn-lumber business and was doing pretty fair. The Ouchita River runs right near Anadarko, and Charlie had channeled off a piece of the stream and built him a raceway that would turn a saw blade, and he was settin' there turning out sawmill lumber and selling it as fast as he could cut it. There was considerable pine trees around that part of the territory, and he had him a regular crew cutting timber and hauling it to his sawmill. Well, he was right pleased to see me. Had him a house built right there next to his sawmill. Nice house built out of his own lumber, three or four rooms. Had him a mighty pretty . . ."

He stopped.

"What?"

"Nothing," he said. "Swallowed some tobacco juice. Went down the wrong way." He made a big show out of coughing. There was something about it that struck me strange, like he was covering up something, though for the life of me I couldn't guess what.

I said, "He had him a mighty pretty what?"

He cleared his throat. "What? Oh, I was just going to say he was mighty well set up. Good business, good house—made that dugout seem like the place you'd keep the hogs in. Anyway, we visited and I stayed the night and then the next day I put it up to him. I told him about what the cattle market had done and I begged him to come back with me. Of course he didn't want to, as well fixed as he was. But I reminded him it was our chance to make the dream come true we'd left Georgia with. We could own the biggest ranch anybody had ever seen. All I needed was him and about ten cowhands and we could make a sweep through the country and arrive in Galveston with a thousand head. But he wouldn't do it. I said I didn't have the money to hire the hands. I could see he must have made some cash with his saw, and if he'd come in with me we'd clean up. Well, I stayed around a few more days, eating his grub and drinking his whiskey, but he wouldn't budge. He finally said that what he'd do, me and him being old friends from when they laid the chunk, what he'd do was he'd loan me the money to hire the cowhands. Of course I didn't want to do it, hadn't come there for charity, but he piled five hundred dollars on his kitchen table in twenty-dollar gold pieces and it weakened me. Weakened me until I done it. I took the money and I went to San Antonio and I hired the cowhands. First one I hired was Tom Butterfield. And of course I've already told you the story of how Tom and I started the ranch, about that first big drive, that first payday. So there it is, son, there's the real beginning to the Half-Moon ranch."

I looked at him, confused. "But you said you stole the money."

"I did."

"He loaned it to you."

"I never paid him back. That makes it the same."

I sat back and looked at him. Either he was pulling my leg or he wasn't telling me all of it. I said, "And this is what is weighing on your conscience, owing some man five hundred dollars for thirty years or whatever it is? This is what you want me to go through all this silly rigamarole for? Carry up not five hundred dollars, but twenty-five thousand dollars in gold? On horseback? And deliver it as your substitute because I'm your eldest son?" I leaned toward him. "Howard, have you reckoned you've raised a fool?"

He looked uncomfortable again. "Justa, I'd just as soon not tell you the rest."

"And I'd just as soon not make that damn fool trip. Especially by horseback."

He seemed to kind of collect himself. "Charlie came after me not long after I got back. We were right in the middle of the cattle roundup and he showed up one day."

"What for?"

Howard looked at that far-off object he'd been studying through most of the conversation. "Come to get what belonged to him."

"He came for his money that soon?"

His voice got an angry note in it. "How the hell do I know, damnit! He came, that's all. And there was a showdown between me and him." He flipped out his hand. "Right out yonder, about where that far barn stands. That was close to where my dugout was. I was still living in it."

"And he came for the money he'd loaned you before you even made your drive to Galveston? That don't make a bit of sense. He was a cattleman. He would of knowed you didn't have his money then, that you would have paid some of it out for supplies and to your hired hands. Tell me the truth, Howard. What the hell happened?"

"I told you, there was a showdown 'tween him and me."

"Over the money?"

"No. I said it weren't over the money."

"Then what the hell did he come all this way for?"

"Something that belonged to him, that's what for."

"And he thought you had it?"

"I reckon."

"But it wasn't the money?"

"Hell, Justa, he had just loaned me the money. He'd of knowed I couldn't pay it back that soon."

"That's what I just said. What I want to find out is what he came all the way from Oklahoma for?"

He got that far-off look in his eyes. I couldn't tell if he was seeing the prairie out in front of him or the years in the past. He said softly, "Charlie was a gentle man. Wasn't no fighter. Would rather laugh than argue. Go ten miles out of his way to avoid a fight. But he was a firm man where something counted with him."

It was worse than pulling teeth. I said, "What the hell happened?"

He shook his head sadly. "The whole thing was a mistake, a misunderstanding on Tom Butterfield's part."

"What the hell has Buttercup got to do with it."

"Me and Charlie was faced off about ten paces apart, arguing. Not really raising our voices, but an observer could have told we was arguing. Tom Butterfield was holding some cattle about two hundred yards away, maybe a little further, maybe three hundred. Course you know what kind of shot Tom is with a rifle . . ."

Of course I did. Even with him as old as Howard, he could still take his old Hawken buffalo rifle and outshoot any of us. I said, "Yeah."

Howard said awkwardly, "Charlie went to take his revolver out of his holster. Was an old cap-and-ball percussion. One of the first. He said he was going to lay his gun down on the ground so there couldn't be no mistaking he'd come in peace. Well, Tom had been watching. Hell, Charlie hadn't been here thirty minutes, half an hour. I hadn't even offered the man a cup of coffee or a drink of whiskey. Tom seen Charlie pull his pistol and he acted. Too sudden, but it was too late for me to stop him."

"What happened?"

Howard swallowed and looked pained. "He fired from that distance. I reckon he was trying to kill Charlie, but he didn't have the quality of a gun like he does now. So the ball hit Charlie in the right arm. The upper part. Broke the bone. Hell, it shattered the bone all to smithereens." He took the chaw out of his mouth and threw it over the railing. "Course there wasn't no doctors here then. It's a wonder Charlie didn't die. We had to cut off his arm. Cauterized it with a running iron. Took four men to hold him down. After that we took care of him as best we could. Took about two weeks, but finally he was able to get on his horse and left. Went back to Oklahoma." He looked around at me. "I ain't never seen the man since."

"And you owe him five hundred dollars plus interest, plus one right arm."

"That's about the size of it."

I said evenly, "What else you owe him, Howard?"

"Nothing." But his voice was weak.

"What did he come to get back from you? What of his did you have?"

He wouldn't answer me, just looked away.

"Howard, what did you really steal off the man that you're trying to repay with twenty-five thousand dollars? You know it ain't the five hundred, no matter what kind of interest you want to add. Or the arm; that was Buttercup's doing. What is it you stole that you don't even feel twenty-five thousand dollars covers?"

He suddenly turned around and faced me. "I'm not going to tell you. He probably will and I think you got a right to know. I ain't got the nerve to tell you. That's why I want you to find Charlie Stevens. It's as much for your sake and the sake of your brothers as it is for me."

Well, that made me blink. I said slowly, "I don't exactly know how to take that."

"Take it for the gospel. It's been eatin' away at me for better than thirty years. I'd like the truth to get out, but I ain't going to say it. I ain't got the stomach for it. And I ain't right sure I'm doing the right thing. I couldn't be sure if I told you. This matter has got me all balled up. I finally decided I'd just leave it to Providence and the Good Lord.

If you go and if you find Charlie and if he tells you, why then, I'll figure you was supposed to find out. That's said and I'm not gonna open my mouth about the subject again. You can go or not go. Please yourself."

I thought about it for a long couple of moments. Then I said, "And you want me to ride horseback all the way to Oklahoma."

"Yep."

"You know how far it is to Oklahoma horseback?"

"Ought to. I done it twice. I don't reckon it's got no further away in thirty years."

"With trains running up there every day you want me to load a horse with twenty-five thousand dollars in gold and waste all that time on a damn fool trip?"

He gave me a look. "You may not think it was a damn fool trip when you get back."

"But how come it has to be in gold and how come I got to go horseback?"

"It's a thing I can't explain. It's just fitten, that's all. Fitten. I can't explain it no other way. I brung Charlie's gold down here on horseback, gold that was the making of this place. Without that gold there wouldn't be no Half-Moon ranch. And Charlie come down here on horseback. And went back on horseback, left his arm here. Most of it."

"Got to be gold? Bank draft won't do?"

He shook his head. "I told you, no. Now if you don't want to do it, why, I'll find some other way."

"If I go I'm taking Ben with me. That much gold is just too much temptation. All the road agents ain't in jail."

Well, a look of plumb horror came over his face. "No! Not Ben! My Lord, no! You can't take Ben."

It perplexed the hell out of me, him taking on like that. "Hell, Howard, keep your hat on. I only said I wanted to take Ben because I want a good gun with me and Ben's the best."

He was shaking his head vigorously. "No. Not Ben. And not Norris."

I laughed. "I said I wanted help, not hindrance. I guess I'll take Ray Hays."

"Ray is fine." he said. He nodded. "Just no family."

Ray Hays was a kind of special case. Several years back he'd pretty well saved my life by helping me get out of some trouble I was in up in the hill country of Texas around the town of Bandera. In gratitude I'd brought him back to the ranch and put him to work. Supposedly he was assistant to Ben in managing the horse herd, but he and Ben had got to be close friends and there was some question as to just how much work he actually got done. He drew wages, but he pretty much considered himself a member of the family. But for all of that, he was worth having around because he was a mighty good man to have on your side in a fight. Next to Ben I calculated him to be about the best gun in the county. He was also good company. He had a nice, easy way about him and was generally good for a laugh. You could josh him until you ran out of things to say and he never took offense.

So I sat there thinking about the trip as the time ran on toward noon. And noon meant lunch and lunch meant Nora, and I didn't have the slightest idea how I was going to go about telling her the details of such a damn fool trip, a trip that would take me away from home for at least two or three weeks. Hell, if it didn't make sense to me how was I going to explain it to Nora?

I got up. "Dad, I got work to do. I got to see Harley about cutting the herd, shipping some cows."

He said anxiously, "But you'll do it?"

"Howard, how come you didn't pay the man back thirty years ago? How come you waited all this time, and for me to do it?"

He was silent for a moment. Then he said, "There were reasons."

"Like what? Didn't want to ride all that way to Oklahoma?"

"I said there were reasons. I was ashamed to face the man again." He looked away.

"On account of his arm?"

He didn't answer me.

I went halfway down the steps. I stopped and turned back to him. "Well, I reckon I'll do it. Though I hope you know what you're asking with a herd to cut and this trouble with the Jordans."

"I know," he said.

"And I don't know if I'm doing it because you asked me and you're my pa, or because you got my curiosity up about what I might find out from this Charlie Stevens. That is, if I can find him."

"You'll find him," he said.

"How do you know? How do you know he ain't dead?"

He shrugged. "I don't. I just got a feeling. But either way, I need you to try."

"Shit!" I said. I gathered up my horse's reins and swung aboard. "Howard Williams, you have got a nerve, I'll say that for you. You want to come help me explain to Nora why I got to be gone for all the time this trip will take?"

He shook his head. "No, sir. I don't think I'd care to do that."

Neither did I. But I turned my horse and started for my home. Lunch would be just about ready. Maybe I'd have time for a couple of drinks before I set to work on Nora.

CHAPTER 3

"When are you going?" We were laying in bed. I hadn't told her all about it until after supper and after J.D. was in bed asleep. She'd agreed with me that it was a strange request and a strange errand, but she'd found it perfectly understandable that Howard had considered he'd stolen the money. I'd said, "How the hell can you figure that? It was a loan. Just because Howard has let hell's own kind of time pass before paying it back don't mean he stole it. He made it sound like he'd either robbed it out of the man's strongbox or thrown down on him with a gun and took it off of him."

Nora had said, "It was an honorable debt and Howard would think he had not treated it in an honorable fashion."

I'd said, "Well, I wish to hell he had. I guarantee you I ain't looking for no long trip to Oklahoma. I'm about halfway tempted to take the train."

She'd said, "But you promised him you'd take it on horseback. I think it's important to him that it be done in a certain manner."

I'd said, "Well, I wish the damn gold had come down on the train. No, I can't take the damn train because I'd get back too soon. I could do the whole deal in four or five days on the train. And if we done it sensible it could be done in half a day by wiring a bank draft."

Now she said, "How are you going to find this Charlie Stevens?"

There was a good moon out and the room was kind of half glowing. I shook my head against the pillow. "Beats the hell out of me. Go up to that town, Anadarko, and go to asking around. Bet you doughnuts to dollars I'm going to spend a week and come up with nothing. I'll bet this Charlie Stevens is either dead or disappeared and left no forwarding address."

"You haven't said when you're going."

I said grumpily, "Not any sooner than I have to. Damn, Nora, there's a hundred matters need tending to around here. And I don't want to go off and sleep by myself for three weeks."

She was laying right beside me, wearing a small light cotton sleeping gown. She moved her hip harder against mine. I had my left arm around her with her head kind of tucked into my neck.

She said, "Justa, you've got to do it. You promised."

I turned my head a little in her direction. It didn't allow me to look into her eyes, but she got the idea. I said, "What is this? Near as I can recall, this is the first time you've ever wanted me to go off on a trip. Always before you had about ten different reasons I couldn't go. How come the big switch? You got you another Kansas City drummer waiting at the hotel in Blessing?"

She gave me a punch in the ribs. I said, "Owww."

She said, "Justa, this trip is a little different, don't you think? I objected, and still object to those trips you took where there was every chance you'd be coming home with a bullet in you. Now all you're doing is running an errand for your daddy."

I gave a dry little laugh. "Darling girl, a saddlebag with twenty-five thousand dollars can draw more attention than a hundred-dollar bill in a whorehouse. And if you think this part of the country ain't civilized, you ought to see Oklahoma."

"Nobody will know you have it if you don't go to flashing it around. That seems like a simple enough thing to do."

"You know how much that much gold weighs? Right around sixty pounds. How are you suppose to lug it around? Put it in a sack and tell folks it's hymnals?"

She ignored that. "What do you suppose Howard means about what Charlie Stevens can tell you that he won't?"

"That's got my curiosity up also." I turned toward her. "Probably the main reason I'm going."

"Well, I suppose if you have to . . . Justa, what are you doing?"

"You don't know by now?"

"Mister, you certainly have your nerve going around . . . Ooooooh!"

I went into town the next morning, going straight over to the bank. Bill Simms was the president. I eased into his office and as soon as we got the necessary remarks out of the way I told him what I wanted. It kind of took him by surprise. He took off his glasses and wiped them and said, "Mister Williams, let me get this straight. You want twenty-five thousand dollars in gold coins or bullion by day after tomorrow?"

I nodded. "Yes, Bill. And I want you to do it yourself. I'll pick it up after the bank closes. What I'm trying to say is that the fewer people know about this the better."

He put his glasses back on. He was a small fussy man in his early forties who'd been running the bank for at least ten years. "Mister Williams, I'm not even sure we've *got* that much in gold coins. We don't have any bullion. You couldn't take part of it in paper money?"

I shook my head. "Bill, I know you feel like you ought to get an explanation and I'd like to give you one. But I can't. The business I'm going to be doing has got to be done in gold. Let's just say the parties don't trust paper money."

He looked perplexed. "Who wouldn't take U.S. government currency? It's recognized all over the world. I—"

"Bill," I said, "don't worry your mind about it. Just get it. Today is Wednesday. I'll come in after three o'clock on Friday and pick the money up. I'll bring my own containers."

He looked as disapproving as a banker could. "You plan to go riding around with that amount of money? In gold?"

I looked at him.

"Well, of course, Mister Williams. It is your money. Far as that goes, it's your bank. What, ah, what account do you want it debited against?"

I hadn't thought about that part of it. By rights I should have talked to Norris first, but I hadn't. I gave it a moment's consideration. Ben wanted some blooded Thoroughbred stock. Animals like that ran high. I said, "Charge it to the horse herd account. If there's not enough in it, bleed off the rest out of the general funds account."

He said, "Yes, sir." I got up and went up to the second floor to Norris's office.

Norris was behind his desk wearing a gray summer seersucker suit. Even though it was fall, it was ninety degrees outside and not a hell of a lot cooler in the building. I pulled up a chair, and Norris obliged me by looking up from his work and giving me his attention. I said, "I'm taking twenty-five thousand dollars out of the bank. Out of the horse account if it'll stand it. The money is coming out after banking hours on Friday. I'm taking it out in cash."

He leaned back in his chair. "Why?"

"Norris, I didn't come up here to explain but to let you know for your book work."

"Is it for those Thoroughbred studs that Ben wants?"

"No."

We looked at each other.

"I see," he said. Then he made a half smile. "No, I guess I don't see. You're taking money but you don't want to tell me what it's for."

"Can't tell you."

"You mean you won't. Justa, you know as well as I do

I've got to record this money some way. Don't you agree it's a little too large of a sum to account for as coming out of petty cash?"

I sighed. I'd seen this coming when Howard had first laid out the situation. I said, "It's personal. How's that?"

"In other words you are making a loan from the company for twenty-five thousand dollars?"

I pulled a face. Now Howard was going to owe me some money. I wondered if he'd take thirty years paying me back as he had Charlie Stevens. I said, "Yes, I guess you could say I'm borrowing it from the company."

We were a company, the Half-Moon Land and Cattle Company. I was the president, Howard was the chairman of the board, Ben was the vice president, and Norris was the secretary and treasurer. We paid ourselves salaries. I got two hundred a month, Ben a hundred and fifty, and Norris a hundred and seventy-five. Howard didn't get anything. Of course we all got a bonus at the end of the year that Norris carefully figured out, depending on profits. All told, not counting the actual land of the Half-Moon ranch, which was willed personally and separately in whole to us boys, the Half-Moon Land and Cattle Company was worth about two and a half million dollars. Of course that included the hotel and the bank and various parcels of land and different securities and stocks.

And of course, it was Norris's business to keep up with all that, but it still kind of irritated me, him asking me so close what I wanted the money for and pressing me like he had. Hell, it wasn't as if we were broke.

He said, "So you want me to treat this like a personal loan from the company? What account do you want me to charge it to?"

It made me angry. "Charge it to the same account for the money we spent when me and Ben and Lew Vara had to come down and get you out of jail in Monterrey all because you was too damn stubborn to pay a Mexican official a hundred-dollar bribe. I believe that bribe cost the company around five thousand dollars. How'd you chalk that one up? What heading did you put that one under, muleheadedness?"

He picked up a pen and fiddled with it for a second. Then he said, "No call to bring that up, Justa. I'm simply trying to keep the books straight. Tell me, will this benefit the company in any way?"

I got up. I was tired of the conversation. Norris was my brother, but his accountant's ways could make me mad as hell. I said, "Yes, I expect it will benefit the company. I know damn well it ain't going to benefit *me*."

He said, "Fine. I'll enter it under General Maintenance."

"You can enter it under General Custer for all I care." I turned and walked out the door. But just before I started down the stairs I stopped and turned back. I was going to have to find a way, somehow, to get along better with Norris. I went back to his door and stuck my head inside. I said, "Norris, I'm going to cut out all the crossbred steers over four. I figure to get around eleven hundred head. So you can figure whatever they bring to buy those Treasury bills or whatever it was you wanted to do."

"When you starting the cut?"

"Harley should be bunching them right now." I hesitated. "I can't be here for the work, but it ought not to take more than ten days, two weeks to get them to market."

"You going somewhere?"

"Yeah. I'll have to be gone about two or three weeks."

"Any of my business where?"

I hesitated and gave Howard a good cussing in my mind. He was always wanting me to make a better effort to get along with Norris. And then he puts me in a position where I've got to hold out on my own brother. I said, "It's that personal matter."

"That's going to benefit the company?"

I gave a little half smile. "Yeah. Let's hope so."

He suddenly stood up. "Justa, I want to ask you something and I want a straight answer."

I looked at him. He was being firm. I said, "If I can."

"Is this some dangerous project that you are shutting me

out of because you don't think I can handle myself? The way you always do?"

I wanted to laugh, but I knew better. "No, no, it isn't. And I have never felt like you couldn't handle yourself. And I have never held you out of a dangerous situation for that reason. The few times . . . the *very* few times I've sent you home when there was threat of gunfire was because you are the only one can do your job. Ben and I can be replaced. You can't."

He was not mollified. Mainly because what he'd said was true. I didn't want Norris around in a gunfight because he'd be someone else I'd have to watch out for. He said, "Is Ben going? On this trip?"

"No," I said. Then I decided to hell with it. I'd tell Norris just enough to salvage his feelings and let Howard do the lying. I said, "This trip is for Howard. It's one of his last pieces of business. Probably the last he'll ever handle. I'm just the errand boy. But I'm breaking a confidence by telling you this. Anything else you want to know you go and ask him, but that will hurt him because he told me flat out that he didn't want another soul to know about it until it was over."

He looked down at his desk for a second. Then he looked back up. "I'm sorry, Justa. I shouldn't have asked so damn many questions."

"It's your job," I said. "Just keep in mind I told you this in confidence. Howard would hold me responsible if he knew I'd told anyone else."

"I understand," he said. "What are you going to tell Nora?"

"Oh," I said, lying, "some kind of cattle trip. Looking at a ranch. It doesn't make much difference. She never believes me anyway."

He said, "Thanks for moving so quick on the steers. We'll make some nice short-term money on these bonds."

I started to leave again, and then stopped. "Oh, in case the mercantile delivers something up here you think ain't supposed to come to your office, don't think anything about it. Just have them set it out of the way. In a corner or something."

His eyes narrowed. "What would the mercantile be delivering up here that I wouldn't think belonged up here?"

"Kegs of nails," I said.

"Kegs of . . ." Then he stopped. "I'm asking too many questions again. I guess I can't help it."

I guessed he couldn't either. Just as he couldn't help himself about every little detail he had to know about. He was worse about details than a drunk about how many drinks were left in the bottle. But I was trying to get along with him. He'd asked if I was taking Ben because he knew I always took Ben if I was going into a serious situation. I didn't tell him I would have been taking Ben if Howard would have let me. Me taking Ray Hays wouldn't tell him anything because I used Ray for all sorts of errands. I said, "You still be here late Friday?"

"If you want me to."

"I'll let you know."

I gave him a little salute, and then walked down the stairs, out of the bank, and over to the general mercantile store that was owned by Nora's daddy, Lonnie Parker.

It was cool and dim inside, just as it was always cool and dim inside every mercantile I'd ever been in in my life. Lonnie was standing by the front counter, by the cash register, where he could nearly always be found. I figured his motto was "Stay close to the money and then you'll never have to wonder where it is."

He give me a big hello just like he always did. I wasn't just his son-in-law; as the head of the Half-Moon I was his biggest customer. I didn't know which cut more ice with Lonnie. Folks said that Lonnie had been known to close up before midnight and on days other than Christmas and Thanksgiving, but I couldn't honestly say I'd ever seen it happen. No, that was a lie. He'd closed half a day when Nora and I had gotten married.

He said, "Well, son, just in town for a bit?"

"Had some banking business to do."

"Just stop by to visit or was there something you was needing?"

"Two kegs of nails."

He took out the little stub of pencil he had behind his ear and crouched over his order book. "What weight?"

"Tenpenny will be fine," I said.

I watched as he laboriously wrote out the order. When he was through he said, "What else?"

"That's all. Except I want you to deliver those kegs over to Norris's office. You know, on the second floor of the bank building. Just shove them over in a corner of his office."

He frowned. "Justa, if you need 'em before yore regular Friday delivery, why, I could send them out special. Wouldn't be no extra charge."

I shook my head. "No, no, that's not necessary. Just taking them over to Norris's office before Friday will work fine."

The whole idea worried him. Lonnie was a tall, skinny drink of water who was fast losing all his top hair. For the life of me I never could figure how he stayed so skinny when his wife was the best cook in Matagorda County. Worked it off counting his money, I figured. But then, I didn't want to be making fun of Lonnie's ways. He was a merchant and that was the way merchants were. Besides, if it hadn't of been for him I wouldn't have Nora. He said, "Justa, them kegs are pretty heavy. Weigh close to fifty pound apiece."

Yes, I thought, and they were going to maybe weigh a good deal more than that when I got through with them. I said, "Don't matter. But listen, Lonnie, make sure your delivery man takes his mallet and loosens the tops on both kegs. They are hell to get off if you ain't got the right tool."

"Oh, so you're going to be doing some work right there in the bank?"

I said, "I've got to get going, Lonnie." I was trying to get away before he could think of anything else to ask me, like what were we going to do with two kegs of big nails inside a bank. It appeared that when a party set out to take $25,000 in gold to Oklahoma it called for questions from all sides. And I hadn't even told Ray Hays yet about the trip. The way he was, with more curiosity than a pet raccoon, he'd likely nail me to the ground with questions. And of course, I wouldn't be able to answer them, not and keep to Howard's wishes. But it was going to seem damn strange, even to one of Hays's turn of mind, that we were carrying two kegs of tenpenny nails to Oklahoma.

Lonnie said, "Here! Don't run off. It's just now going on for ten o'clock. Couple more hours it'll be lunchtime. Always room for another plate."

"That's tempting, Lonnie. But I got to see the sheriff and then I need to get home. We're gathering cattle."

I went on out, turned right, and walked down the board-walk to Lew Vara's office. The sheriff was in, sitting behind his desk with his boots up on a corner, his arms folded, and a cigarillo in his mouth. I said, "Don't you worry about them voters, Lou. They can see you're on the job even if you ain't got your spurs on."

"I'm thinkin'," he said. "Job requires a certain amount of that."

I sat down in a wooden chair across from him. "Well, you'd want to take it careful on such a practice. Man could hurt hisself."

He brought his boots down to the floor with a thump. "What the hell you doing in town?"

Lew and I went back a lot of years to a time when we were both about nineteen and had done our level best to kill each other in the worst fistfight I'd ever had. He'd left the country after that, and had almost gotten on the other side of the law. He'd gone up into the Oklahoma Territory, where I was headed, and fallen in with bad company. Of course, there wasn't no shortage of that commodity up there then, or now as far as that went. But he'd come to his senses and come back home before he'd gone too far. As a favor for some well-appreciated help he'd given me and my family, we'd backed him for sheriff some seven or eight years back, and had had no cause to ever be sorry.

But just looking at him you'd be more likely to take him for a bandit than a sheriff. You looked at him from one direction he looked like a Mexican. From another side he looked like an Indian. And in some ways, he didn't look like either. He was about two inches shorter than I was, but about the same weight. Most of that weight was packed in his upper body, his shoulders and his arms and his big hands and neck. Lou was not anybody to take lightly. He wasn't particularly good with a handgun, but then he didn't have to be. He had a presence about him that could usually stop trouble before it got started.

I said, "Oh, getting some business set up I've got to tend to."

"I help?"

"Yeah," I said. "Friday afternoon I'll be coming out of the bank with twenty-five thousand dollars in gold hidden in two nail kegs. Be me and Ray Hays. We'll leave town riding north. I'm trying to keep this as quiet as I can, but I wish you'd back-trail me for about three or four miles. Make sure nobody in town has got wind of it and is looking to make a payday. Hang back about a mile, mile and a half."

"You don't want me to go further?"

That was Lou. Tell him you're riding out of town with $25,000 in gold in two nail kegs, and he don't even raise an eyebrow, much less ask any questions.

I said, "Naw, we're going a pretty good ways. I don't think the voters could spare you as long as I'll be gone."

He raised his arms and stretched. "I'm sorry to hear that. I won't have anybody to drink with. At least anybody that pays their share."

I got out a cigarillo and lit it. "You still remember the geography around Oklahoma, don't you?"

"Palm of my hand. That where you're headed?"

"Yeah. Anadarko. Any idea where that is?"

He leaned his elbows on the desk. "Smack dab in the

middle of the Indian Nation. My people, Cherokee."

I said, "I wish you'd get it straight. One day you ain't got no Indian blood, next day you do."

"Hell, I've always thought you had more Injun in you than I do. I swear there's a war chief somewhere in your background."

"Never mind about that," I said. "How far you figure it is up there?"

He gave me a look. "You don't mean by horseback?"

I nodded. I didn't know what there was to say.

He said, "A hell of a long ways. You make fifty miles a day, and that's pushing it over some parts of the country between here and there, and you'll be on the trail ten days at least."

I winced. God, ten days going. Then God only knows how long it would take me to find Charlie Stevens and get my business over with with him. And then the trip home. At least that could be by train. Still, it was a hell of a long time away from home. I said, "If you were to go and try and locate somebody up there how would you start?"

He let out a breath and thought. After a moment he said, "Well, if they was Indian, I'd go to the Tribal Council right there in Chickasha. They got records on everybody. An' even if he ain't Indian, they know more about what goes on in the whole state than the governor. Naw, I'd check in with the Tribal Council before I did anything. Of course you're not telling me you're going horseback all the way to Oklahoma to see somebody you don't know where is. You wouldn't do that, not even you."

I got up. "You're right. Even I wouldn't do that."

"You got time to go down to Crook's, get a beer?"

I shook my head and said I'd better get on back to the ranch. I started to turn for the door, but on a thought came back to Lew. I told him what Norris had said about Shay Jordan coming to his office and advising him there was more than one way to settle a land dispute outside of a lawsuit. I said, "Lew, I wish you'd keep an eye and an ear on this business. I've warned Ben to stay clear unless somebody actually starts shooting, but it worries me, me going off like this."

"Aw, hell, that Shay is just a smart-aleck kid."

"He ain't no kid. And that gun he's always packing is full growed."

"You want me to ride out there and talk to Rex Jordan? Tell him to hobble the boy?"

I thought about it a minute. I finally said, "Naw, it's liable to cause more trouble than help. They're liable to think we're picking on them, running to the sheriff. Let's just let it lie. Maybe nothing else will happen. Get the damn matter in a courtroom and get it settled."

Lew just shook his head. "Them Jordans must be damn fools. Hell, yore daddy has *occupied* that piece of land for thirty years. That's a proven fact. Do they really think they can come along now and make a real claim?"

I shrugged. "I think they're just shaking the money tree. Hoping some will fall off. They know they can't win, but they're hoping we'll give them something just to get rid of them. Of course if we did that, then everybody and his brother would be trying the same game."

"Well, don't let it plague you. I'll keep a close eye on the situation, and if any of them Jordans so much as spit on the sidewalk I'll find a place for them to have a good long think on the matter."

I told Lew I'd see him Friday, and then went out the door and down to the bank, where my horse was. I was still riding the sorrel gelding and liking him better every day. He was a good traveling horse, and I had pretty much made up my mind to use him for the Oklahoma trip. He was a long three-year-old, nearly a four, and he had a gait that just ate up the ground. I got on him and turned him east, toward the gulf and toward home. If I hurried I could get there in time for lunch with Nora.

I was just a bit out of town when I heard someone calling my name. Whoever he was, he was just leaving town and coming toward me on the little wagon track that ran due east. The rider was still a good quarter of a mile away so

I couldn't see him clearly, but I could hear him yelling, "Williams! Williams! Williams, damnit, stop!"

I pulled up, turned my horse, and waited to see who could have such important business with me they had to shout my family name all over the prairie. The rider came on, bringing his horse at a hard gallop. I sat my horse, waiting, watching him come on. At a hundred yards I thought it was Rex Jordan. At sixty or fifty yards I was sure it was, though I'd only seen the man a couple of times. About forty yards away he started pulling his horse up, but the animal was hot and was fighting his head and didn't want to stop. I watched Jordan sawing on the reins, ruining the horse's mouth, standing up in the stirrups and using his weight on the horse's mouth. Finally he got him down to a sideways canter, the horse still flinging his head every which way, doing his best to tell Jordan to quit yanking on the goddam reins, and then finally down to a nervous, fast-footed walk. He came straight at me, his right arm pointed out, a finger sticking out of the fist he was pointing at me. He yelled, even though we were only a few yards apart, "Williams, I want to talk to you, by gawd!"

He was red in the face. I didn't know if it was from anger or from trying to cold-jaw his horse. I said, "Well, here I am. Talk."

He pushed his horse right up next to mine, so close we could have touched. Jordan was a tough-faced man with a scar under his eye. He might have been in his late forties, but his body looked hard and thick. He was a good deal shorter than me, but he was beefy and bullnecked. I noticed, as I had before, that he wore the narrow-brimmed hat of a man who wasn't native to Texas.

He jabbed his finger at me and said, "I'm gonna warn you an' I ain't gonna warn ya but this oncet. . . . That high-hat brother'n of yours, that fancy-pants Norris er whatever his name is—he goes to pullin' them bullyboy stunts on my boy Shay a'gin an' we goin' to war, you unnerstan' me?"

His finger was coming a little closer to my face than I cared to have it. I reached up and knocked his arm away with my left hand. "Jordan, I don't know what the hell you are talking about. You got a complaint with me you calm down and make some sense. Don't come riding up to me yelling your fool head off about goin' to war. I don't have the slightest idea what you are talking about."

He was still so mad spit was flecking out of his mouth when he talked. "I'll by gawd tell you what I'm talkin' 'bout. I'm talkin' 'bout all you goddam Williams and your goddam bullyboy ways. You don't own this goddam country n' it's about time you—"

"Get off your horse."

"An' you messin' with the wrong bunch of folks you come courtin' trouble with us. Tellin' my boy you's gonna run us outten the country. Lis'sen, by gawd, I'm gonna tell you a thang or two. I—"

"I said, GET OFF YOUR HORSE!"

He stared at me then. "What'd you say?"

"I said get off your horse."

He spat. Not at me, but closer than I cared for. "Mister, you can go screw a mule tellin' me when to git on er off my horse. Lis'sen, I'm by gawd—"

My gun was suddenly in my hand. "I'll tell you once more. Get off your horse."

His mouth closed as abruptly as if he'd closed it to keep a bug from flying in. He stared at the revolver in my hand. He said, a little unsteadily, "That a pistol in yore hand?"

"That's damn good, Jordan. Next you'll notice there's a hat on my head and a shirt on my back. Get off your horse. Now!"

I could see he wanted to ask me what for. I didn't want him to ask me that because I didn't know the answer. I was angry, bad angry, and I was trying to calm myself down before I did something I'd regret later. I watched as he pulled his horse back to give himself room, then dismounted. I said, "Drop them reins."

He said, "My horse'll run off."

"Shit," I said in disgust. Man didn't even know how to train a horse to ground-rein. I eased out of the saddle. We were standing between our two horses. Jordan was about three feet away. He was wearing a sidegun, but he was carefully keeping his hands wide of his sides.

"Pull a gun on a man," he said. But he was all eyes for the .42/.40-caliber Colt revolver in my hand. "By gawd, it'll be murder. They'll ketch you."

"Shut up, Jordan," I said. "I'm not going to shoot you. I pulled the gun because you wouldn't shut your big mouth. And you were putting it on my family. Now I'm going to tell you something. You ever bad-mouth my family and I hear about it, I *will* pull a gun, only I'll use it next time. You understand that?"

He just stared at me, pure anger and hate in his eyes. "I unn'erstan' any sonofabitch can talk tough when he's holdin' a gun on a man ain't got one in his hand. You put that sonofabitch up and see how tough you talk."

"Jordan, you are trash. I was hoping you wouldn't turn out to be so, but I see, on short acquaintance, that you are." I shoved the revolver back in its holster. "There. Now what do—"

He charged me with his head down like a billy goat butting a stump. It happened so sudden that it took me off guard. He smashed into me and the momentum knocked me backwards. I was just able to wrap my arms around his back and carry him over with me as I fell. As we hit the ground I whipped up my right boot and got it in his belly and gave a hard push. Even as heavy as he was, and I figured he outweighed me by ten pounds, he went flying off to the side and landed on his back in the dust. I jumped to my feet. He was scrambling, trying to get up. I let him get almost erect, and then I hit him flush in the face with a hard, driving right. I didn't care if he was a forty-year-old man. He and I were going to have to reach an understanding and damn quick or I was going to beat him to death.

The right hand knocked him straight backwards. He flailed his arms, trying to keep his balance and not go down. I stepped forward and hooked a left into the side of his head. It knocked him sideways. There was an ugly red splotch in the middle of his face and his nose was leaking blood. But even off balance he got his hands up and drew his right fist back, drawing it way back to throw a haymaker. I said, "That goes back much further you are going to have to put a postage stamp on it." Then I hit him two quick left jabs, rocking him back on his heels, and then hit him a hard, jolting right on the jaw. He dropped down to his knees and then fell over on his side.

I wasn't particularly proud of myself. He wasn't much of a fighter. I could tell from his style that he liked to grab on to somebody and then wrestle around in the dirt and use his strength and size. Well, I'd quit doing that in grammar school.

I said, "Get up, Jordan."

He was trying to push himself up with his arms, but he was still a little woozy. I reached down, got him by the shirt collar with both hands, and dragged him to his feet. He was still unsteady, so I give him a good shaking. I said, "Jordan. Jordan! Jordan, look at me!"

He shook his head as if to clear it, then slowly raised his hand and touched his face, and then looked at the blood on his hand. He said, "Fuckin' son'bitch, gonna kill yore ass." He mumbled it, but I heard it plain. I let go of his collar with my right hand and ripped an uppercut into his belly just below his ribs. The blow almost lifted him off his feet. He went, "Hooooooo," and fell backwards, his collar jerking out of the hold I still had on him with my left hand. He landed on his back, struggling for breath. I stood over him watching him gasp and heave. I was patient. I knew it'd be a moment or two before he could get his breath back.

Finally his breathing got somewhere near normal, and he struggled up on one elbow and then sat up. One of his eyes was starting to close and his nose was bleeding worse. Every lick I'd hit him had raised a lump. I squatted down where we could be eye to eye. I said, "You just threatened to kill me. You want to try it here and now?"

He didn't answer, just sat there panting, one arm resting over a knee. I noticed he'd lost his revolver. It was laying in the dust about five yards back of him. I also noticed his horse had run off. It hadn't gone far, just a few yards off the wagon track and into some tall grass, where it was grazing. My horse was standing where I'd left him.

I said, "Jordan, I asked you a question. You threatened to kill me. I'm not planning on letting that pass. You look like a bushwhacker to me, and I don't plan on riding around this country looking over my shoulder. You want to settle it here and now?"

He made a little surrender move with his hand. He said, lowly, "Didn't mean it. I was mad as hell. I ain't no bushwhacker. I jest got mad about my boy Shay and what yore brother tol' him."

"Happens I heard a different kind of story. And it happens I know my brother Norris a hell of a lot better than you or your son. Norris don't threaten. That ain't his style. And he wouldn't threaten to run anybody out of the country. The way I heard it was your boy, Shay, come in my brother's office, uninvited, and showed him that revolver he likes to flash around so well, and told Norris there was more than one way to settle a land dispute."

He looked up at me. He was still breathing hard. "Then why would the boy come and tell me what he done for? I was goin' in to see yore brother Norris when I seen you coming out of town. I know you be the boss. I thought I'd take it up with you."

"You got a damn strange way of going about things. I don't know where you're from, Jordan, but folks around here don't take to having their kin bad-mouthed and they don't take to a lot of yelling and threats. Now, I don't know why Shay told you what he did, but I know what Norris said passed in that office. So far nothing has come of it but a scuffle between me and you. But if it gets to picking up speed it might get out of hand. You understand what I'm saying?"

He put his jaw in his hand and worked it back and forth for a minute. "Maybe Shay overtol' it. He puts on the dog ever' once in a while."

61

I started to say, "Maybe Shay lied," but I didn't. You've got to leave a man a little pride. You push his face in the dirt too hard and he'll never be clean with you. I said, "The matter is going to court. We're satisfied to let a judge rule."

He worked his jaw again. "I'm willin' to let it be over. You hit mighty hard, Mister Williams."

I stood up. "Then let's let it be at an end. I've got to leave the county for a few days, and I'd like to know there ain't going to be no flare-ups about this. My youngest brother Ben tends to be a hothead. I'd hate to have any trouble start while I'm gone."

He pushed off the ground and got to his feet. "Suits me," he said.

I pointed. "Your revolver is back behind you. I'll catch up your horse."

I deliberately turned my back on him, knowing he was picking up his pistol, and walked to my horse and mounted. Still without looking back, I rode over to his horse, caught up the reins, and took him back to Rex Jordan. He took the reins without a word. He hadn't apologized for bad-mouthing my family, so I was damned if I'd say I was sorry for punching his face in. But I said, "Your brother . . . I ain't ever met him."

He swung into the saddle. "Luther? He's younger than me. By a good ten years."

"I ain't seen him around."

Jordan said, "He just got outta jail. Down in Mexico. Been kind of enjoyin' life. Know what I mean?"

"Yeah," I said. I nodded and turned my horse for home. I wasn't all that pleased to hear that he had the kind of brother could get himself thrown in jail in Mexico. But by the same token I couldn't make too much out of it because Norris had done the same thing. But I somehow doubted it was for the same reason.

I rode along, flexing my right hand. I'd hurt it on Jordan's hard head when I'd hit him on the side of the jaw. The first time I'd hit him his hat had flown off and I could see he was mostly bald on top. But I didn't figure it was on account of age. Some men I had known went bald in their early thirties. And there wasn't nothing old about Jordan's strength. I'd felt it when he'd charged me, butting me in the chest and trying to get his arms around me to squeeze me like a vise. You didn't want a man like that to get too close to you. Fortunately, my arms were long enough to hold him off.

But even though we'd both said the matter was settled, I was still troubled. The family was trash. I didn't like to go around calling people a name like that, but I didn't know any other that fit.

And then there was the brother, Luther. I didn't know anything about him, but I did hate to be going off for such a long time with an ex-resident of a Mexican jail lined up on the side opposite my family.

But then, we weren't exactly defenseless. Ben was worth any four men they could bring up against him, and at least half of our dozen regular hired hands could use a gun to some good effect. And there was still Buttercup and his shoulder-held cannon. He was no bigger than a dried frog, and yet able to make a shot at 500 yards that few men half his age would attempt, much less hope to make a success.

And there was Lew Vara to keep an eye on the situation.

I decided to hell with it. If a man set out to worry about all the possible trouble that could come his way, he'd never get anything done but worry. Still, I couldn't help but think that Howard had a hell of a nerve asking for his little errand at such a time. I glanced at the sun and kicked the sorrel into a lope. I might still make it in time for lunch, though I didn't know how I was going to explain my skinned knuckles to Nora. I couldn't tell her the truth because it would just cause her to worry and to also give me a good scolding for not handling things in a more civilized manner. Nora was never going to learn that there were some people and some situations that just did not respond to a civilized approach. All they did was take it for a sign of weakness.

CHAPTER 4

I didn't get home for lunch with Nora on account of I swung by the big house to have a word with Ray Hays. I knew the men would be in for the noon meal because they were working close to headquarters, holding the "cut," the steers we'd be shipping, in a little pasture right up next to the barns.

As I rode up toward the house I spied Hays lallygagging around the bunkhouse, and I rode up and dismounted. Hays said, "Hell, here's the boss. What have you got to say for yourself there, Mister Williams?"

I said, "Let's me and you walk off a little ways and have a talk."

It kind of alarmed him at first, but when I assured him I wasn't about to fire him, not that he didn't deserve it, he relaxed a bit. Ray was a slightly built man with sandy hair and a pleasant, open face. You could josh him and you could kid him so long as you were his friend. If you weren't, it was not a smart thing to push him too far. We walked along and Hays said, "Boy, Boss, feel that fall air? Don't it make the sap just rise in yore tree? Boy, howdy! This is my kind of weather."

I looked sideways at him and shook my head. Ray was from west Texas, and out there mid-October meant crisp, cool weather. The fact that it still felt like August must have gotten past him somehow. But that was the way he thought.

It was October, it was fall, and it was time to howl.

He said, "Can't wait fer Saturday night. Hear Miss Maybelle has got some new girls. Ah'm goin' in an' have me a ripsnorter of a time. If I don't feel like I need a doctor Sunday morning ah'm gonna feel like I been cheated."

We'd walked far enough away from the other cowboys hanging around the door of the bunkhouse so we couldn't be overheard. I stopped us. I said, "Hays, me and you are fixing to take us a little trip horseback. Cross-country. Pick you out a good traveling horse, a good stayer, because we're going a pretty good piece. We'll be leaving the ranch right after the noon meal Friday. Day after tomorrow. We'll be gone the better part of two weeks."

His jaw was hanging open. "What about Saturday night?"

"Oh, there'll still be a Saturday night. Only thing is that me and you will be spending it out on the prairie somewhere."

"Aw, hell, Boss . . . I was countin' on goin' in to Miss Maybelle's place Saturday night and washin' off a little of this hard work."

I didn't pay him any mind. I said, "Now this is strictly between you and me. When you go to gathering up supplies and folks start asking you questions, you don't know nothing. All you're doing is what I told you to do. You understand that?"

"Yeah," he said kind of listlessly.

"Pick out a good packhorse. I know we ain't got no regular packhorses, but do like that time I was headed for Del Rio. Get one that is solid and gentle and won't spook and that can keep up with us if we have to run. Get a big horse because it'll be carrying a pretty good load."

Hays said, "Boss, you sure I'm the right one for this job? I mean—"

"Hush," I said. "I may need a gun and I may need a steady man in a fight. You recommend anybody else outside of Ben?"

He sighed. He knew there was no way out. "I reckon not." Then he suddenly brightened. "We wouldn't be headed for any hot spots, would we? Like Dallas or Houston or Galveston?"

"Might pass some along the way," I said. "Doubt we'll have much time to frolic."

"Well . . ." he said, looking dejected.

"I want you to go to the cooks and get some trail grub. Get a bunch of smoked beef and some cheese and as much bread or biscuits as won't go stale. And get a bunch of canned goods. And locate a ground sheet. And get several of them big canteens. You can spend Thursday morning getting it all rigged up. I'll tell Ben I got you busy at something else. And you don't want to forget your carbine or extra cartridges. Hell, you know what gear to pack. And what grub."

"Where we goin'?" he asked.

"Why, Ray, I thought you'd be happier than this about the trip. You are always complaining about being stuck here on the ranch. Well, I'm giving you the chance to be stuck out on the prairie."

"Yessir," he said, but without much spirit.

"You get us all packed and ready and then eat with the crew. I'll come along about one o'clock and we'll take off. Understand?"

"Yessir. I'll get her done."

That was Ray. He'd grouch and slouch for a little, but then, come Friday, he'd be as anxious to go as if it had been his own idea.

He said again, "Where we goin'?"

"Why Ray, you ought to know me well enough by now to have known that if I was going to answer that question I'd of answered it the first time."

"So you ain't gonna tell me? Jest drag me off 'crost the prairie no idea where ah'm bound for?"

"No, I'm not going to tell you. And the reason I'm not going to tell you is because you would probably tell somebody else and I don't want anybody else to know."

"Awww, Boss," he said, "I ain't gonna tell nobody else."

I started back toward my horse. "I know you're not because you ain't got anything to tell anybody."

I mounted up, leaving a disgruntled Ray Hays in my dust, and rode home. I put the sorrel up, unsaddling him and turning him into the corral. I wasn't through work for the day, but I wanted him to start getting rested up for the work he had ahead.

I was too late to eat with Nora, but she laid me out a meal of cold beef and tomatoes and onions with some light bread. She made a fresh pot of coffee and sat down to have a cup with me. I told her what I'd been up to.

"Friday, huh?"

"Yeah," I said, busy eating. "I'll have lunch with you and then take off."

"Must you be gone all that time?"

I shrugged. "If I do it the way Howard wants. Hell, it's a long ways. He's got a calendar. I can't show back up here in a week and claim we just kind of pushed the horses a bit."

She sighed. "It's just such a long time." She looked up at me. "Now that I've gotten used to sleeping with you I can't sleep by myself as good."

"Why don't you go in and stay with your parents? You know how much your mama and Lonnie enjoy having J.D. to make over."

"Yes, and they just spoil him rotten. What happened to your knuckles?"

I gave them a quick glance. "I barked them on some kegs in the back of your daddy's store. Dark back in that part. I was looking for the right size. Anyway, I hate the idea of you staying out here by yourself all that time. I know you got Juanita, but she ain't no company. Go in and stay with your folks. It would make me feel better."

"Did you drop a keg on your knuckles?" She reached up and took hold of my right hand. "This hand is swollen. Justa, have you been fighting?"

"Nora, one of the kegs got loose and slid around and slammed my hand against another one. A keg of nails weighs a ton. What's the matter with you? Who the hell would I get in a fight with?"

She gave me her look that said she knew something wasn't quite right, but since she couldn't prove it she'd let it go . . . this time. But don't figure to keep on getting away with these stunts, mister.

I said, "Hell, honey, I've got to go off for a good long time. Let's don't have no unpleasantness at a time like this."

She gave me an appraising look but, since she didn't have proof, she had to say, "You're right. I swear, I'm turning into a worse nag than my mother. But Justa, you have to admit I never know what you are liable to get into next."

I gave her a half smile and shook my head. "You just can't quit being the schoolteacher, can you? Of course if you want to act like a schoolteacher, I wouldn't mind staying after school and dusting your erasers."

She blushed. "Justa, it's the middle of the day. You ought not to talk like that."

I reached under the table and got my hand on the inside of her thigh. "What kind of talk? I'm just talking about dusting your erasers."

"You know very well what you meant. And get your hand out of there."

"I've got to get me enough to hold me for the next two weeks. That's going to take a lot. Reckon we could start now?"

"Justa, you are getting awful! Do you want Juanita to hear us? My heavens!"

"Juanita can't even speak English, much less understand this kind of talk. But if you're worried, we could go out into the barn."

Now she did blush. She put her hand to her cheek and said, "Justa Williams, what has come over you? Do you hear yourself talking? My heavens above!"

Of course I was just joking, knowing I didn't have no more chance than a Catholic fish at Friday night supper. Not that Nora wasn't nearly more than I could handle when we got right down to it, but she no longer was that sassy girl I used to court now she was a wife and a mother. And wives and mothers didn't fuck in the daytime, especially if there was anybody else in the house.

She ran me off pretty promptly and I got a different horse, a little bay mare, and went out and worked the rest of the afternoon with Harley getting the herds shaped up for the final cut. After that I came home just about dark, took me a cold shower in my little stall outside by the barn, and then had supper with Nora while J.D. watched and drooled over a piece of hard candy he didn't have the teeth to bite with.

After supper I went up for our usual drink and meeting. Dad was up and appeared to be feeling good. Looking at Howard, I told my brothers that if they had anything to get settled with me they'd better get it done then or the next night because I was leaving on a long trip Friday afternoon. I said, still looking at Howard, "And I mean a *loooong* trip. Maybe three weeks." Howard wouldn't meet my eye. Instead he leaned over to spit tobacco juice in a spittoon. I didn't blame him. If I was doing to him what he was doing to me, I couldn't face him either.

Ben said, "Three weeks! Where the hell are you going?"

Norris gave me a little half smile. He said, "I hope you're back when that land trial with the Jordans comes up."

I said, "No court date been set yet, Norris. I saw Huggins three or four days ago."

Jake Huggins was our lawyer. He didn't live in Blessing, but business brought him down often enough that we stayed in close touch.

Ben said, "Where the hell are you going?"

"North," I said shortly.

"What for?"

I looked at Howard again. I said, "I'm going to investigate the sawmill business."

"Sawmill? We going to set up a sawmill? Hell, I can't see us doing that. What the hell do we need with a sawmill? Why don't we stick to what we know, cattle and horses?"

I said, "It's Howard's idea."

The old man cleared his throat. He said, "One of you boys want to hand me another drink? That first one was so weak I didn't know whether to swaller it or wash my hands in it."

Ben looked over at me. I shrugged. While he took the old man a watered drink I said, "Norris, we have given Huggins every available paper we have, haven't we? Every title, every grant, no matter how old?"

Norris said, "I'm not a lawyer, but we've got proof about four times over that we own that land. And that's not counting the law of constant usage."

Ben said, "Hell, Justa, there's gonna be a hell of a horse sale in San Antonio in two weeks. Listen, we've got to have some new blood. They are going to have some damn good horses there. Stock from clean up to Kentucky and Tennessee. Hell!"

I said, "Then go to San Antonio and buy some new breeding stock. I never told you you couldn't."

His face lit up. "Now you're talking, big brother. What kind of money I got to work with?"

I looked at Howard, but said to Norris, "Oh, anything up to twenty-five thousand dollars. Norris can set it some way on the books so it'll look like it's benefiting the company."

Ben gave me a puzzled look. "What the hell are you talking about? Of course it will be benefiting the company. It'll improve the horse herd, and the horses are part of the ranch, and the ranch is part of this here company Norris is always talking about, ain't it?"

"Yeah," I said. "Twenty-five thousand be enough?"

"Lord, yes," he said. "I wasn't hoping for anything like that."

Howard cleared his throat again and said, "Appears to me that one of my sons is tryin' to make a point without comin' right out and sayin' it."

Of course it went right over Norris and Ben's heads.

Ben looked at Howard and then at me. He said, "What the hell's going on here?"

I said, "Ben, I'm taking Ray Hays with me."

"Naw," he said. "Hell, Justa, I need Ray in San Antonio with me to look at that horseflesh."

I said, "You can get drunk enough on your own. You don't need Ray Hays to help you run around them San Antonio *cantinas* and whorehouses. By the way, tell him to take some cold-weather clothes. I just told him we were heading north. I didn't say how far."

"Well, how far?"

I shrugged. "Till we find somebody in the sawmill industry we're interested in." I changed the subject before anyone could say anything. "I ran into Rex Jordan this afternoon. And I mean I literally ran into him." Without making any more out of it than had to be told, I described what had happened. "So I want to be damn sure that we don't give them any kind of provocation. Stay clear of the whole family. And if you can't avoid them, walk as lightly as you can."

Norris had been about to come out of his chair ever since I'd told the part about Rex saying that Norris had threatened Shay. He waited until I'd finished, but then he said, "Why that lying little punk! If there was any bullyboy tactics they were on his part! I've a good mind to see Jordan on the street and straighten him out about the matter."

I said, "No, you've a good mind to let the matter lay. We know the truth of what happened and so does Rex Jordan. But they have a weak case in court and they know it. They're looking for trouble, so you stay the hell away from Shay Jordan. And all the Jordans for that matter."

Norris said, "He *came* into my office. I didn't invite him. What am I supposed to do the next time he comes swaggering around making sure I can see he's wearing a gun, get up and leave my own office?"

I said, "No. Tell him to leave. If he doesn't, then send for the sheriff."

Norris said, "I'll just be damned if I'll let some little punk like that force me to call the law. I can take care of Mister Shay Jordan!"

I ran my hand through my hair and shook my head tiredly. "Norris, don't give me no more grief than I already got. You're not a gunman. You're—"

He said, "I can take care of myself, whether you and Ben think so or not."

I said, "Let me finish. You're not a gunman, neither am I. You're a businessman and I'm a cattle breeder. Shay Jordan ain't a gunman either, but he's trash and he's a smart-aleck kid that thinks it makes him a man to go shoving around and bragging and acting like a jackass. All you can get out of a scuffle with Shay Jordan is trouble. If you win you lose because you'll be the big, mean, rich ol' Norris Williams who not only is stealing land from the poor Jordans, you've got to beat him up or shoot him in the bargain. You got to realize that everybody around here does not love us. There are more than just a few who are a shade past jealous and who wouldn't like anything better than to see us taken down a notch or two. Right now we don't need no more public sentiment against us, not with a land dispute case coming up."

But Norris was still being stubborn. He said, "I won't kowtow to any such as that Jordan fool."

I sighed. "Norris, your manhood is not being challenged here. You are good enough to handle Shay Jordan, but you are not good enough to handle him in the right way, and that way is to put him out of business without him getting hurt or you getting hurt. I doubt that I am. I even have some doubts that Ben is. Ain't none of us in this room a Wilson Young, so let's stay the hell away from trouble."

Norris said, "I will take whatever steps seem appropriate."

Ben said, "Oh, hell, Norris, listen to Justa. Dammit, you can't be satisfied with being smarter and having more book learning than me and Justa. You want to be just as tough."

Norris said, "Taking sides again. That's the way it was when we were kids and that's the way it's always been. Sometimes I feel like I'm not even related to you two."

Howard said, "Boys, don't fight! This is family."

I said, "Norris, I have given Ben the exact same instructions. Last night. You heard them. I told him to stay the hell away from the Jordans. You heard me say that, didn't you, Ben."

"I did."

I said, "So both of you listen. I've got to go off on this damn fool trip, and all I'm asking is that you keep the lid on the kettle until I can get back. Don't send me off worrying about what might be happening while I'm gone."

Norris looked sour, but he said, "Very well. Very well, I'll tuck my tail between my legs and cross to the other side of the street if I so much as meet a Jordan on the boardwalk."

I looked at Ben. He said, putting his hands up in the air, "You ain't heard me saying a word. I'm minding my own business."

"Thanks," I said. I drained my tumbler, set it on the floor, picked up my hat, and got up and started for the door.

Howard creaked out of his rocker. He said, "Son, I'll just walk with you to the door."

I gave him a look, but he just shooed me on ahead. I turned out of the room and walked down the long, dark hall to the back door. I opened it and stepped out onto the small back porch. Howard came as far as the open door. He said, "Son, I know you're having terrible thoughts about me for asking you this favor."

"Howard, I am way on past terrible."

"Son, you'll understand it when you see Charlie Stevens and talk to him. I'm carrying a parcel that's got to be opened up or I'm going to bust."

"There you go with that mystery hoopla again. Why can't you just tell me what all this is about and let's mail this man a check care of General Delivery in Anadarko, Oklahoma, and save me one hell of a lot of trouble."

He looked plain miserable. "Justa, there's things he can tell you, about me, about what I done . . ."

"Why don't you tell me yourself?"

He shook his old head. "I can't. I done told you it ain't in me to do it. I can't make the words come out of my mouth. But it's important that you know. And when you know, then you can decide if your brothers ought to know. At least I won't have that burden. Took me long enough to decide *you* should know."

"Now wait a minute. This is something new. First you didn't want me even mentioning much about this trip to my brothers. Now you tell me I might find out something that they ought to know. Now just what in hell is going on here, Howard?"

But he was shaking his head and pulling back into the house. "I've said all I better say. I maybe ought not to have said what I did, except I wanted you to understand I wouldn't send you off like this unless it was mighty important."

I stopped him from closing the door in my face. Holding it with one hand, I pointed with the other in the general direction of the office. I said, "I hope to hell you do understand that this is not the right time for me to be leaving. We do have that land dispute, and we've already had two run-ins with the Jordans. I don't see why you can't wait until this business is cleared up and settled."

He was shaking his head again. "Court cases can drag on and on. And then something else would come up. There ain't no real good time for something like this to get done. But I know I'm going fast. I can feel the strength leaving me."

It wasn't like Howard to talk about his health. But I still felt like he was using it on me like a quirt. I said, "Aw, hell, Howard, you'll probably outlive the lot of us. But I promise you this, old man. If I make that long, cold, weary, lonesome trip to Oklahoma and get your business done, you better damn well die quick. If you don't I'm liable to kill you myself."

He at least had the good grace to smile a little. "You got to indulge an old man a little, Justa."

"Fine." I pointed in the direction of the office again. "But you better sit on them two hotheads while I'm gone or you are liable to see all your work go up in smoke. Or at least nine thousand acres of it."

"I'll tend to 'em," he said.

"Of course you will," I said. "Just like you only have one whiskey a day like the doctor ordered you. Good night, Howard. I don't know how well a man that lies as much as you do sleeps, but get as much as you can."

Nora was still awake when I got home, but she was in bed with the overhead lantern on. She said, "Well, did Howard have any more surprises for you?"

I was sitting in a chair taking off my boots. "No. Fact of the business is, I got in a few licks myself. Said things to my brothers that were intended for him. He walked me out to the door and said I'd understand when it all got done."

"What do you suppose he's talking about?"

I shook my head. "Beats the hell out of me. Even with this trouble with the Jordans coming up, he's still dead set on me going."

"Are you worried about that?"

I shrugged and stood up and took off my pants and shirt. "I'm always worried about leaving Ben and Norris to their own devices when there's any thinking to be made. Norris is still taking his visit from Shay Jordan personally. All I can hope is that Ben can hold him down while I'm gone."

"That's certainly different."

"Ain't it," I said. I went over, and was fixing to turn the lamp off when Nora reminded me I hadn't cleaned my teeth. I said, "Aw, hell, teeth don't need cleaning all that often. I done it this morning."

"March in that bathroom and do like you are supposed to."

So I went in and put a mixture of baking soda and salt on my toothbrush and gave my teeth a good working over. Then I rinsed out my mouth good because baking soda and salt ain't the best-tasting stuff in the world. When I went back in the bedroom and slid in beside Nora I said, "Well, at least one good thing about this trip is I won't have nobody around correcting my grammar or telling me not to cuss in the house or to brush my teeth twice a day. Lordy, that'll be a relief."

She got over next to me, next to my bare skin, and I could tell she wasn't wearing her nightgown. She said, "Yeah, but I bet I know one thing about that trip you're not going to feel so good about."

I turned toward her. I said, "I'm already thinking about it."

CHAPTER 5

I wasn't able to get away without Howard getting one more lick in on me as to how important the trip was to him. I'd had lunch with Nora on Friday and then kissed her and J.D. good-bye. After that I'd saddled the sorrel gelding and ridden up to where Hays was waiting with his own mount and the packhorse. It was already going on for two o'clock and I didn't have a hell of a lot of time to spare, but Howard was out on the front porch in his rocking chair and he waved me to come up. I rode up to the porch, expecting him just to wish me a safe trip, but nothing would do him but to dismount and come up and sit down.

"Son," he said, "I appreciate this. I want you to know it."

"Then let me get on with it," I said.

"I just want you to be sure and tell Charlie Stevens how sorry I feel and how I hope he can find it in his heart to forgive me."

"Hell, twenty-five thousand ought to speak real loud for you. If he can't hear that he ain't going to be able to hear anything I've got to say."

"I'm just a-fear'd that Charlie won't understand why I done what I did. See, down here by myself things had gotten mighty tight. I mean, I was so hemmed up by troubles that I didn't have room to cuss a cat."

"All right. I'll tell him that."

He reached out and clutched at my upper arm. "Son, you've got to make him understand it took a power of temptation to do what I did. To steal from him like that."

I frowned. "Howard, has all that whiskey you've drunk all these years finally reached your brain? First you stole the money, then it was a loan, now you're back to stealing it."

He cut his eyes away from mine. "I ain't talkin' about the money."

I stood up. "Aw, hell, Howard, you are one too many for me. You and your mysteries. Only mystery to me is your memory. I'm probably going to get about halfway there and it's going to come to you there ain't no Charlie Stevens."

"Now, Justa . . ." he said.

But I was going down the steps. I said, "We got to get kicking. It's a hell of a long way to Oklahoma." I waved over my shoulder as I swung my horse and mounted. Hays was waiting about a hundred yards away, and he turned and took the packhorse on lead as I came up even with him and his mount.

As we rode into town I was feeling a little guilty about the hard time I'd been giving Howard. I knew most of the irritation was caused by the particular way he wanted me to carry out this job, but I was also frustrated by him insisting it be done at a time when I felt I should have been home. But hell, if I matched that off against all that he had done for me through the years, he was way out in front on the giving. Still and all, I thought he was using his age and his time of life as a sort of lever on me. But that was Howard. And after all, I could have refused. I was the boss.

But I decided there was no point in being mad at him for the whole time the trip was going to take. If I did that I was going to be feeling pretty miserable for a long time. Best thing to do was just to get after it and get home as fast as possible.

Hays said, "Boss, when you goin' to tell me where we be goin'? Ben told me to take some warm clothes, so I packed a sheepskin jacket in with my gear, but time of the year being what it is, I could need that in a lot of places."

"Hays, I'll make a deal with you. I'll tell you where we're going when we get there. How's that? That way you won't be wondering every time we make a camp if we've arrived at our destination."

It took him in for a moment. "Hell, that seems pretty fair. I . . ." Then he caught himself and looked over at me. "Boss, that don't sound right."

"Why not?"

He studied on it a moment, and then he said, "I dunno, but it don't. Let's say we make our third camp. How am I gonna know if that's the next to last one or if they's a half a dozen more to go?"

"You got a point there."

"Well?"

The roofs of the buildings of Blessing were just starting to rise out of the prairie. I said, "Well, what?"

"Well, when you going to tell me? Where we're going?"

"When we get there."

"Aw, hell."

We rode in silence for a few minutes, and then he said, "How come I can't know? Don't seem fair to drag a feller off on a trip an' not tell him where he's headed."

"Yeah, you're right. It don't seem fair."

"So I am just supposed to shut up and not worry about it?"

"Ray," I said, "now you are getting the idea."

As we jogged along I looked over at the packhorse. Under my directions Ray and a couple other of the hired hands had taken a wagon sheet, doubled it, and sewn it together and then made big pockets on both sides. I wanted each one of those pockets to hold a nail keg so too much weight wouldn't be on one side of the horse or the other. And the pockets were big enough to also hold our own gear—our grub, bedrolls, ground sheet, cooking utensils, and other paraphernalia. It was a much better arrangement than it would have been using a packsaddle that would have thrown all that weight right on the horse's back. The pack was girthed forward and back, so that the two pockets wouldn't swing and slam into the horse. I figured the horse wasn't carrying any more than 160 pounds. But of course, dead weight like that is heavier than, say, a 190-pound man who, if he's a fair hand at riding, works with the horse and ain't too big of a strain on the animal. Ben had about the lightest seat of any man I knew. You could take two similar horses, and put Ben on one and another man of Ben's weight on the other, and send them off across the prairie, and Ben would get ten, fifteen miles more out of his mount. It was a gift. You couldn't learn it and you couldn't teach it. You were either born with it or you weren't.

We finally got into town. I looked at my watch. It was ten minutes after three. The bank would have closed at three o'clock, but I slowed us down and we made our way through the streets at a slow pace. I wanted to make sure any lingering customers would have gotten through with their business and out the door before I went in. We got to the bank, and the shades were drawn over the two big front windows. I got down off my horse, telling Ray to just wait right there on the street. Coming into town I had caught sight of Lew Vara sauntering along the boardwalk, and now I looked and saw him heading casually in our direction. I figured he'd take him a position so as not to be noticeable and hang around while we got the gold loaded.

I went up to the door of the bank. The shade over the half window was pulled down. I knocked and, in a moment, the shade was pulled back and Bill Simms peered out at me. As soon as he recognized who it was, he unlocked the door and pulled it back and I stepped in. There were still a few clerks and tellers tending to their business, but they never paid me no mind. A lot of folks don't know that the business of a bank goes on a long time after they hang up the CLOSED sign. They got to count the money and balance their books and, in general, get their accounts straight.

I said to Simms, "You get it?"

He nodded. "It's in the vault. But Mister Williams, it was a close squeak. I had to send to the Columbus bank for the last five thousand."

"You did good," I said. "Help me carry it up to Norris's office."

We went into the vault, which was really just a big old six-foot-high safe where they kept the money. The gold was in four cloth bags. I picked up two and Bill Simms got the other two. Climbing the stairs to Norris's office, I figured each sack weighed somewhere between fifteen and twenty pounds. They were a little heavier than I'd expected.

Norris was at his desk when we entered his office. He looked up, but didn't seem interested or surprised. The two kegs of nails were in the corner. I thanked Bill Simms and then let him excuse himself, and closed the door and locked it after he'd gone. Norris leaned back in his swivel chair. He said, "So, that's the gold."

"Yeah," I said.

"Need any help?"

"Not right now. Will in a minute."

The wooden lids of the nail kegs were loose just like I'd asked Lonnie to have them. I took one and dumped out better than half the nails on Norris's floor. He said, "Here, what are you doing?"

"Making room for the gold."

I picked up two sacks of the gold and stuffed them down in the keg, and then picked up a double handful of the nails and spread them on top of the sacks. They covered the gold nicely. Anybody opening one of the kegs would just think it was nails. I put the lid back on the keg and hammered it down hard with my hand. It was a friction lid and the harder you hammered, the tighter it got.

After that I took the second keg and did the same to it as I had the first. I straightened up. "There. That's that. Now you can help, Norris. I don't want to make two trips out of this, so if you'll shoulder one of those kegs we'll take them downstairs and load them on a packhorse I got out front of the bank."

"What about the rest of these nails?"

There were about twenty pounds of tenpenny nails that the gold had replaced that were left on the floor. I said, "Oh, you don't mind a few nails on your floor, Norris."

"A few! Hell, you could build a fair-sized house with that many nails."

"Then don't let them go to waste. Get a sack somewheres and pick them up and carry them out to the ranch when you go home this evening."

I reached down and shouldered a keg and unlocked and opened the office door. Norris did the same, but he was still grumbling about the nails I'd left on his floor. I said, "Tell you what, Norris. I'll clean up the nails and you take this two-week cross-country trip for me."

He didn't say anything after that, just followed me down the stairs. When we got into the bank Bill Simms saw what we were up to, and jumped up from his desk and ran and opened the door for us. I thanked him and we passed out into the street. Hays was still there, sitting his horse. I said, "Get down, Hays, and give us a hand."

He jumped off his horse and came around to the pack animal. As soon as he saw what I wanted, he held open one of the big pockets and I eased my keg in it. Hays said, "Nails? Tenpenny nails?"

I took the keg from Norris, and Hays and I went around the packhorse and did the same on the other side. It took a moment longer because that was the side where our grub was stored and Hays had to move it out of the way before I could load the keg in.

When we were finished I stepped back and eyed the rig critically. It looked fine to me. I could tell from the way the big dun packhorse was standing that it wasn't much of a load for him. Hays had picked out a well-worked seven-year-old that was even-natured and not likely to spook. He couldn't be as fast as our two horses, carrying the kind of load he was, but he wouldn't be slow like a mule would be. I said, "That looks fine."

Hays said, "Why in hell are we packing nails?"

CHEROKEE

I said, "Ever done any carpentry, Ray?"

He got that overwhelmed look on his face and said slowly, "Well, not in some time. In fact not any that I recall right off."

I shook hands with Norris and reminded him that I was counting on him and Ben to handle matters while I was gone. He reminded me to get off a telegram now and then to let them know my progress, and I mounted my horse and Hays and I turned and started north out of town on the road to El Campo, which was kind of on the road to Austin. I was still resolved to sleep in as many hotels as we could on the trip and do as little camping out as was possible. But El Campo was thirty miles away and, if we were going to make it in time to get a night's sleep, we were going to have to push.

Just before we got to the edge of town I looked back. I could see Lew standing at a corner near the bank. He raised his hand as I looked. I nodded back. He'd be mounting up in ten or fifteen minutes and backing our trail, making sure we didn't have any company trailing us.

A couple of miles out of town, while we were walking the horses to let them rest from the pretty good pace I'd set leaving town, the curiosity bug bit Hays again. He said, "Boss, I don't understand this. Are we going someplace they ain't even got *nails*? I mean, hell, what kind of uncivilized place would it be you had to haul yore own nails to? Have they got whiskey? Hell, I only packed three bottles."

"Three? Two for you and one for me?"

"Naw. I jest throwed in what come to hand. Hell, if I'd knowed we was goin' to someplace you had to pack in yore own nails, I'd of added another horse just to pack the whiskey. My gawd, Boss, we ain't got near enough grub. How long is it gonna take to build whatever it is we're a-buildin'?"

"At least two weeks," I said.

He shook his head mournfully. "I know we is headed for some gawdforsaken prairie in west Texas where they ain't nuthin' between us and the North Pole but a bob-wire fence." He shuddered. "Makes me cold jest thinkin' on it. Burnin' cow chips to make a fire. Say, where we going to get the lumber? It already there?"

"Yeah."

"Well what about tools? Hammers and saws and such?"

"We'll make do," I said. "Come on, let's kick these horses up a little. I want to make some miles."

"We are gonna pick up some more grub, ain't we? Boss, I swear we ain't got enough for more than a half a dozen meals."

"You should have got more," I said. He said something back, but I couldn't hear him because we already had the horses in a canter. The packhorse was leading along with us nicely, staying right up on the off side of Hays's horse. I watched the way the kegs acted in the pack rig he was wearing, and they seemed to be traveling just fine. Ahead the prairie stretched out far and wide and coloring toward ripe wheat. Only here and there did a scrub oak or a mesquite or cedar break the level sweep of grass. There were clumps of cattle, but they were not Half-Moon cattle. Most of them were still old mossy-backed Longhorns or shallow-bred range cattle. They didn't look a thing like the prime beef we were raising on the Half-Moon.

I looked back, but never saw anyone behind us. Of course I didn't expect to see Lew Vara. The only time I would have been aware of him would have been if he'd signaled with a shot or two that he'd caught someone suspicious on our trail. We rode on, and a few hours passed and it commenced to get dark. It was going to be a good, moonlit night, and the road to El Campo was plain to see and smooth riding, so I was content to just travel along as we were.

We rode on into the night. The moon commenced to get up, just barely showing in the western sky. About seven o'clock Ray Hays said, "Boss, course I don't know what our timetable is, or when we got to be where-at, at what time, but my stummick is startin' to dispute me."

He was right. We'd gotten a late start out of Blessing, and we'd be lucky to get to El Campo much before nine-thirty.

I'd been determined to sleep in a hotel bed the whole trip, but it appeared that plan was going to go awry the first night out. By the time we got to El Campo the only thing that would be open would be saloons and whorehouses, and we'd likely not find even the worst cafe open. I said, "Yeah, well, we'll pull up pretty quick. Let's try and make Pecan Creek. Least that way we can water the horses and find some downed wood for a fire."

About an hour later I could see the straggly line of trees that bordered the little creek come rising out of the prairie. In ten minutes we were there, pulling up the horses and turning left to get away from the road and to find a good place to camp. Pecan Creek wasn't much of a creek. In some seasons, like late summer or winter, it nearly went dry. But now it was bubbling along, about four or five feet across and maybe a foot deep at its worst. We rode along the tree line about a quarter of a mile or so, and then pulled the horses up and got down right by the tree line. The trees were mostly willow and mesquite, with a big cottonwood or sycamore scattered here or there. We unloaded the packhorse first because it took the both of us to do it. Not that one of us couldn't handle the weight; it was just the unwieldiness of the thing. The wagon sheet that Hays and his helpers had made the pack out of was good heavy canvas. They'd sewn it with heavy twine using a punch and an awl. So far it was working good. I felt the packhorse's back and he didn't seem at all tender, which was a good sign that the pack wasn't working back and forth and rubbing him raw. That meant that the two girths had been placed correctly and were holding the pack in place.

Once we got the pack off and on the ground we unsaddled the other horses, took their bridles off, and then tied picket ropes to their halters. After that we led them down to the creek and let them take their time watering while Hays and I gathered up downed wood for a fire. I left the building of the fire to Hays, and took the horses a little way from our camp and tied their picket ropes together. I didn't want to tether them to the trees along the creek because, given that kind of opportunity, a horse will just insist on winding in and out of the trees until he's got himself as tangled up as it's near possible to get.

By the time I come back to the campsite Hays had the fire going good so I could see what I was doing. I unrolled a slab of bacon from its oilskin, trimmed off some of the rind with a butcher knife Hays had packed, and then cut off a bunch of thick slices. The fire was starting to make coals, and I got out the big cast-iron skillet and slid it in among the coals, setting it on top of some, and banking others up around the sides. After that I opened up two cans of beans with my pocketknife and waited for the skillet to get hot. When I judged it had heated properly—and a cast-iron skillet heats slower than a steel one—I laid in the slices of bacon. They commenced to sizzle as soon as they hit the bottom of the skillet. Hays had filled up the coffeepot out of one of the canteens and thrown in a handful of ground coffee. He smelled the bacon as it began to cook and said, "Oh, my, don't that smell good! Boss, reckon they is anything smells as good as bacon frying?"

"Well, there's women's perfume."

"Aw, I meant stuff you got to smell on a regular basis. Not somethin' you just get a whiff of now and then."

"Well, bread baking. Or a pie."

"Them are good too. But I don't see how you can beat the smell of coffee and bacon fryin' in the pan."

Hays had brought a big sack of biscuits that the cook must have made up special for him because they seemed middling fresh. I set the sack by the fire with the top open so you could just reach in and get a biscuit when you felt like it.

Hays had made the fire out of dry mesquite, which cooks uncommonly hot, so I was obliged to keep turning my bacon with the point of the butcher knife to keep it from burning. I finally pulled the skillet back a little and then dumped in the two cans of beans. Of course the beans were already cooked. They come that way in the can. Same way you got tomatoes or peaches or whatever. Some day, I thought, I was going to have to find out how they did that. They couldn't put the beans in the can and then seal them up—and I didn't even know how they did that—and then cook them, or else the pressure would build up in the can like steam in a boiler and blow the whole damn thing apart. They had to cook the beans first and then put them in and seal them up. But Nora said that wasn't the way they did it. She said they did it the same way she put up preserves in the glass bottles with the wire hooks that pulled the lids down tight and clamped them.

The water was starting to bubble in the coffeepot, and Ray pulled it back from the fire so it would just simmer. Then he got up and went over to the pack right behind me to get out tin plates and forks and tin cups. I could hear him rattling around and heard him mutter, "Nails. *Damn.* Carrying nails."

I smiled to myself in the dark. I'd tell him sooner or later, and then he'd wish it was nails we were carrying. If he knew we were camped out on the bald prairie with $25,000 in gold, he'd get so jittery he'd never go to sleep. And not because he was worried about the money, but because he'd be worried that someone would know about the gold and come and try and take it and feel the need to kill him in the process. No, I was very definitely doing Ray a favor by letting him think we were hauling kegs of nails around the country.

He came back and handed me my plate and cup and utensils. He said, "Say, ain't we kind of close to El Campo?"

I said casually, "Yeah. I figure we're about ten miles short of it. I was planning on making it tonight and staying at a hotel."

He looked surprised. "You wuz?"

"Yeah."

"How come us to draw up?"

"You went to complaining about being hungry. I have never mistreated my hired hands yet and don't mean to start with you."

I could see his face pretty good in the light of the camp fire. He was kind of chewing at his lip. I knew what he was thinking. He said, "Well, I never meant to interfere with yore plans with my stummick. I'd of just as soon rode on."

"No, a man has got to see his men are well fed."

He said, kind of clearing his throat, "Uh, uh, don't guess you'd want to ride on in once we've eat?"

I smiled at him. "What's on your mind, Ray? You're not thinking about that whorehouse in El Campo, are you? Or ain't there two there?"

"Three," he said.

I said, "Well, la-de-da. Ray Hays. You mean you are thinking of being unfaithful to Maybelle's girls? Even the two fat ones? Give your business to an out-of-town establishment? Hell, El Campo is three times as big as Blessing. They don't need your money near as bad as Maybelle's does."

He got a kind of longing look on his face. "Don't reckon we'll be stopping there for any amount of time as we pass through tomorrow?"

"We ain't even going to be passing through there, much less stopping. We'll go around El Campo to the east. I figure this time tomorrow night we'll be camped near La Grange somewhere on the banks of the Colorado River." Of course it was my intention to be camped in a bed in a hotel in La Grange, but I wasn't telling Hays that. It was much more fun kidding him, making him think he might not see the inside of a town for however long the trip took.

He said, "Whyn't maybe we could make it to La Grange by tomorrow night? Can't be but fifty miles up there. Maybe not even that far. Might even be less."

The beans were starting to bubble, and I knew the coffee was ready by the aroma. I took a big spoon and filled Hays's plate and passed it to him. He was filling me a tin cup of coffee. I said, "Ray, you might as well make up your mind that there is gonna be damn little fun had by either one of us on this trip. Now eat them beans and bacon and be happy you got that. Here's the biscuits."

The beans and bacon were just about all a man could want. That was all I could say about the business of camping out on the trail—it made the food taste so much better. If Nora had tried to give me a plain dish like bacon and beans at home, I'd of thrown a fit and demanded a steak or a roast or at least fried chicken. But out on the trail, with the night air getting a little nippy, wasn't anything that tasted quite as good as what you were eating sitting around the fire with the stars for your roof and the moon your lantern.

We cleaned up the bacon and beans, even wiping the skillet clean with pieces of biscuit, and then Hays took the plates and the utensils and the skillet down to the creek to give them a wash. I put a little more water in the coffee, added a half a handful of ground coffee beans, and set the pot back in closer to the fire. The fire had burned down until it was just glowing coals. We had some extra wood on hand, and we'd use that for light when we got ready to locate our bedrolls. The night was so quiet I could hear the sound of our horses grazing. Hays came back and I got out the bottle of whiskey. We poured the cups half full of coffee, and then I added some whiskey to mine for "sweetenin' " and passed the bottle across to Hays, who did likewise. After that we both leaned back against our saddles and sipped coffee and whiskey and thought our own thoughts. Mine were mainly concerned with the long trip ahead, and missing Nora, and how in hell I was going to find one man in the whole state of Oklahoma. Maybe he'd been elected governor and then he'd be easy to lay hands on. But other than that, I had no idea of how to go about the chore except start with the Tribal Council as Lew Vara had suggested.

After a time we finished our second cup and Ray threw the balance of the dry wood on the fire. As soon as it blazed up we set about unrolling our sleeping bags and putting down the ground sheet so as not to be sleeping with the chiggers and ticks and whatnot. I took off my boots, loosened my belt, took my revolver out of the holster and put it handy, and then laid back on my blankets with my head on my saddle. Ray was just beside me, to my right. I closed my eyes and tried to get comfortable on the hard ground. Just about the time I was starting to relax Hays said, "Boss?"

"What?"

"Gimmee a thought to chew on so I'll drop on off to sleep."

It was a habit he had that I had always found the strangest notion a grown man had ever come up with. But we'd been doing it for a number of years. He claimed if somebody else gave him a thought, it would keep his mind off his troubles and then he could relax and drift on off. He said if he came up with the thought it would invariably be about some of his troubles, and then he'd just agitate himself the whole night through.

I said, "Hays, you beat anything, you know that?"

"Come on, Boss, you'll be wantin' to git off early in the mornin'. I need my sleep."

"Who does this for you in the bunkhouse?"

"Oh, first one and then the other."

"They don't make fun of you?"

He sounded surprised. "What fer? Ain't nuthin' funny 'bout a man tryin' to get a good night's sleep."

I sighed. "All right, give me a minute."

I had been thinking about the Jordans and all the trouble they could make before I got back and just how Norris and Ben would handle it. I said, "You can pick your friends, but you can't pick your enemies."

He took it and got quiet. Hays slept on his back with his hat over his face. The fire was dying down, but I glanced over and saw him settling his hat more securely over his face. I never could understand how anybody could sleep with their face inside a smelly old hat.

I was just starting to get relaxed again, and could feel sleep working its way through my body, when Hays said, "Boss?"

"What!"

"That do be true. An' I never even thought of it before. You can't pick yore enemies. They jest happen. If you could pick 'em, why you'd pick little old folks that couldn't be much of a bother. Ain't that so?"

I said, with a threat in my voice, "You are damn well fixing to find out."

It took him a few seconds, but then he said, "Oh. I ain't sayin' another word. Not one word. You've heard the last out of me tonight."

"Fine."

"Unless they's a commotion of some kind. Or it comes on to rain. Or—"

"HAYS!"

"Yessir. Not 'nother word."

We got a good early start, just taking time to make some coffee and eat a few biscuits and then we were back on the road. We jogged along, making El Campo around nine of the morning, and skirting it to the southeast, then turning back northwest once we were by it, and picking up the road to La Grange. Weren't many travelers out and about. Before noon we met one farmer heading into El Campo with a load of pigs in his wagon, and a couple of solitary horsemen trotting along. They were just ordinary folk, going about their business, and ordinarily I wouldn't have paid them the slightest mind. But there's something about running around the country carrying $25,000 in gold that causes you to look at people in a different light.

Just before we nooned Hays said, "Boss, that pack is working around."

I looked over at the packhorse. We were in a rack, a gait somewhere between a trot and a canter, and I could see that the weight of the kegs was causing part of the pack, the middle part, to slip and slide over the horse's back. It wasn't much, but it didn't take too much of that kind of action to get a horse sore-backed. And a sore-backed packhorse is as useless as a sore-footed running horse. I said, "Damn! I was afraid of something like this." And I had been afraid of using the nail kegs because of their unwieldy weight, but it had seemed like such a good place to hide the gold and hide the weight of the gold. But the nails I'd left in the kegs had just made the whole proposition too heavy. It wasn't too heavy for the horse; it was just too heavy to keep from swinging around and pulling the pack all over the horse's back.

Up ahead I could see a little grove of trees, oaks, off to the left side of the road about two hundred yards. I swung us into the grass and pointed. "Let's make a nooning in those trees and see what we can figure out."

We pulled into the trees, and Hays and I got down and loosened the girths on our riding horses so they could have a good blow, and took the bits out of their mouths so they could crop a little grass. Then together, we unfastened the girths on the packhorse and lifted the pack off. I ran my hand along his back, running it against the grain of his hair. "Yeah," I said. "Seems to be chafing him, all right." I could see little spots where the hair had worn down to the skin. That stiff canvas the pack was made of wasn't an ideal material to put up next to a horse's skin.

Hays said, "Appears as if the pack is workin' front to rear. You can see from the sweat marks on the girths, see how they movin' backwards. Maybe a martingale might help."

"Might," I said. I dropped the packhorse's lead rope so he could graze along with the other two horses and said, "Let's eat a bite and think about it." Of course I was thinking about dumping the rest of the nails out of the kegs and just leaving the gold in the kegs. That would lighten each keg at least twenty pounds. The problem with that was we didn't have a mallet to loosen the tops of the kegs, and they were hell to get off even when you did have a mallet.

While Hays sliced off some smoked brisket and cheese I stood there staring at the horse's back and looking at the pack and trying to think of a way to fix the problem. The biggest part of it was that folks just didn't take kegs of nails and hang them on a horse and not expect trouble. Finally I turned and sat down on the ground where Hays had lunch all laid out on the ground sheet. We ate biscuits and cheese and the smoked beef and washed it down with water. Hays said, "I figured you was in too big a rush to build a fire so I didn't figure on coffee."

"Who said we was in a rush."

He gave me a look. "Well, it's either that or they is a hell of a wind at our backs judging from the pace you be a-setting."

"Maybe if we tie that pack off across the horse's chest it will keep it from working backwards."

Hays was chewing. He said something I couldn't understand.

"What?"

He swallowed and said, "Couldn't hurt to try."

We finished the meal, and then got the saddle horses ready and turned to the packhorse. I said, "We ought to put some kind of saddle blanket on him, protect his back from that stiff canvas."

Ray looked around like somebody was fixing to hand him a saddle blanket.

I said, "You didn't think of a saddle blanket for this packhorse?"

"Well, no, not actually."

"So we just got the two saddle blankets for the horses, the saddle horses?"

"Well, yeah, I reckon you could say that."

"Let me ask you. If you'd been putting a packsaddle on this horse wouldn't you have used a saddle blanket?"

He swallowed. "Well, yeah, of course. But it didn't seem necessary on account of all the pack we was using was cloth, not leather like a packsaddle."

"Canvas, not cloth. Stiff, hard cloth. That's canvas. Would you wear a shirt made out of canvas?"

"If I had to."

"Would you put an undershirt in under it?"

"If I had one."

"Uh, huh. You are the assistant boss of the horse herd, right? That is who I'm speaking to. I mean, you draw wages for knowing more about horses than anyone except Ben, ain't that about the size of it?"

He swallowed again and just blinked at me, not speaking.

I said, "And we just have the two blankets?"

"Just the two horse blankets. Saddle blankets."

"None others?"

He looked uncomfortable. He looked around the grove of trees as if the answer to my question might be written on one of the trunks. He finally said, "Well, they is the blankets in our bedrolls . . ."

"Reckon one of them would help this horse's back if it was between the horse and the hard canvas?"

"Well, yeah . . ."

"Then why don't you get one?"

We were facing each other across the back of the pack-horse. I could see him shift from one foot to the other. He said, "Gonna kind of mess up the blanket. That horse is gonna get pretty sweaty. Wouldn't be much use to a man at night."

"That's all right, just get one."

"Whose?"

I just looked at him.

He said, "I know, I know. Let ol' Ray Hays get his sleepin' blanket and put it on a smelly horse. Let that poor sonofabitch get his blanket ruined."

He was kneeling by the pack, hauling out his bedroll and stripping one of the blankets out of it. It looked like an old olive-drab army blanket. I said, "Well, who was it forgot the saddle blanket?"

He came back, waving off the words with his hand. "I know," he said. "I know, I know. Don't matter if old Ray Hays has a choice of sleepin' cold or usin' a blanket some horse has smelt up with horse sweat. Don't matter, it's jest ol' Ray Hays."

"Hays, if you get any dumber we are going to have to cut you into cordwood."

He adjusted his blanket to the right size and then smoothed it over the packhorse's back. Then we took the pack and hung it on the horse. While Hays was pulling the girths tight I went up by the horse's neck and took out my pocketknife. First I cut a couple of three-foot lengths off his soft lead rope. Then I punched a hole in each side of the pack just below the horse's neck. I ran one end of one of the lengths through one of the holes, tied a knot, and then did likewise with the other end, pulling it tight but not so tight that it would bother the horse, just tight enough to hopefully keep the pack from sliding backwards. I did the same thing a little lower down, making another hold-back right across the middle of the horse's breastplate.

When I was done and Ray was done, I stepped back and looked at our work. We had that pack cinched in about as many ways as we could, but I still had the feeling it was going to work around and gall that horse's back. See, you set a saddle on a horse and the leather skirts go down on each side and hold the saddle in place. The canvas was stiff but not like saddle leather skirts. And the weight hung too far down on each side. The pockets should have been snugged right up nearly to the horse's back. As it was they drooped down nearly below his belly.

I said to Hays, "I don't like it, but it'll have to do."

Hays said sourly, "Hope the damn horse appreciates my blanket."

"Oh, I'm sure he's going to be mighty grateful."

We got mounted, and Hays took the packhorse on lead and we started for La Grange. But even as we rode I could see we still had trouble. If we tried for any speed at all the packs on each side of the horse would get to swinging back and forth, sometimes out of time with each other, and the poor old horse would get so confused he wouldn't know which foot to put down first. By mid-afternoon it was becoming clear we weren't going to make La Grange by dusk or by any time within reason. The poor old horse that had been pressed into service as a packhorse was well on his way to getting so confused on account of his burden that he was going to be ruined forever. The whole situation just made me angry all over again. Here I hadn't figured to spend a single night out on the prairie, and now it was beginning to look like that was the only place I was going to be sleeping. Well, it just wouldn't do. Besides, even if we did get to a hotel in time, how were we going to get the pack up to our room? One man couldn't carry it; it wasn't too heavy, but it was too unwieldy. And we couldn't just take the kegs out and carry them through the lobby. Might as well carry a sign that said we were hiding something because I didn't believe any two men had ever taken rooms in a hotel carrying a keg of nails each. And of course, we couldn't leave the pack with the kegs in them in the livery; it was too risky. Ninety-nine times out of a hundred nobody will mess with your gear in a stable. But when you're carrying $25,000 around with you, you just can't take the chance and leave it unguarded. Of course I could always sleep in the stable, or make Hays do it, but that would just be like raising another flag. Here is the hotel and here are a couple of prosperous-looking men and one of them is sleeping in the stable with his gear.

Hell, it was a quandary and no mistake.

We rode on until it began to get dark. I knew there was no chance we could make La Grange at any decent hour. Consequently we veered off the road, and hunted around until we found a grove of mesquite trees and made camp.

It was like a thousand other camps I'd made before. The ground was just as hard, the Gulf Coast mosquitoes were just as big. You couldn't get cleaned up; you couldn't clean your teeth without going to a hell of a lot more trouble than it was worth. The food had to be the same because you had to pack food that wouldn't spoil and there wasn't just a hell of a big selection of that. When I'd been fifteen it had been fun. By the time I was twenty I was beginning to think it wasn't all that big of an adventure like I'd thought it was at an earlier age. By the time I was approaching thirty and was making a lot of money, I figured I'd done my share of that kind of living and it was somebody else's turn. Then, after I got married, I was completely convinced that I deserved a good bed in a pleasant house with a pretty woman beside me. And then had come Howard with his simple little request.

While we circled the horses around and around in a tight little area to tramp down the grass I mentally gave Howard a damn good cussing. But it wasn't doing any good; I was still out in the open with a chill wind starting to kick up and Howard was home in bed.

We ate beef and bread and canned tomatoes, and finished off with some canned peaches, mainly just punching a hole in the can and drinking off the juice and then sucking the peaches dry. After that we sat around with coffee and whiskey. Off to the north of us I could see a dim glow. I figured it was either a prairie fire or La Grange. Hays thought that more than likely it was La Grange.

I said, "Yeah. I reckon."

I figured we were about ten miles short of it. But on beyond it, on the road to Austin, which was the general direction we were taking, was the town of Bastrop. I figured it to be about thirty miles from La Grange, maybe thirty-five. But cutting cross-country we could make it closer, maybe just thirty or thirty-five miles from where we were camped. There was no railroad line that ran through La Grange, but I knew there was a northbound line out of Bastrop, a line that ran to Austin and then on the Fort Worth, and from there, I figured a man just about had to be able to get a train from someplace in Oklahoma.

I knew Howard didn't want me to do it that way, for reasons known only to himself. But Howard wasn't stuck with a bewildered packhorse and a rig that didn't allow us to make much more than thirty miles a day. Besides, we were probably going to spend so much time looking for this Charlie Stevens that we'd spend the extra time it would have taken us to go all the way horseback.

Still, I knew I was thinking angry and that a man ought not to make decisions in that frame of mind. I'd told Howard I'd horseback his gold to Charlie, just as it had been horsebacked away from him, and I was going to do my dead-level best to stick to that line of agreement.

Hays said, "Boss . . ." He kind of hesitated. Then he said, "This gonna be a real long trail?"

"Your bones getting old, Ray?"

"Well, no, you just ain't give me no indication of when it's gonna end."

I tilted my watch toward the glow of the fire. It was a little after nine. I said, "We better get to bed. Maybe if we start early enough we can get out of our own shadow."

Hays lifted his head to the wind. He said, "Damned if that wind ain't gettin' colder. You don't reckon we could be gettin' a norther this early, do you?"

"I hope not." But we were in Texas, and a blue norther could come swooping over those flat plains and drop the temperature forty degrees before you could get into your coat.

Hays got up. He said, "I reckon I maybe better borrow my blanket back from that damn horse. Ain't gonna make me smell no better, but that's better than freezing."

"You ain't going to be anywhere where it's going to much matter how you smell."

"I wish you wouldn't say that. Just takes the heart plumb outten me."

We got settled down for the night. I could see clouds scudding across the night sky, blotting out the stars. It was getting colder. Even through my blankets and my clothes I could feel it. I was starting to wish I'd put on my sheepskin-lined jacket, but I was just too sleepy to get up and get it. Hays was laying right beside me, and he was right about the blanket he'd loaned the horse. It smelled like hell.

It came on to rain about midnight. Hays and I rose as one, grabbing our bedrolls and the ground cloth and dashing into the thicket of mesquite. We made another trip back as the cold rain started to pelt down to bring in our saddles and the pack. We dragged them in under our feet and then squatted there under the ground cloth, half wet and all cold and miserable as hell.

We'd been sitting there, listening to the rain hitting the tarp we were holding over our heads, for about an hour.

We'd got a whiskey bottle out of the pack, and were passing it back and forth to ward off the cold. I said, "Hays?"

"Yessir?"

"You remember before we went to bed asking me how much longer we might be on the trail?"

"Yessir."

I took a swig of whiskey. "Well, if we can make it to Bastrop by tomorrow night, this is the last goddam night we camp out like a couple of fucking poor-ass Injuns."

CHAPTER 6

Even with the rain keeping us up half the night, we were still able to be up and bustling around before dawn. We were both still about half chilled to the bone, and Hays somehow stumbled around and found us enough dry wood to get a pretty good fire going. We didn't want it so much for cooking breakfast as for making coffee and getting warm and drying out our damp clothes. After what I'd said the night before, about if we could make Bastrop by that night it would be our last night on the ground, Hays was all for mounting up and taking off without fooling around with anything. But I knew we were going to make good time on account of I'd decided to do something he didn't know anything about. So I bade him just to bide his time and get himself comfortable and to fry up some bacon while I got the coffee going.

We'd built a pretty good fire. Once the dry wood had worked itself up we'd been able to put on some of the wet wood, and it had caught and dried out while it was burning. As a consequence we had a fire that would warm a body through and through.

But it burned down pretty quick, and I got out the coffee-pot while Hays went to work on the bacon. We hadn't suffered much damage from the rain other than having to sit up and be uncomfortable for a couple of hours. The biscuits had somehow managed to get damp but, as Hays said, that just made them easier to chew.

We made a pretty good breakfast, and then Hays got the horses in just as it was coming dawn. The wind was still pretty chill, but it wasn't blowing near as hard as it had been the night before, so we knew it had just been a mild thunderstorm come through. If it had been a norther, a blue norther, we'd of had on every speck of clothes we'd brought and would be looking for several more days of the same misery. There ain't really nothing quite as cold as that first Texas norther of the winter. Hays said he'd once known a lady in Abilene who could match it for just plain old bare-ass cold. He said they could get this lady to sit on a keg of beer in the warmest days of the summer, and after no more than an hour and a half of sitting they'd have beer so cold it would make your teeth ache to drink it.

We got the horses saddled and bridled, and then I directed Hays to fetch me over one of the kegs of nails. I was standing pretty close to the fire, still getting warm. He give me a kind of a funny look. "You want one of them kegs over there?"

"Yes," I said. "Bring me a damn keg. What's the matter with you?"

He went over to the pack, worked out one of the kegs, and then lugged it over and set it down on the ground in front of me. I wasn't about to fool with the top. With no mallet and with the wood having swollen even tighter with the wet weather, I didn't figure there was any way to get the top off. Of course a nail keg is made just like any other kind of barrel, big or small, with staves held in place by wires pulling them together. I picked up the keg at each end, raised it over my head, and smashed it to the ground.

Hays said, "Boss, what in hell!"

Some of the staves had bent and separated, but not enough. I picked the keg up again, lifted it as far up as I could, and flung it straight down to the ground with all my force. It burst open and nails came spilling out in all directions. In amongst the nails and the broken wood I could see the two canvas sacks of gold. I pulled them out and laid them on the ground beside me. On each white canvas sack the letters were clearly printed: U.S. MINT.

Hays was staring at the sacks. He said, "What in hell is them sacks doin' in a keg of nails?"

"Hand me the other keg, Ray."

He brought the keg over, still staring at the sacks on the ground. I repeated my process with the second keg, and soon the two sacks had turned into four. Hays said, "Boss, what in hell be goin' on here?"

I didn't answer him, just picked up two of the sacks and carried them over to my horse. I put one sack in each pouch of my saddlebags. They didn't weigh much over fifteen pounds apiece, so I didn't figure the extra thirty pounds was going to be any hardship on my animal. I said, "Ray, are you blind? Can't you see those two sacks need to be put in your saddlebags? Or do you want me to carry all the load?"

He went over, still wearing that puzzled look, and picked up the two bank bags. "Damn," he said, as he picked up the two sacks, "these here are shore heavy for they size. They as heavy as . . ."

He stopped and looked at me. He said, "Is they what I think is in these sacks?"

I nodded.

He just stood there. "Boss, this here is gold. An' you had it hid in them kegs so nobody'd know. Ain't that right?"

I nodded.

"Only the packhorse couldn't carry it on account of it galling his back, what with the weight of this an' them nails that is scattered all over the prairie."

"That's about the size of it."

"Is they as much in here as it feels like?"

"Twenty-five thousand dollars worth."

"Oh, lordy!" he said. "Oooooh, lordy! Boss, right now I feel like ever' *bandito* 'tween here an' Mexico can smell this here gold. We are gonna be shot, get robbed, get our throats cut, maybe get burned alive all on account of we carryin' all this here gold. Boss, this is frightful!"

"How come you reckon I didn't tell you what was in them kegs?"

"How far we got to carry this here death notice?"

"Oh, for God's sake, Ray, you can take on worse than anybody I know. We're seventy or eighty miles from where we got this gold. Nobody around here knows we got it."

He was putting one of the sacks in one side of his saddle-bags. As he came around the end of his horse to put the second bag in the other side he just waved his hand at me. He said, "Say anything you're a mind to. Just go on in yore innocence. But I'm tellin' you they is thieves and murderers can *smell* this here gold. I jest want to know when I'll git my next hour of sleep. A week? Two weeks?"

I stared at him and shook my head. "Hays, you are some piece of work."

"I'm jest askin' how long I got to hold myself in mortal terror. How far we goin' to pack these here coffin makers." He put up his hand. "I know, I know. What right has ol' Ray Hays got to be askin' a question that only concerns his very life. I'm jest askin' where I might can expect to be buried."

"Oklahoma," I said.

He turned into stone and stared at me. "Oklahoma? Oklahoma? Oklahoma!" He sighed and looked away. "Hell, if I'd knowed that back at the ranch I'd of shot myself in the laig or somethin'. I'd a never refused the job, but a man's got a right to disable hisself if he takes a mind to."

I just shook my head. There wasn't anything I could say. "We better get that pack on the packhorse. And don't forget to use the saddle blanket."

"You mean *my* blanket."

"Listen, if you don't get a move on we won't get to Bastrop by tonight and you'll get to use that blanket again on yourself."

That speeded him up.

We set out and, without that awkward weight to contend with, the packhorse could make pretty good speed. Of course he was just about as good a pony as either of the horses Ray and I were riding. He'd just gotten a little old for the hard and fast work we put cow horses through during busy times of the year.

After we'd been riding about an hour Ray said, "Nail kegs, huh. You know, I must be gettin' kind of slow upstairs. I ought to've figured out right away that they was somethin' jest not quite right about them nail kegs. Man wouldn't be goin' off carryin' kegs of nails to some kind of job. You need nails for lumber. So it jest natcherly makes sense that whoever was brangin' the lumber would brang the nails. I don't see how come I didn't catch on to that and see that you was up to somethin' else."

"Well, Ray, you know you've been hitting the bottle pretty hard here lately. Could be it has something to do with that. I know that the old Ray Hays wouldn't have been fooled all that easy. But you put a few years on a man, add a few too many drinks . . . it all adds up." I looked over at him. He was sitting stiff in the saddle, a worried look suddenly coming over his face.

I said, "You reckon? What are you now, Ray, forty? Few years older"

He turned his face to me, his mouth open. "What are you talkin' about? You know blame well I ain't no forty year old. Hell, I'm a year younger than you!"

I shrugged, trotting along in the saddle. "All the same, wasn't me didn't know what was inside those kegs. I wasn't the one took it for granted that a man would be hauling kegs of nails cross-country horseback."

"Well of course not." Then he said, "Hell, you knowed what was in them kegs besides nails. Quit tryin' to mix me up. I'm already worried as a tick on a smokin' dog."

"I was hoping you'd stay in the dark about the gold the whole way just on account of the way you are carrying on now. Hays, ain't nobody but us knows we got this gold. If you keep your mouth shut or don't go around wearing a sign it will stay that way. Of course, knowing you, you'll blurt it out the first saloon you're in."

"Won't have to," he said complacently. "They's outlaws can just look at you and tell you are holding deep. They might not 'zactly know what it is, but they'll know we are packing heavy."

I looked over at him. Sometimes his conversation made me want to drown him in the nearest river. I said, "All right, supposing that is so. You think I just plan to hand them this gold? What the hell you think I brought you along for? We are supposed to *guard* this gold. You and I are supposed to know how to shoot a gun. You *sabe*?"

He just nodded knowingly. "Won't matter. They'll take us from behind some dark night. Catch us unawares. You should have never taken that gold outten them nail kegs. If I'd knowed what was what I'd of made shore you didn't bust them kegs. It was a mighty fine idea."

"Hays, it made you suspicious. Think what it would have caused somebody with any sense to think."

I kicked up the pace and we rode on. The country was beginning the gradual change from the flat plains of the coastal area to the rolling grasslands of south central Texas. When we turned north we'd begin to see some chopped-up country with a few hills and some valleys and more underbrush and bigger trees. It would be a less gentle country than our home country, but nowhere near as rough as that further north and to the west.

We got into Bastrop about a half an hour before dusk. True to my prediction we'd made good time once we'd fixed the packhorse so he could keep pace with our saddle horses. Once into town we headed straight down the main street toward the depot, which was on the north side of town just at the very outskirts. I got down, leaving Hays to watch the horses and the gold, and went into the depot. From the ticket clerk I found out there was a northbound train out the next morning for Fort Worth through Austin with no changes. He didn't know about connections on into Oklahoma because a different line served the country in that direction. I made arrangements for us to have a stock car added to the train, with preparations for the care of our horses such as water and hay and such. We would also ride in the stock car with our animals. The clerk was willing that we do so, but he said, "I reckon you know it's gonna get a little brisk as you head north and they is going to be a pretty good wind blowing through the slats of that stock car."

I told him I didn't care. As a matter of fact I had always preferred to ride with my animals rather than the chair cars, which were generally crowded and noisy and too hot. With the MKT that operated through Blessing, I could generally get half a car rate even though there was just our animals. But that was the Missouri-Kansas-Texas, a line Howard had considerable influence with. This clerk worked for the Denver and Rio Grande, and he not only had never heard of the Half-Moon ranch, he didn't give much of a damn. Consequently he charged me for a full car, and insisted on me buying two passenger tickets for me and Hays. He said, "I don't care where you ride, but you got to have a ticket to ride." The matter cost me $68, which was a considerable sum for a train ride for two men and three horses just to Fort Worth. Fortunately, I was carrying better than $500 in cash and could stand the price, but much more of that and we were going to have to go to drinking cheaper whiskey.

With the train arranged me and Hays rode back down the street to what appeared to be the best hotel in town. They advertised the best meals in town and baths on request. It was starting to chill up again, what with night coming on, and I figured a good hot bath and a shave would be just the ticket. We put our horses and the packhorse in the stable, leaving the pack in one of the stalls, and then swung our saddlebags over our shoulders and went on into the hotel and got a big room with two beds. Bastrop was a pretty big town, running, I figured, close to four thousand inhabitants. It appeared to be a pretty lively place judging from the number of saloons and dance halls. I'd seen Hays taking special note of the dance halls as we rode through the town. Didn't take no Gypsy fortune-teller to figure out what was on his mind.

They had baths in the room, though you had to get boys to bring up hot water from the kitchen if you wanted a hot bath. I arranged with the desk clerk for two baths and told him to add two dollars to my bill for the boys carrying the water. I also ordered up two quarts of the best whiskey they had and inquired about supper.

The clerk said, "Open until nine, sir. Best steak around. Special tonight is fried chicken with cream gravy and hot bread and honey. And it ain't boardin'-house style. You can sit right down at yore own table and be served by yoreself. I can tell you're a genn'lman is the only reason I mention it."

We had a room on the second floor and, climbing up the stairs, Hays said, "See? What'd I tell you?"

"What are you talking about, Hays?"

"Why the way that room clerk treated you, calling you a genn'lman and tellin' you how they served supper."

"What's that got to do with anything? What makes you think I ain't a gentleman? At least by some standards."

"Ain't got nothin' to do with it. It's the gold. This much gold kind of puts out a power, kind of power you can practically feel. It draws like a poultice."

"Why don't you keep talking about it? Maybe everybody in the hotel didn't hear you first time. The reason he called me a gentleman was partly because of the size of room I ordered and partly because I told him to add something extra on my bill for the boys lugging the water. Most folks thinks when they order a bath that the labor of the boys is included in that. They don't know that the boys are working for what the customer is willing to pay them."

"Oh," Hays said.

We went in the room and dumped our saddlebags down. I got the last bottle of whiskey out of mine and got a glass and poured myself out a drink. There was a pitcher of water setting on the washstand and I added a little water in the whiskey. I had plans for us both to take it a little easy on the liquor while we were in charge of so much gold. While Hays was getting himself a drink I said, "Now, I know what you got on your mind and here's the way we'll work it. It's plain that one of us has got to stay in the room at all times?"

"Why?"

I gave him a look.

He said, "Oh, yeah! I forgot."

I just shook my head. I did that a lot around Hays. "So what we'll do—I'll take a bath and get cleaned up and then go downstairs and eat supper while you are getting cleaned up. Then, when I come back you can go out and get your ashes hauled or whatever you got in mind."

His face lit up. "I taken note was some pretty likely-looking places a man could find what he was looking for."

"Well, that's all right. But you better not do one thing. You better not get drunk and go to letting your mouth run."

He looked hurt. "Awww, Boss."

"Don't 'awww, Boss' me. I know you, Ray. Don't get confused in your mind that this is a holiday. We got a job of work to do and we ain't going to do no celebrating until we get it done. You understand that?"

He was still acting hurt. "Well, of course. I ain't no idjit."

"Just watch the drinking. You can fuck all you want, but you do your drinking up here with me behind a locked door. Now, you got enough money?"

He shrugged. "I think I got about ten dollars."

I gave him a twenty. I said, "That ought to be plenty. You spend more than that you are having too good of a time."

There was a knock at the door. It was the boys with the buckets of steaming water. There was a built-in galvanized tub in a little alcove in the room. It had running cold water, probably from a cistern on top of the hotel. I went over and turned on the tap and started taking my clothes off as the boys came in.

I had the fried chicken and cream gravy with the hot bread and honey for supper. It was all right, but it wasn't much threat to put Nora out of business. Still, if a man is hungry enough his own cooking will taste pretty good. I didn't hurry, but I didn't tarry either, knowing that Hays was upstairs chomping at the bit ready to get out on the town. I climbed back up the stairs and knocked on the door and he let me in. He was all slicked up with his hair combed and the dust knocked off his boots. Fortunately we'd thought to bring a clean change of clothes with us to the room, so we were both clean at the same time.

I said, "Now, Ray, it's half past seven. You eat a good supper and then go on out. But I want you to bear in mind we are going to be turning out early in the morning. We'll have to be down at that depot by seven to get the horses loaded and taken care of, and that means we'll be needing to turn out of bed before six. So you better not be staying out until all hours. I ain't going to be able to get any sleep until you get in, and I don't want to be setting up here until all hours."

"Hell, I can jest take the key. Let myself in."

I shook my head. "You forgot what is under my bed in them saddlebags? You reckon I want that key floating around some whorehouse?"

"All right, all right," he said. "I'll cut 'er short. Won't play no cards, won't be sociable with nobody at the bar. Jest get out there an' git my business done and get on back."

"I ain't sayin' you can't have no fun. I'm just telling you to get back at a reasonable hour."

"You're the boss," he said. He put on his hat.

I said, "You ain't going to wear a gun?"

He looked down at his waist. "I kind of figure it's safer in a strange town. I ain't armed, I don't give nobody no trouble, nobody gives me no trouble. You can always run into a drunk thinks he's tough. But it's less likely if you ain't packin' a revolver."

I shrugged. "I apologize, Hays. I never thought you give that much thought to anything."

After he went out I took my boots off, got up on my bed, poured myself out a drink of whiskey, and then watered it down some. I figured it was going to be a late night. Ray's intentions might be of the best, but you turn him loose in a whorehouse with money in his pocket and he wouldn't be back until the money ran out. I couldn't really blame him, though. Now that I was married I didn't see how them cowhands of ours, or cowhands that worked for anybody, could get by just getting into town once a week or even if they were lucky. Sometimes, during a particular seasons of the year, we worked seven days a week. I'd let a man off to go to church, but he better come back knowing the sermon by heart. Of course it had practically been the same for me. I hadn't gotten away that much myself unless I was traveling on business, and it had even been harder on me because I never got much out of being with whores. Not that I had anything against them. I just didn't like the idea of all them tracks that had been laid down before me. Any man that had ever rented a stable horse would know what I meant. Of course I had chances to meet women my hired hands never would, but they were so quick to sigh and giggle and say yes. Getting into some of their britches had required a good deal of time and effort and money. And then there'd been some you were sorry about later. They were the ones who swore you'd mentioned something about marriage or love or maybe both. Sometimes it had gotten mighty complicated.

Hell, I'd of probably been better off and saved a hell of a lot of trouble and bother and expense if I'd of done like Ray and his cohorts. But it was Ben, I figured, that was heading for trouble. I knew for a fact he was lifting a lot of skirts and getting in amongst a lot of silk and lace, and one of these days his antics were going to backfire on him.

It was hard just laying there waiting. I was wishing I had something to read, but I'd searched the room over and there wasn't so much as a religious tract. I figured there ought to be a newspaper of some kind in the lobby, but I hated to leave the room that long. I got up and went to the window. We were on the second floor at the front of the hotel. I could see right down on the main street, and even get a pretty good look at some of the intersecting streets. Nearly all the businesses appeared to be on the main street, but there were some nice-looking residences on the side streets. It was a quarter until nine by my watch and the town appeared to be going pretty good. Right across the street was a saloon. I could see a little movement over its batwing doors, and hear some laughter and now and again the sound of a piano playing some tune. It would have been nice to have been over in that bar, having a drink and watching the people. I was a little sorry now that I'd given Ray so much rope. I should have told him, "Just go get on the first girl you can find, and as soon as you buck off get right back on over here." Then maybe I could have gone out and sampled a little of the sociability of the town myself.

I went back and laid down on the bed, propping myself up on the two pillows that had been provided. My gun belt was laying right beside me, and I took out my revolver and worked the action and spun the cylinder, making sure it was in good working order. I carried a .42/.40 Colt. That was a .40-caliber bore on a .42-caliber frame. The .40-caliber slug was big enough to stop anything you hit in the right place, and the heavier frame gave the gun a better balance with less barrel deviation. I had the one in my hand that had a six-inch barrel on it, and the one in my saddlebags had a nine-inch barrel. I never carried the nine-inch barrel when I thought there was the slightest need for some quick work, because that extra three inches could cost you a precious fraction of a second clearing the leather. That could get you killed. But that extra three inches was also mighty handy for accuracy in a long-range gunfight. I shoved the revolver back in its holster and put my hands behind my back and yawned. That damn Hays probably wouldn't get back before eleven o'clock, and if he did, I was going to make his life miserable.

I was still laying there thinking dire thoughts when, about fifteen minutes later, I heard a light tap on the door. Obviously we'd kept the door locked so somebody couldn't just come busting in and catch one or both of us unawares.

And naturally, I hadn't let Ray have a key. I got off the bed saying, "Hold on," and walked across to the door. I twisted the key to unlock it, then turned the knob and pulled it backwards toward me. There was Hays, and I was fixing to say something about him getting back before dawn when he suddenly came stumbling into the room and I saw there was a man right behind him holding a steady-handed revolver. The man was a tough-looking middle-aged *hombre*—about forty, I reckoned. For some reason he reminded me of Rex Jordan. In the instant I had to think I calculated it was because they were both kind of short and stout. The man wasn't dressed like a cowhand, but then neither did he look like a businessman either. He had on a gray wool coat and khaki pants. He was wearing a narrow-brimmed Stetson. He was just a step into the room. Hays had come to a stop to my right and just behind the door. I glanced over at him, my eyes telling him what I was going to do to him if we got out of this. He looked miserable. But he said, "Boss, it ain't—"

But the stocky man cut him off. Motioning with the fingers of his left hand he said to me, "All right, Mister Big-Wad-of-Money, let's have it! Get it out! Now!"

I glanced at Ray. He was nodding vigorously. He said, "Boss, the man wants your *cash*. For gawd's sake, let him have it."

The man said, "Hurry up, goddammit! I'll put one through you."

Then it hit me. What Ray had meant wasn't what I'd thought. The man wanted the cash in my pocket. I slowly put my hand in my right-hand pocket and pulled out the roll. The man said, "Hurry up. Give it here!"

He switched his revolver to his left hand from his right and stuck out his right to take the roll I was holding out. He was just starting to stuff it in his pocket and to back out of the room when Ray suddenly kicked the door hard with his boot. The door hit the man's gun hand and he yelled and the gun flew out of his grasp. Before I could react Ray had reached around the end of the door and grabbed the man by the hand in both of his. He jerked the man into the room and flung him. The man went staggering across the room, off balance. I was standing there, still about a fraction of a second behind, when Ray charged across the room and hit the man and knocked him to the floor. Money went flying everywhere, but Hays wasn't paying any attention. He'd got the man turned over on his back and got astraddle of him and was whaling away with both fists. I just stood there watching. I had never seen Ray Hays so furious. He was hitting the man with long, hard punches, timing his words with the blows. He said, "TRY ROB MY BOSS YOU BAS-TARD! GIT MY ASS IN TROUBLE SONOFABITCH!"

I said, "Ray. Ray! Stop!"

"BEAT THIS FUCKER TO DEATH! SONOFABITCH ROB ME AND—"

I went over and got him under the arms and pulled him back until he was clear of the man laying on the floor. Ray hunkered down there panting. I looked at the would-be robber. He was knocked colder than a tombstone and his face was all-over blood. Ray had nearly beat him to a pulp. Now Ray just squatted there panting. I went around the room picking up money. I had misjudged Ray and I was going to owe him an apology. It was clear what had happened. The man that had tried to rob me had seen me at the desk with my wad of money out arranging for our bill and our baths and the extra couple of dollars for the bath boys. Or maybe he'd seen me paying for my supper in the dining room. He hadn't known anything about the gold; all he'd known was that I was carrying enough cash to make him a pretty good payday. No doubt he'd seen Ray go out, and had come up and tried the door so quiet that I hadn't heard. When he'd found it was locked he'd waited on Ray, and then followed him upstairs and stuck a gun in his back as soon as he'd knocked. There was no way Ray could have done any more than he did. And I had thought Ray had been running his mouth about the gold and had brought me some company I didn't want. I was going to have to apologize to Ray and I didn't have the slightest idea how.

Just then I looked up. Ray was opening one of the windows facing onto the street. There was no screen. Before I could think what he was doing he'd gotten the robber to his feet and half carried, half dragged him over to the window. I saw him stick the man's head out into the cold air and I figured he was trying to bring him around. Only when I saw him lift the man's legs and start him out the window did I realize what he was doing.

"Ray!" I said. "Wait!"

I got to the window just in time to see the man fall the few feet to the slanting, porch roof, roll down that, and then fall to the street. Because of the overhang of the verandah roof I couldn't see how he'd landed in the street. I stood there staring as Ray shut the window and then, still panting, went over, sat down on my bed, and took a big gulp of the whiskey I'd just fixed for myself. He swallowed it down, still panting, and said slowly, "Too much wa—water."

I went over, picked up the bottle of whiskey, and poured him out a straight shot. He had it down before I could upright another glass and pour myself one. I gave myself a drink and then poured another one for him. Then I crossed the room and sat on the side of his bed. He was still sitting there trying to get his breath, his elbows propped on his knees, his hands and his head hanging down. I could see his knuckles were skinned and bruised. I lit a cigarillo and waited for him to come back to himself.

When he got ready he was good and ready. He jumped that last drink down his throat and then started at a run. "Justa, I know how it musta looked to you, but I swear that man wasn't after what's under the bed. I swear I never said a word to nary a soul about what we're packin'. Fact of the business is I never said nothin' to nobody 'cept the woman, an' that was jest to ast her how much. See, I wuz really tryin' to git back quick's I could, 'cept I had to have seconds with 'nother one I seen I hadn't seen when I walked in the place, and I—"

I kept trying to interrupt him, trying to let him know that I understood what had happened. But he had to keep on going with the head of steam he had up. He went ahead and told me what I'd already figured out, that the robber had followed him up from the lobby and put the gun in his back just before he got to the door, and he'd of warned me if he could've thought of any way to do it without gettin' himself shot, but that he already knowed the man was after the cash on account of he'd said somethin' 'bout did I always carry as big a wad as—

I yelled, "RAY!"

He stopped and looked up at me, startled. "Huh?"

"I already had it figured out."

But he said, "I kept tryin' to give you looks, let you know he was after your roll so's you wouldn't say anything about what was under the bed. I mean, I was tryin'—"

I said, "Hays, you beat all. Do you reckon I'd of taken him by the hand and led him over to the bed and got down and pulled out the saddlebags for him so he wouldn't have to stoop over?"

He said, looking a little hurt, "Well, I didn't *know* what you wuz likely to think, not after them instructions you give me 'fore I left. I jest figured I was through if he got the notion was something other than yore roll. Hell, I could have made that up outten my salary in about a year."

"Ray, now listen to me. Are you listening to me? Look here at me."

"Yeah?"

"It was my fault."

He looked a little puzzled. "What?"

"I knew this was a rough town and I shouldn't have been flashing that roll down there in the lobby, either when we were getting the room or when I paid for my supper. There were plenty of hardcases sitting around and I should have had better sense. Maybe I was thinking about the gold. Maybe I was thinking who'd be interested in the five or six hundred dollars I had in my pocket when I was worrying about a hell of a lot more than that."

"Now let me git this straight. You be sayin' that this was yore fault?"

I sighed and looked away. I knew what was coming. I had just given Hays enough ammunition to use on me for the balance of the year. I figured to never hear the end of it. But I said, "Yes, Hays, it was my fault."

He looked at me blankly for a moment and then said, "Well, I'll be damned. I never thought I'd hear them words come out of yore mouth."

I gestured at his hands. "You better soak them fists of yours or you won't be able to hold a knife and fork by breakfast."

"You ain't blamin' me fer that fella bustin' in the room like he done, comin' in here with the you-know-what, even if he didn't know about it?"

"Now, listen, Hays, I have already said I'm to blame. Do not keep on with this or I'll bring up a few things in the past that were your fault. Now look here, go on down to the desk and make that clerk get you some salt out of the kitchen. He won't want to, but you tell him if he don't that I'm coming out to talk to him. Go on now."

He got up. He glanced toward the window. He said, "Wonder if that old boy comin' out the window will fetch the law?"

I got up and raised the window and leaned out as far as I could. As near as I could tell it was business as usual. Hadn't been five minutes since the man had tumbled into the street, and so far, he hadn't drawn so much as a crowd of one. I said, "I reckon they got so many drunks laying around one more don't draw no notice." I turned away, shutting the window. I looked at Hays curiously. He was up and putting on his hat. "Ray, you were well on your way to beating that old boy to death. I never knowed you to have such a temper."

"Wasn't *my* temper was poundin' that man. Was *yours*. I could just picture the hell I was fixing to catch from you and I reckon I took it out on him."

"You moved pretty quick jamming that door against his gun arm. Especially considering you couldn't see around the end of the door."

"Uh, uh," he said. "I could see his revolver an' his wrist. I knowed what I was doin'."

"Yeah, considerin' that gun wasn't pointing at you."

He sighed in that way he had. "I might have knowed it. Might have knowed it. Should have knowed I wadn't gonna get off scot-free. Now I'm bein' blamed 'cause I didn't let him run off with your money." He sighed again. "I should have knowed."

I had to laugh a little. "Hays, go get the salt. You done a good job. I'm serious. I'm going to prove it to you by not cutting your wages like I'd been planning on."

He opened his mouth to say something, but then thought better of it and closed it and went out the door.

I smiled. Hays always made me smile. There was something about him that struck my funny bone. I glanced over and saw the blood on the floor. But there was nothing funny about the way he'd hit the robber. I'd seen Ray in gun fights and knew he could hold his own, but I'd never seen him use his fists. He could hit a hell of a lot harder than I'd thought.

I locked the door and then got my revolver and waited. I didn't want a repetition of what had just happened. Next time we threw somebody into the street it might not go unnoticed. Pretty soon there came a knock at the door. It was a kind of a dull thump. I went over to the door. I said, "Ray?"

He said, "Yeah. Open the door, will ya?"

I turned the key and then twisted the knob. Ray came in carrying a big saltshaker. I said, "Just the one of you this time?"

He ignored it. "Boy, my hands are *already* sore. I had to knock on the damn door with my head."

I said drily, "You should have used that on that feller. Then your hands wouldn't have got hurt."

He give me a sour look. I took the saltshaker out of his hands, unscrewed the top, and then dumped the biggest part of the salt into the big washbasin that was sitting on a stand with a pitcher and some fresh towels and other things. I poured the basin about half full of water out of the pitcher, and then kind of stirred it around and took it over and set it on Ray's bed. I said, "Sit down there and stick your hands in that water. It works better when it's hot, but there ain't much we can do about that this time of night."

He put his hands in the brine and said, "Awwh!" and immediately took them out. "That stings like all get out."

"Ray, put your hands in there. We've got to get to sleep sometime tonight. Just soak your hands for half an hour."

"How am I gonna have a drink if I got both hands in here?"

"Well, the answer to that is that you're not going to have a drink. Now sit there and soak your hands and don't say anything. I need to think."

"I ain't goin' out again without a weapon. I was a damn fool to do it tonight."

"That ain't not saying anything. That's talking."

"Course I don't know what I could have done even if I had had a gun. Ol' boy jest come up behind me, and next thing I know he's proddin' me in the small of the back."

"You're soaking, but you're still talking."

"Wasn't as if he come at me from the front where a pistol would have done me some good. Never gave me no chancet."

I ignored him and poured myself a drink.

"You gonna drink in front of me when I got both hands in this brine an' can't have one? It's still burnin' like sin in case you be interested."

I continued to ignore him.

"Well, you see any way I could have avoided lettin' happen what happened?"

"Yeah," I said.

"What?"

"Stayed in the room."

Next morning we got away in pretty good style other than the usual trouble I had with railroad people. It seemed as if when you asked them for something that wasn't right down on their list in block letters, it just threw them completely off track. I had to explain to the crew that was handling the freight cars that, yes, a stock car got hay and water even if there was just three horses going in it, and yes, since I'd paid for the whole damn car it was my car and they couldn't put any other stock in it even if I didn't have but three animals. And yes, we were going to ride in there with the horses and it was legal because we had tickets that said so, and if they wouldn't bust up all the bales of hay we could sit on a couple of them until it came time to feed them to the horses.

But we'd finally gotten rolling, pulling out of Bastrop no more than fifteen minutes late. Some day I vowed to find out why railroads went to all the trouble to print up timetables since they didn't seem to pay the slightest bit of attention to them.

But finally the town was behind us, and Ray said something about he could now relax from worrying about the sheriff coming looking for him for throwing the man out the window. He said, "That ain't generally like me, you know. I've had to use a gun, but I don't generally just cold-bloodedly fling a body out a second-story window."

"You didn't seem so cold-blooded to me. In fact you appeared a touch hot under the collar."

I didn't know about Ray, but I hadn't slept so well. Seemed like, after the little scuffle, I was more conscious than ever of the gold in the saddlebags under the bed. So I'd just more or less dozed, listening for every sound and coming full awake if anything sounded the least suspicious. Hays yawned about the same time I did. He said, "Boy, I didn't sleep so good last night."

"Hands hurt you?"

He looked down at his knuckles. They were skinned up and red-looking, but they hadn't swollen much. He said, "Naw. Reckon it was that damned gold."

"Yeah." We were rolling through open countryside now. The land was starting to get more woody and broken. "Well, we can't nod off now. Ain't more than an hour till Austin and I don't like the idea of us both being asleep while we're going through there. There's about a thirty-minute layover, according to the clerk at the depot, and I imagine this train will get shunted off to a siding or do a lot of backing and starting and stopping before we get lined out for Fort Worth."

We were both wearing leather jackets. Mine was my sheepskin-lined one that reached halfway down my thighs. Ray had on a big one that was lined with what looked like an Indian blanket. We were both huddled up pretty good. It was getting colder and colder and, as the train picked up speed, that wind just came whistling through the car. Ray said, "Hell, I'm about halfway too cold to sleep."

"You get a couple of drinks in you and drag out your sleeping blankets, you'll sleep. I'll bet on it. We ought to have a good three or four hours on the run from Austin to Fort Worth."

"I can stay awake. Besides, I ain't seen Austin in a long time. I used to work for a cattle outfit had a ranch not all that far out of town. Of course that was a long time ago. Used to have me a right pretty girl I was courtin' then."

"What happened to her?"

He shrugged. "Beats the hell out of me. I was mighty young and on the move. I reckon she figured she could do better."

"You ever think about that, Ray? Finding the right woman? Settling down and getting married?"

He shrugged again. "I dunno. Man don't get much chance to meet the right kind of girl in a cowhand's life."

"You ain't a cowhand."

He made a motion with his hand. "Well, you know what I mean. Far as I can remember, that girl in Austin was the last nice girl I was ever around much. I mean in a courtin' fashion."

"I never cared for Austin. Still don't."

"Why not?"

I shrugged. "Don't know. Capital of the state and all that and I just never cared for it. Something kind of made up about it. Don't seem real."

CHAPTER 7

By the time we started getting into Austin Ray Hays was doing a pretty good job of nodding off and then jerking back up awake. But I had the sliding door open and had a bale of hay pulled up, and was sitting and looking out at Austin as it rolled by. I hadn't been there in a while, but it still had that kind of temporary look about it as if everybody in the place was all fixed up to move on at the drop of a hat or the sound of a cannon. Which was just about right. Houston had been the first capital of Texas, back in 1836 when it had won its independence from Mexico and become a republic. But Houston was on the very east coast, and it was a hell of a trip for most folks to go to the coast to transact business that involved the government. So the powers that be decided they needed a more central location for the seat of government, and they sent out a bunch of surveyors and whatnot and decided, based on the then-settled parts of the country, on a spot that was just about in the middle of everywhere. So right then and there, right on the bald-ass prairie, right there without so much as a house in sight, they drove a stake and said that this was the site of the new capital.

Which seemed to me like a kind of haphazard way to set about establishing a city, let alone a capital. As far as I knew, most towns had a reason for being. Either they were a port or on a river, or at a railhead or on the border or in the middle of a big bunch of cattle country or some other such thing. I had never heard of somebody just driving a stake in the ground and saying, "Well, let's unpack. Here she be."

Of course the whole plan of the capital being in the center of the settled areas as they were then was a good idea. It meant nobody had to go any further to see the government about some business than anybody else. The only problem with the plan was that the forefathers hadn't figured on Texas continuing to go west and north and southwest the way it did in the next fifty years. Now the capital was one hundred fifty miles from the coast, but it was near four hundred miles from the New Mexico border in far west Texas.

And watching it as we slowly rolled into the depot and switching yards, it still appeared to me to not quite know what it was except the place where the capital was located. Of course it was a big city of about twenty thousand souls, but a good many of them were transients, and I wasn't just talking about the legislators and the governor and his wife. Of course Austin grew up around the capital. It just being there created a town overnight, drawing mercantiles and hotels and saloons and grocery stores and churches and blacksmiths and every other kind of business you could name. But they always seemed to be changing. Seemed like nothing ever stayed the same, nothing was ever in the same place as it was when you last were there.

The train shuddered and jerked as we come slowly to a stop. I looked back over at Ray. The jerk had jolted him off his bale of hay and he was sitting on the car floor looking around, still about half asleep, trying to figure out where he was.

I said, "We're in Austin, Ray. Short of the depot. I figure they'll be switching around and adding some more freight cars before we pull in to pick up the passengers."

"Yeah," he said. He got up, kind of groggily, and sat back down on the bale of hay and leaned back against the slats of the car.

I leaned out the door and looked up the tracks. The depot appeared to be no more than a few hundred yards away. I figured to have plenty of time to walk up there while the train was switching around and getting itself made up. I said to Ray, "Hays, I'm gonna walk up to the depot and ask about what train we can get out of Fort Worth on into Oklahoma. You hear me?"

"Yeah," he said. But his eyes were closed and he had his hands in his lap.

"Ray, goddammit! I'm going to get out of the car! Now wake up and stay awake!"

That roused him. He sat up, blinking his eyes. He said, "What? What?"

I told him again what I was going to do. "Now, damnit, you stay awake. You hear me? I'll be gone maybe fifteen minutes. See to the horses."

We'd left the horses saddled with the stirrups tied over the seats of the saddles so they wouldn't swing around and bother them when the train motion got rough. And of course, we'd slipped the bits out of their mouths so they could eat hay. They didn't seem to be minding the ride too much, though they hadn't had but an hour of it.

Ray was rubbing his eyes. He said, "I'm fine. I'm fine. Go right ahead."

When the train made a stop at a junction switch I jumped down. Just to be on the safe side I slid the door to. There was something wrong with the lock so that it wouldn't shut tight, but I didn't figure that mattered. I set off up the tracks.

The depot was just running awash with folks, most of them carrying little bundles of their clothes or carpetbags, with here and there some gentry with leather luggage and a hired hand to carry it for them. I finally got up to the window, and the ticket agent was good enough to look up the change for me even though it didn't have nothing to do with his line. It turned out there was a train that very night at eight P.M. that left Fort Worth on its way to Oklahoma City. En route it passed through Chickasha, and I knew that Anadarko wasn't but a good horseback ride from Chickasha. The agent said the line out of Fort

Worth was the TP&O, and that we ought to be in there in plenty of time to get our car hooked on to the eight o'clock train. He told me he'd tell the conductor of our train to spot our car, when they unhooked us, so as to make an easy connection with the TP&O line. He said sometimes the brakemen and the conductors could get kind of ornery if they was carrying a grudge for some reason or another against another line, and would sometimes try and hide a whole string of freight cars.

I left the depot and started back up the tracks toward our train. It was good luck and a good break and no mistake. The way things had been going, I'd fully expected to get to Fort Worth and then get to sit for a couple of days before we found any kind of train going anywhere near where we wanted to go. Or at least where we *thought* we wanted to go. For all I knew we'd get to Anadarko and I'd find out I'd wanted to go to Ohio or Georgia or some other such place the whole time.

There were several other trains in the yard being made up, but I'd marked ours carefully and now I stepped along, trying not to trip, over the rails and between the ties and switches and all the other clutter that you find in a railroad yard. It appeared our train hadn't moved, and I headed about catercorner toward where our car ought to be. I had counted it to be the seventeenth car from the caboose, but walking along, when I counted again, the seventeenth car had its door open. Either the train had indeed moved and the door had slid back, not being latched good, or else Hays had gotten out. Only I didn't see him anywhere. I quickened my pace. Maybe he'd opened the door just to see out. I couldn't for the life of me figure he'd get out of the car and wander off with all that gold in there for any reason under the sun. If he'd had to head for the bushes I knew he'd of waited for me or bust first.

When I got near our car I got up next to the train and went slipping along. I had no reason to expect trouble, but when there's $25,000 involved, you don't take nothing for granted. I got to the end of my car and peeked in between the slats. It was a little darker inside, but I could clearly see a man I didn't know up by the horses at the end of the car. I couldn't see Hays because of the angle and the horses in between.

I watched the man while he untied the bridle of a horse and then slipped the bits in. It was, I noticed, Hays's horse. But I figured the man had just picked the horse that was the easiest to get to. When he had the horse properly bridled he took the reins and turned the horse around and started for the open door. I hunkered down and crept along just under the car so the man couldn't see me. When I got to the bottom of the door I drew my revolver. Looking up over the edge of the floor of the car, I could see the man get to the door and jump down. What he was going to do was to jump the horse out of the car, which, for the horse, was a pretty risky matter, especially in a railroad yard with tracks and ties and switches running all over the place. Normally you used a wooden ramp to load and unload a horse out of a stock car. But what the hell, if the horse made it the man had him a fine animal. If it didn't he'd just steal one somewhere else. Only this one happened to be carrying $12,500 in gold in its saddlebags.

The man hit the ground with his back to the door and the reins of the horse in his hand. As soon as he landed he turned around to face the horse, and as soon as he turned around he saw me. His jaw dropped. I put a finger to my lips with my left hand and stuck my revolver in his belly with my right. I took a quick glance in the car. Hays was slumped on the bale of hay, leaning back against the side of the car, his arms hanging down and his chin on his chest. He was either asleep or he'd been knocked out. If he hadn't been knocked out he soon was going to be. As soon as I got my hands on him.

I turned back to the fellow. He was a kind of young-looking man, maybe in his mid-twenties. He was wearing cattle-working gear, boots and jeans and a hat. He was sort of run-down, looking like he hadn't been making much money lately. But if that was the case, he could always sell the fine-looking Colt .44-caliber revolver he was wearing at his side. I reached over with my left hand and eased it out of his holster. He was still staring at me with his hands raised and his eyes big and round. I pitched his revolver under the train. I didn't figure it landing amongst all the rocks and iron was going to do its new, shiny finish one bit of good.

I said, whispering, "Now I want you to get back up in that car. You understand me?" I prodded him with the barrel of my revolver in case he was hard of hearing. "Just nod your head."

He swallowed and nodded. He said, "Now?"

I said, through gritted teeth, "Goddammit, keep your voice down. You better not wake that man up in there. Now get up in that car and lay flat on your belly until I get aboard. That's all right. I'll tend to the horse."

I waited until he'd climbed quietly into the car and gone flat on his belly before I followed him up into the car holding the horse's reins. Hays slept on. I got up close to the man and said, "Now I want you to get up and take hold of the reins and go over there and wake that fellow up."

"What?" he said. "Hell, he'll shoot me."

"No, but I damn well will if you don't do exactly like I say. You try to make a break for that door—" I was interrupted by a loud snore from Hays. I waited until it had subsided. "You try anything and you can believe I'll shoot you. Dead center. Now go over there and wake him up. When he's awake you hold out the reins and say, 'Here's your horse.' You got that?"

He gave me a kind of funny look, but he took the reins to Hays's horse. He said, "Tell him here's his horse?"

"That's right."

He got up to a kind of crouch and started toward Hays. Then he stopped. He looked back at me, looked at that big black eye in the barrel of my revolver. "Whata you gonna do with me?"

"One thing at a time. Right now you're a horse thief. Let's see if you can do a little acting also."

He straightened up and took the few steps over to Hays. He said, in a kind of low voice, "Mister. Hey, mister."

I said, "You got to yell at him."

He looked at me and then came back to Hays. "Mister!"

"Louder."

"Hey! MISTER!"

Hays suddenly came bolt upright, shaking his head and looking around. He said, "Jus' dozin', Boss, jus' dozin'."

He was still only half awake.

But then the man held the reins in front of his eyes and said, "Here's yore horse."

It got him. His eyes went wide and slowly traveled up the man's arm to his face. He said, "By gawd what in the hell's goin' on in—"

I said, "You awake, Hays?"

He stared at me for a second and then blew out his breath. He said, "Whew! You nearly scairt me to death with that little prank."

I said, "It ain't a prank." I said to the man, "Now go tie the horse where you found him."

I followed him to the end of the car and made sure he secured the horse properly. He'd untied the stirrups and I directed him to do them back up. All the while Hays was watching us and trying to think of something to say. I paid him no mind.

When the fellow was through with the horse I prodded him toward the other end of the car. It was empty back there. I said, "Just go back there and sit down and don't say nothing."

He said, "What are you gonna do with me. Mister, I'm mighty sorry about this but, see, I was in kind of a tight."

I said, "I ain't going to tell you again. Get back there and sit down and shut up."

Hays said, "Boss, I—"

I looked at him and said, with plenty of force, "Shut up, Hays. And keep it shut. Was I you I wouldn't even think, much less talk."

He swallowed and sat back on his bale of hay. I got up, still holding my revolver on the horse thief. The train was starting to move. I got a bottle of whiskey out of the saddlebags on my horse and sat down on the bale of hay I had pulled over next to the door. I pulled out the cork with my teeth, let it fall in my lap, and had a long pull out of the bottle. Neither Hays nor the horse thief asked if they could have a drink.

We sat just like that, not a word out of either of them, until the train had pulled into the depot, taken on some new passengers, and then begun to pull out. One of the horses turned his head around and nickered as if to say, "When in hell we getting out of this little bitty barn that won't hold still?" I guessed it was hard on horses riding on a train and not having the least idea what it was all about. Of course I guess they'd rather have walked to Oklahoma. The only thing I knew was dumber than a horse was Ray Hays.

Once out of the station, the train commenced to pick up speed, gradually at first and then, gaining momentum, faster and faster. By the time we'd left the last of the raw-looking buildings of Austin behind we were rolling along pretty good. I calculated we were doing about thirty miles an hour, which is about as fast as a horse can run full out. Of course he couldn't do that for very long, while a train could do it all day long and some into the night. And I knew we'd get to going even faster. Norris said there were some trains could run sixty miles an hour, a mile a minute, but I didn't much think I cared to ride on one.

As soon as we got into open country I shoved the bale of hay past where Hays was sitting and over toward the horses, placing it further away from the door. I motioned with my revolver. I said to the horse thief, "All right. Get up and come over here and stand in front of the door."

While he made his way forward, staggering a little what with the motion of the car, I sat down on the bale of hay and cocked my pistol. The man heard the sound and looked at me with the fear plain in his face. He had his hands about half raised, but he stopped short of the door. I motioned him further. "Get right in the door."

He took a couple of more steps forward until he was in the opening, but was careful not to get too near the edge. He swallowed. "What're you gonna do? Shoot me in the door so I fall out?"

I shook my head. "I ain't going to shoot you. Not unless I have to."

He nodded his head toward Hays. "Then he gonna shoot me?"

"He ain't gonna shoot anybody. Unless he shoots himself in the foot."

The man said, his face still worried and uncertain, "Then what you gonna do with me?"

I said casually, "Let you go. You can jump any time you're a mind."

He looked outside, at the ground rushing by in a blur. His eyes got scared all over again. "Mister, I didn't aim to steal yore horse. I climbed in this car to ketch me a ride north. I was hopin' it was headed fer Fort Worth. I figured maybe I could get me a job in the stockyards there, maybe save enough money to buy me a good horse."

"I seen that new Colt you had. You could of swapped that for a horse."

He looked back the way we'd come, like he could spot his revolver laying back there in the yard between a couple of tracks. "Man needs a gun," he said.

"Needs a horse more. Where'd you get the Colt? Steal it?"

He shook his head. "Nosir. I bought that second-hand off an old boy. Give him twenty-five dollars and meant to hold on to it."

"Looked new to me."

"I kept it that way. Was practically new when I bought it."

"New Colt costs forty dollars. Buy a halfway decent horse for forty dollars."

"Mister," he said, "I was never thinkin' on stealin' yore horse. But I got in here an' I seen my chance and it just come on me in the spur of the moment to take the chance."

"I don't see where it makes any difference whether you studied on it for a week. Stealing a horse is stealing a horse. I think I'm letting you off light."

He was looking mighty miserable. "I know I done wrong. See, I've had me a bad run of luck lately. Lost my job an' then I lost my horse an' saddle in a poker game. But hell, I do ranch work an' you can't walk out to no cattle ranch an' ast to get on workin' cattle when you're afoot. They'd laugh you off the place."

Out of curiosity I said, jerking my head at Hays, "How come you didn't ease his revolver out of the holster before you untied the horse? If he'd of come to and seen you with his horse he'd of shot the shit out of you."

"I studied on it. But the way he was sleepin' he kind of had his elbow down over the butt of his pistol. I figured he might be a light sleeper and I'd wake him up if I tried to move his arm."

I looked over at Hays, who was staring at the floor. I said, "No, you wouldn't have waked him up. You might could have exploded some dynamite under him and that would have done the trick, but nothing less." I glanced by the thief at the countryside rushing by. We were really traveling. I calculated we were doing upwards of forty miles an hour. I said, "You want to jump on your own or you want me to give you the word?"

He looked out and swallowed hard. He looked back at me. "Mister, I jump off this train at this speed it's liable to break both my legs."

"That's what would probably have happened to that horse if you'd of jumped him out that door on top of all those rocks and all that iron."

He looked down. "I know it. Fact of the business is, I was just studyin' on that, thinkin' 'bout gettin' back in the car and tying that horse back up when you come out from under the train at me."

"Sure you were," I said.

He gave me a look. "Mister, I ain't no horse thief. Not as a general thing. I admit I was thinking of stealing your horse, but that ain't no reason to leave me layin' beside a railroad track forty miles from nowhere with two broken legs."

I looked at him, thinking it over. "Well, I guess we could wait for the next town and then turn you into the sheriff. Course they hang horse thieves."

He looked miserable and didn't say anything.

I felt the train begin to slow, just a little at first, but then it slowed enough I could tell it wasn't slowing for just a crossing but was coming into a town. I dug in my pocket and came out with a few bills. I didn't want to expose my whole roll. I'd had enough of them kind of tricks. I held the money out to the man. It appeared to be about forty-five dollars. He stared at it. I said, "Come over here and get this. Then go back and sit in the door with your legs hanging out. It appears we're coming into a town. When the train slows enough you jump. That money is to help you get a horse, not to buy another revolver. I don't think you're a horse thief, but I do think you're a damn fool. Next man you try and steal a horse off of might not be so easygoing as I am."

He took a hesitant step or two toward me and stretched out his hand. I made him come closer by not moving. Finally he kind of snatched the money. "I am much obliged, mister. That was a mighty Christian thing to do."

"Well don't count on no more acts of charity. Now get on over there and sit in the door. And I'd get off just as quick as I could before I come to my senses and remember you and that horse."

The train was slowing up at a rapid rate. Way up the line I heard the long sound of the steam whistle, waking the people up in whatever town we were arriving at. Just then the young man said, "Maybe someday I'll get a chance to repay you."

Before I could answer he'd jumped. I stood up. He'd jumped onto a slope that led down from the tracks toward what appeared to be a creek. I got up in time to see him rolling over and over in the grass. I took a step to the door and looked back. He was getting up. I went back and sat down on the hay bale. Behind me Hays cleared his throat. I said, "Not a word, Hays. Not one damn word!"

I waited until we'd come in and left the little town of Denton before I said anything. The train was back up to speed, the car rocking and swaying and the rails going by under us, going *clickety-clack* as the wheels ran over the rail joints. I said, still looking out the car door, "All right. We're even. I done the wrong thing back at the hotel and liked to have lost some cash. You done the wrong thing here and like to have lost the gold and a horse. Half the gold I mean."

He said, "Just the horse."

I looked around at him. "What?"

He cleared his throat again. "Just the horse. I would have just lost the horse."

"Hays, when you're wrong you're wrong and you ought to admit it. There was twelve thousand five hundred dollars in gold in each of them saddlebags. The man takes your horse he takes half the gold. He don't know it until later because he thinks he's just stealing a horse, but later on he finds out he's rich."

Hays had a look on his face I couldn't quite place. He looked hurt and determined and insulted and triumphant all at the same time. He said, "Gold wasn't in the saddlebags no more." He thumped the bale of hay he was setting on. "I got concernt when you left I might nod off, so I up an' took the gold off'n the horses and put it under this here bale of hay I'm settin' on."

"What?"

He got up and raised the big bale until I could see the U.S. MINT sacks. He said, "Thar tha' damn gold." He let the bale fall back with a thump. Then he sat back down and gave me a look.

Well, for a minute I didn't know what to say. He figured he had me and he damn near did. I finally said, "Well, you almost got your horse stole. So we are even. Was I you I'd let the matter drop."

But he said, "When was the last time you hear'd 'bout somebody comin' up in a stock car an' makin' off with a horse? They is lots easier places to steal a horse than outten a stock car."

"Ray, if I was you I would let the matter drop."

"That's all right with me," he said.

I turned around and faced the car door. I heard him mutter, "Set some dynamite off under me might wake me up."

I looked around. "What?"

"Nothin'," he said.

I turned back around and, in another moment, I heard him muttering something else. I turned around again and said, "Goddammit, Ray, now what are you mumbling about?"

He gave me a stubborn look. "I was jest wishin' folks would give me money every time I took it into my head to steal a horse. Wouldn't ever have to work a day again. Just go around lookin' like I was goin' to steal a horse."

"All right, all right. You've made your point, dammit. Now get over and open up the pack and see if we've got anything left to eat. I'm about to starve to death. Ought to be some beef and cheese left."

He got off the bale and went over to the packhorse. "Notice you didn't offer me no drink when you had one. Surprised you didn't offer that horse thief one."

Just for plain out long-distance pouting Hays was a world's champion. I figured I was in for a long ride.

He didn't say anything else until right before we got into Fort Worth. He'd got a bale of hay and pulled it over to the open door to watch the beginnings of the big city. I was a few feet behind him taking little bites off the bottle of whiskey every now and then. He said, "Man didn't ast me if *I* wanted to go to Oklahoma. Jest said, 'Git on yore horse!' " He was still looking straight ahead, talking just loud enough for me to hear, but trying to act like he was talking to himself. "Other man he ast if he wanted to jump or did he want a shove. Didn't ast *me*! Ast me an' I'd of tol' him didn't *need* to ast me. I'da jumped on my own. Yessir! Jumped off and *walked* home. Would have walked home *barefoot*. Course nobody ever asts me if *I* want to do sompthin'. They jest *tells* me I want to do it. Never ast me. Pretty soon they be tellin' me what I want for breakfast."

Oh, he was in good form.

We had good luck in Fort Worth. The agent in Austin had wired ahead for us, and the TP&O had everything set to switch our stock car onto the train that was leaving that night for Oklahoma City. Us and the car would be dropped off in Chickasha at six the next morning. The amazing part was that it only cost $40 to go to Chickasha, which was about twice as far as it was from Austin to Fort Worth, which had cost $68. I didn't say nothing or ask any questions. For some time I'd been convinced there was probably a woman at the head of every railroad company. It was the only way I could explain or understand how they thought.

The business got done so easy that it left plenty of time for me and Hays to walk downtown and have dinner in the dining room of the famous Cattleman's Hotel. As near as I knew, every cowman who could get a shine on his boots and get his hat brushed had to take a meal at the Cattleman's whether he owned one cow or ten thousand. It was a nice enough place, but I'd have never thought of bringing it up in conversation that I'd eaten there. Hays and I even got to poke a little fun at the waiter when he come over. It was advertised on the menu that they had a special on oysters, two dollars for a dozen. Since oysters were about as common as fleas where we were from, Hays asked the man if the two dollars was what you got if you was willing to eat a dozen of the slimy things. Of course the waiter didn't think that was too funny. And he probably thought we looked like a couple of yahoos who'd been riding in a stock car all the way from Bastrop, Texas. But it didn't make me any mind. We ate a steak dinner and then had some coffee, and I polished it off with a glass of brandy in a kind of left-handed salute to Wilson Young, who claimed the stuff was the only liquor a civilized man ought to drink. I'd always thought it would be best used for tanning hides, but I was about halfway wishing I had Wilson with me, especially sitting there with a saddlebag on the floor under my feet with the whole $25,000 in it. I'd decided to just put it in the one place, combine it, until we got back on the train. It wasn't that I didn't trust Hays; in fact I dared not even look like I was thinking I didn't trust him if I didn't want him to start pouting again. But we'd swapped off carrying it from the depot down to the hotel, so it hadn't been too much of a burden.

Hays was sitting back with some coffee and a whiskey and looking mellow. Getting out of that stock car for a while and getting a good dinner down had done wonders for his state of mind. He said, "Boss, how come you pick me to fetch along on this trip?"

Well, I was damned if I was going to let him fish me for compliments. "Because we ain't got no dog."

But he wouldn't rise to it. "Naw, I didn't mean of all the hired hands. I meant, with all this money involved it would look like you'd of kept it in the family. Norris or Ben."

"Hays, if you don't know by now that you're a better hand in a tight place than Norris, I'm not going to tell you so."

"I was thinking more of Ben."

I didn't say anything. It was a question I'd of liked answered myself. But I couldn't very well tell him Howard had forbidden it without giving me any reasons. Hell, I could understand why Hays was curious as to the sense of it. So was I. I finally said, "Ben was needed on the ranch. We're cutting the herd for market and I want him to learn a little more about the cattle end of our business. Knowing horses ain't enough to run a ranch."

"You planning on going somewhere?"

I shrugged. "Running around the country with what we got in this saddlebag is a damn good way to make a job come open."

"*That* makes me feel good," Hays said. "Now that jest makes me feel plumb wonderful. Oh, yeah!"

"You can always cut and run. Ain't your money."

That could have hurt his feelings since he liked to think of himself as family, but instead he said something he'd said before. "You and Ben is shore different from Norris. You ever take note of that?"

I just looked at him and shook my head. "Naw! You think so? I thought we was as alike as three peas in a pod."

"You said oncet you figured he must have favored yore mother. What was she like?"

The memory of losing her was still a little painful, even after all the years. It wasn't something I liked to talk about, but I felt I owed Hays a little leeway. I said, "Oh, she was kind of delicate, ladylike. She was from Georgia. Just like Howard. I don't recollect if she was an old flame of his or if he met her while he was driving cattle up there during the War of Rebellion. The Civil War, as they call it up North." I looked off, trying to remember her. "She made us behave ourselves at the table. Made us wash and such. Fussed at us when we got in fights. Talked a lot about us remembering to be gentlemen." I laughed slightly. "I think Norris was the only one listened to her."

"Was she sweet?"

"Yeah," I said. "Kind of embarrassed me. I was scared to hug her very hard on account of she seemed like she might break." I shook my head again. "She just wasn't cut out for this kind of country. This kind of life. In the end I reckon that's what she died of more than anything else. She was like Nora, always talking about the country getting civilized. Except it was a hell of a lot less civilized then than it is now." I swilled the brandy down and got up. "We better get moving. I damn sure don't want to miss this train."

Everything was as we'd left it in the stock car. The horses were fine with plenty of water and hay. They were just kind of restless, confined to the little space as they were. Every once in a while one of them would stamp his feet, making a loud noise, or fight his head a little bit, sawing his head

up and down and making the hardware on his bridle jingle.
I transferred half the gold back into Hays's saddlebags and
we got ourselves settled. It was good and dark. I had the
car door shut and locked from the inside. Wouldn't be
anybody getting in without making a ruckus. We settled
down to wait. Hays was yawning already, though I could
barely see him and him not three feet away, it was that dark.
He said, "Boy, I'm gonna sleep tonight."

I didn't say nothing about the amount of sleep he'd gotten that afternoon. I figured it was better to let a sleeping
Hays lie.

We got out of Fort Worth about eight-fifteen. After that
it wasn't too long until we were starting to make speed. I
sat on the floor and leaned back against a hay bale. I didn't
feel a damn bit guilty about taking the train and not going
cross-country on horseback as Howard had wanted. Right
about then, I figured, we'd be making camp somewhere
short of Austin with about three-hundred miles left to go.
And it would probably be raining too. I heard Hays get up
and go to rustling around with something. He said, "You
want yore bedroll?"

I yawned. I was tireder than I usually was at such an
hour and I wondered why. Then I remembered I hadn't
gotten much sleep the night before. "Yeah, throw it on
over here."

I felt it thump down by my side. My eyes were starting
to adjust to the dark of the car, and I could make out Hays's
dim form as he went about bedding down. I said, "You light
a smoke, be damn shore you don't go to sleep before you're
sure it's out. This car is full of hay and ain't a fire brigade
in the country could catch us if we catch on fire."

"I wuz jest thinkin' of mentionin' the same thing to
you."

"Sure you were," I said.

I rolled out my sleeping blankets. Then I shucked the
heavy jacket I'd been wearing, took off my gun belt, hat,
and boots, loosened my jeans, and crawled in between the
blankets. Since I didn't have a saddle for a pillow and, as

cold as it was starting to get, didn't want to use a blanket for one, I just wadded up my sheepskin-lined coat and put it to use to keep my head off the car floor. I had the bottle of whiskey handy, and I took a good pull and then sung out to ask Hays if he wanted a drink.

He said from somewhere up near the horses, "I got me one. Piece of one, anyway. Say, you notice it's gettin' right brisk? Where the hell we headed, the North Pole?"

He was right. Rolling along at forty miles an hour like we were, with the cold wind just whipping through the slats of the car, it was more than a little chilly. I said, "I noticed you got up there by the horses so you could suck a little warmth off them."

"Naw, was the horses wanted me to git up here an' keep *them* warm. Hell, they gonna find us froze stiff in the mornin'."

"Shut up, Hays," I said. "I'm trying not to think about it."

I wrapped up in my blankets as best I could, pulling them up to where they were nearly over my head. The wind was still nearly going through me. I finally got up, stumbling around in the dark, and pushed three bales of hay together so they blocked most of the wind off me. Then I went through the chore of getting back in my blankets and getting them adjusted again. It had been a lot of trouble, but it had been worth it.

Hays said, "Boss?"

"What!"

"Will you git up an' take a leak fer me? It's too cold to git out from under the covers an' I'm about to pop."

"Hays, if you bother me again I'm going to make you jump. You was upset you didn't get asked to jump, well, you just let me get relaxed again and open your yap and you'll get your wish."

I heard him rustling around, getting up to take a leak. I said, "You better be damn shore that don't spray back in this direction."

Then I heard him cursing under his breath and stamping around toward the back of the car, getting past me. After a little he came up the side of the car, heading back to his blankets, going "Brrrrrr" and hugging himself, his teeth chattering.

But finally everything settled down. Wrapped up like I was, my own body heat kind of spread around and got trapped in the blankets and I commenced to warm up. I lay there with my eyes shut wishing that I was home with Nora and the rest of my family and my cattle and in my own bed. But of course, wishing wasn't going to do it. I got to thinking about Nora and what a pistol she was and about what had happened the last time she'd dragged me to church. The preacher had been preaching and I was about half asleep. All of a sudden he'd said, "Everybody that wants to go to heaven, stand up. Stand up if you want to go to heaven." Well, everybody stood up but me. I'd still been about half asleep and had missed the whole occasion. Going home in the buggy, Nora had been quiet most of the way. Just before we got home she'd said, in a kind of hurt, uncertain voice, "Justa, don't you want to go to heaven?" Well, it had caught me off balance. I'd had no idea what she was talking about. So I'd said that yes, of course, I wanted to go to heaven. She'd said, "Well, then how come you didn't stand when the Reverend said for everybody that wanted to go to heaven to get up?" I'd looked over at her, figuring I was in trouble, and said the first thing that came into my mind. I'd said, "Why, hell, I thought he was getting up a load for right then and there."

Naturally she'd smacked me on the chest with her little fist and said, "Oh, you heathen! Is nothing sacred to you? I swear, Justa Williams, you are going to joke yourself into serious trouble one of these days. Why, that's almost sacrilegious."

But I'd got her to laughing a little bit later, and she'd admitted that such an interpretation might have been put on the situation. Sometimes I think she acted churchy and religious because it was expected of her. Not that she wasn't a true Christian, she was, but she kind of put on the dog about it like my mother had and Nora's mother and all the good matrons I'd ever known. I'd one time asked her if she knew why Baptists never made love standing up. Naturally she'd acted horrified and righteous about such a question, but it hadn't kept her from saying no, she didn't know why. Why? Then when I'd told her it was because they were afraid God would think they were dancing, she'd done about the same: hit me in the chest and blushed and said I was outrageous and was storing up sin and suffering for myself. But later, I'd caught her in the kitchen giggling to herself.

Oh, Nora was fun to be with. Especially in bed.

I shivered and listened to the creak of the car and the sound of the horses stirring around and the whistle of the wind. It was uncomfortable, but it sure as hell beat making thirty or forty miles a day.

CHAPTER 8

The train didn't get into Chickasha until after seven the next morning. Hays and I were grateful for it running late. The delay at least let the sun get up enough to take the brittle edge off the cold. The station agent told us it was the earliest norther he could remember in his thirty years in Oklahoma. That was small consolation to us, knowing how mild it probably was back home. But then Hays said, as we were going back out into the rail yard to see about getting our horses dismounted from the train, "Boss, you realize this blue norther would have caught us out on the open prairie about twenty miles either side of Austin if we hadn't of took the train?"

I nodded. "Yes, that is something to be thankful for." But I thought to myself that, if the norther had made it all the way to the coast, which it mostly didn't, it would have caught me in my bed or sitting in my kitchen drinking coffee if Howard hadn't come up with this godawful request of his.

We went back to our car, which had been detached from the train, which had already pulled out for Oklahoma City, and stood around waiting for the railroad hired hands to bring down a wooden ramp so we could lead our horses down it. Hays said, "Boss, I'm gonna say something. Might make you mad, might not. But I'm gonna say it just the same. I *still* can't understand what you done. You let that

142

horse thief off scot-free! Not only let him off without puttin' a mark on him, you give him money on top of that! If I live to be a hunnert I'll never unnerstan' that. The man was a thief! I didn't figure he ought to be shot, but I'm damned if I can see you re-wardin' him."

There really wasn't much I could answer to that. I'd sort of surprised myself. I'd meant to make the young man jump off the train while it was running pretty fast and leave it to Providence to punish him. In the jump he could have gotten off light or he could have broken his neck. Instead I'd given him money and then practically let him step off the train. I said, "I don't know, Hays. The way the fellow acted and talked—he said he wasn't a horse thief and I believed him."

"What you think that was he was leading out of here, a big dog?"

"No, I mean I don't think he would have gone through with it. And even if he had, he'd of been sorry later."

"And we'd still been a horse short. But he made out better this way. Got *cash* money for not stealin' the horse."

I smiled and looked down. "Well, I had deprived him of his principal asset. I took his Colt revolver away from him and flung it away."

"Which you've done with other parties without feelin' no need to hand 'em a wad of cash."

I could see two railroad hired hands hurrying our way carrying a ramp between them. I said, "You figure I ought to have shot the man?"

"That ain't far from what you'd normally done. No questions, no answers, just a quick settlement. The man was stealin' the goddam horse!"

I shrugged. "Guess I'm getting soft."

"Not whar I be concerned you ain't."

Well, it was a puzzle, but I didn't have time to think about it. The railroad hands got there and put the ramp up to the car door, and me and Hays went aboard and led the horses down the ramp and out onto the ground. They were rested and frisky in the cold air. We'd already fixed the saddle stirrups and the bridles, so we just mounted up and Hays took the packhorse on lead and we started toward town. Chickasha didn't appear all that big, maybe three thousand souls, but it was a kind of funny-looking town. The depot was on the north end, so we took our time and rode all the way down the main street and then turned back the way we'd come. It seemed to me that the town, the business section anyway, was cut right in two. The northern half appeared to be Indian, while the southern end was white. It wasn't anything announced, it was just something that I felt. There were no Indian words on the stores in the northern end or anything like that; in fact, both ends looked pretty much the same. About the only thing that was noticeable was that there weren't any saloons among the northern bunch of businesses. And no churches either. All that was to the south. But there was one big building at the far end of the town that was built out of logs. It was just one story but it was a mighty big one story, and it appeared old and important and well-built.

After we'd made the tour Hays said, "Well, what now?"

I looked at my watch. It was just half past seven. There weren't many people on the street and not many stores had opened up. Looking toward the north I could see a low range of hills and, it appeared, a number of teepees, even in that late day and age. I said, "Well, let's get some breakfast. I don't reckon that Tribal Council is open yet."

Ray pointed across the street at a cafe. "That looks like a good 'un."

But I said carefully, "Naw, let's go back down to the south end of town. There's a big hotel there. You can't go wrong on hotel grub. Especially breakfasts."

There were surprisingly few customers when we went into the dining room of the hotel. We shucked off our heavy jackets, taking pleasure in the warmth coming from the wood stove in the corner of the place. Hays said, "My goodness, this shore feels good. I swear it's cold enough outside to snow." He dropped the saddlebag he'd been carrying.

CHEROKEE

We got sat down, and a man in a greasy apron came over to take our order. We both just ordered ham and eggs and grits and biscuits. I was surprised to see grits as far north as we were, but there they were on the bill of fare. While the man was pouring us some coffee I asked him if that big building up north was the Tribal Council.

He'd been giving me looks ever since we'd sat down, and now he set the big coffeepot down and give me a good staring over. He said, "You Injun?"

Hays laughed, but I said, "Not that I know of. Why?"

He picked up the coffeepot and filled my cup. " 'Cause Injuns ain't allowed in here."

I said, "How come?"

He looked at me like I'd just fell off a sour apple tree. "You ain't from around here?"

"Never been here before in my life."

He said, "You are smack dab in the middle of the Cherokee reservation. Damn few places left fer white folks around here. We be tryin' to keep it that way."

I said. "I taken notice when we were coming up the street that it looked like it was divided. I ain't got no good reason to think that, but the north end looks Indian. And I don't mean because I saw just Indians there."

He nodded, still holding the coffeepot handle by an end of his apron. "They's a line right through the middle of town. You can't see it, but it's thar. The Injuns keep to they end."

I said, "They can't come down here?"

The waiter said, "They got the money they can come down here and buy a shirt or a saddle or a pair of jeans or a bucket, but they can't buy no liquor or eat down here or use a hotel."

I said, "What about a white man? Can he go up to the north end?"

The waiter was a grim-faced sort of man about fifty who looked like he could use a shave and a bath. He said, "Yeah. Hell, they dyin' fer us to come down there an' spend our money. Yeah, a white man can go all over town, git anythang he wants."

Hays said, "Thet don't seem very square."

I gave him a quick look, but the waiter kind of leaned forward and said, "Talk like that around here gen'lly comes from folks lookin' fer trouble. Messin' in other folks' business."

I jumped in before Hays could say anything. "We're just passing through. I'm lookin' for a fellow and figured to ask at the Tribal Council about him."

The waiter relaxed a little. I guessed he figured we were sticking our nose in where it didn't belong. He said, "Yeah, it's that big building at the north end of town. If yore man's Injun or married to Injun they'll know. Got records go way back. Ah'll say this fer them Cherokees. If I got to put up with Injuns the Cherokees be the best of the bunch. Even if the gummit does mollycoddle the shit outten 'em. All Injuns is lazy, worthless bastards, but yore Cherokee is 'bout the best of a poor lot."

Hays said, "You said they couldn't get a drink this side of town. Ah didn't see no saloons lookin' north."

The waiter said, "Huh! They got they saloons. Jest don't call 'em that is all. They's a place up the street called the Cigar Store. Only don't go in there 'xpectin' to buy a smoke. Place sells whuskey. You kin git all the whuskey you want on the Injun side. Cheaper too than crost the line. Thet's wha'r I buy mine to take home. Course they ain't suppose to have it. Law says they ain't supposed to be none on the reservation 'cept what's controlled by white men. This end of town is knowed as a sutler's store. All of it. The very hotel you a-sittin' in. In fact, oncet, it was jest a sutler's store. Gummit give who owned it hunnert acres. Town growed up round it an' it jest natcherly growed. Line down the middle of town is the property line fer the sutler's place. So all this is private prop'ity. Injuns jest tacked on they part of it at the line."

Hays said, "Well, if the law says they can't have it, where they get it? An' how come it's cheaper?"

The waiter moved away, toward the kitchen. He said, over his shoulder, "Ast them Injuns. Beats the hell out of me."

We ate our breakfast when it came and didn't have no more words with the waiter. I didn't really know what good it was going to do to ask at the Tribal Council for Charlie Stevens since he wasn't an Indian, but Lew Vara said they kept up with just about everybody, and especially anybody that would have had much dealings with the Indians. I figured a sawmill operator would have had to have had a few Indian customers. But it didn't make much difference. The train had brought us here, and it wasn't going to take more than a few minutes to ask and it certainly couldn't hurt anything.

I paid our score and we walked out of the hotel buttoning our jackets. It seemed to have warmed up, though I didn't know if it was the weather or the good breakfast we had in our belly.

Hays said, "That ol' boy wadn't especially fond of Injuns, was he?"

"You got to remember, Hays, wasn't that long ago that an Indian wasn't much different than a panther or a cougar or a bear except they were a hell of a lot more dangerous."

"Yeah, but I've knowed some Cherokees. Even worked oncet with one on a ranch up in the Panhandle. Damned good cowhand. They suppose t' have been a sight more civilized than even some of the whites or Mes'kins round here."

"Yeah, I've heard that," I said. "Howard said they were a far piece from the Comanches or some of them other tribes would just as soon skin you alive as look at you."

"So where does that ol' boy waitin' tables git off actin' so high and mighty about them? I don't see whar he's got all thet much to brag about, hustlin' hash an' pourin' coffee."

"His kind have always got to have somebody to look down on so they won't know how low they really are. Anyway, keep your mouth shut about the subject. We ain't up here doin' good works for the church; we're carrying this here worrisome gold and I'm in a hurry to get shut of it."

While we were putting the saddlebags back on the horses he looked across at me and said, in that sneaky way of his, "You know, I can see whar that ol' boy didn't want to give you no breakfast. You was to let yore hair grow out and braid it an' git a little paint on yore face, why, you'd be right at home in a teepee. I never noticed it before it was called to my attention. I reckon I'd better call you 'Chief' from now on instead of Boss."

I gave him a look. "You better be worrying about what I call you. How about 'out-of-a-job'?"

We mounted up and rode slowly down the street toward the big log building at the end. I could almost tell when we passed the line in the middle of town, though there wasn't a single marker. I guessed it was just something everybody knew about and understood. I agreed with Hays; it seemed like a damn poor way to treat some folks who, from all appearances, were doing a pretty good job of being civilized.

We tied up in front of the big building that I had guessed right was the Tribal Council. I left Hays to watch the horses and the gold and went inside. It was plenty light enough to see. They had a whole rack of windows opening on the north and some back to the east. I went into a kind of outer room. There were three or four desks and some men sitting behind them working over papers. They were all dressed in regular clothes, and only one of the men had long hair in braids. I picked out an older-looking man and went up to him. He looked up as I approached. There was a chair beside his desk. He said, "Howdy."

The man had some gray in his black hair, but his face didn't look much older than mine. I said, "Howdy. I'm looking for a fellow. Hope you can help me. He's an old friend of my father's and I've come up from Texas to find him."

The man said, "Is he Cherokee?"

I shook my head. "No."

"Is he Indian?"

"No."

"Married to Cherokee?"

I smiled slightly. "A friend of mine who used to live up here said the Tribal Council kind of kept up with everybody. I hate to waste your time."

"Oh, you're not wasting my time. That is what I'm here for. Sit down and tell me the name of this person. Maybe he is in our files. Who can say?"

When I sat down he said, putting out his hand, "My name is Joe Slowfox."

I shook hands with him and told him mine.

He said, "So you have come up from Texas. A long distance?"

"Yes," I said. "I live down in the south."

"Then this must be important business to bring you so far. Tell me this man's name and I will do my best to help you."

"Charlie Stevens."

Mister Slowfox laughed. "Oh, I don't have to look in my files for that one. Charlie is an old friend of my people. In fact Charlie was married to one of the tribe."

"He was?" I wasn't particularly surprised, considering where I was and that the bulk of the people, including women, were Cherokee. I was just mainly surprised that Howard hadn't mentioned it. It would have made my job a lot simpler if he had told me. But I reckoned it hadn't occurred to him.

Mister Slowfox said, "The girl was not full blood of the tribe. But her mother was Cherokee, and when the mother is Cherokee we consider that to make the baby Cherokee also."

"Not the father?"

Mister Slowfox shook his head. "The bull casts many seeds but the calf comes only from the cow."

"I see," I said. "If the mother's full-blood Cherokee, then you know damn good and well the offspring is at least

half-blood. I do that with my cattle as a matter of fact."
I suddenly thought I might have given offense. I rushed
to say, "I didn't mean no disrespect making it sound like
I was comparing my cattle to your people."

He smiled. "Why should that bother me? It is a good
way to do it, right? A sure way."

I nodded, glad I hadn't put my foot in it. "Would you
have any idea where Charlie Stevens would be?"

"Certainly. Your father must have told you he had a
sawmill in Anadarko?"

"Yeah."

The Indian held his palms up. "He still has it."

"And he's there now?"

"So far as I know. Charlie was here but a few days ago.
We buy a lot of lumber from Charlie. He said he was going
home and Charlie speaks with a straight tongue."

I gave him a look and he smiled slightly.

He said, "I put that last in at no extra charge."

I got up. "You didn't have to. I believed you were an
Indian. What do I owe you?"

He shook his head. "For telling you where to find an
old friend? Nothing, of course. Do you need any other
help?"

I shook my head. "No, I got a pretty good idea where
Anadarko is. Due west."

"And a little to the north."

"Well, much obliged." I turned to walk out, and then
paused. "One thing I would like to ask you . . ."

"Yes?"

"Well . . ." I was a little embarrassed. "I was kind of
wondering where ya'll got those names. Like Slowfox."

He smiled. "If I told you my real name you could not
write it down. That is my name in English, but it means
the same. My father named me Slowfox because he saw
some dogs catch a fox the night before I was born. Our
names are taken from dreams or from what is seen in
nature. Some people think that a name such as Swiftdeer
would mean the man who is named that can run very fast.

But that is a stupid way to think because the man was named before he could even walk. He might be as slow as Christmas."

"Well, I was one of them stupid people that thought thataway. I appreciate you straightening me out."

I give him a little salute and went on out. Hays was leaning against a post, smoking a cigarillo and waiting. I said, "Let's go," and we mounted up and turned our horses north.

Just a little beyond the edge of town we struck a road running mostly to the west. We took it and started off across the rolling land. The country was so stark it looked like I'd never seen its kind before, even though I'd seen even worse out in west Texas. I figured it had been so long since I'd been away from the gentle land of the coast that I was just shocked by the change. The country looked almost bare. You'd look ahead and see a patch of ground and think it was just yellow clay, but when you got up to it, you could see it was dried grass that had been cropped off so close, either by cattle or game, that it was nearly down to the roots. We saw a good many trees, poplar and elm and osage, and lodgepole pine and even some oak. But except for the pine, they were all as bare as fence posts, and just kind of stuck up in the cold sky like so many skeletons.

The country rolled, as I say, and then made little hills and shallow valleys, with here and there a butte rising kind of stubbornly straight up from the prairie. It just wasn't the most welcoming country I'd ever seen. But then, I had to remember that I was just come from an area where grass nearly grew all year round and a hard freeze was a seldom thing. That was one of the drawbacks of railroad travel; it was just too fast, it didn't give you time to adjust. You get on the train one morning and the weather is mild and every tree is still in full leaf. Then next morning, you find yourself in a country that has suddenly been frozen over and doesn't appear as if it could grow anything but icicles. Of course I knew I could come back to this same place in the spring and wouldn't even recognize it.

Hays said, "Where we a-going?"

"Anadarko. Town about twenty miles away."

"You git directions in that Injun house?"

I shook my head. "Naw. Lew Vara told me."

"Lew Vara? He here?"

I gave him a look. "Of course not, you ninny."

"Call me a ninny! You tell me you got directions to this here place, Anna what?"

"Anadarko. Lew gave me the directions back in Blessing."

He just looked at me.

I said, "Lew knows this country. He knew we had to come to Chickasha on account of the Tribal Council. He said Anadarko was just west of there. You satisfied?"

"I figured you found Sitting Bull in thar and he told you where to go. How'd you get along with them Injuns? You talk sign language?"

I said, "I only saw one 'Injun,' as you call him. And was I you, I wouldn't get in any spelling bees with him. I would reckon he is a little more up on his reading and writing and ciphering."

"Well, never mind about all that," he said. "I want to know if you found out anything about this Charlie Stevens we're lookin' for."

"Man said he was in Anadarko."

Hays looked at me. "You mean we might ride on about fifteen or sixteen more miles and run across this *hombre,* and hand him these sacks of lit dynamite and turn around and head for home? Just like that?"

I gave him a hard look. "Goddammit, Hays, don't you have better sense than to put your mouth on our luck?"

He realized immediately what he'd done. "Damn my mouth! Justa, I'm sorry."

"With you saying that, he will have just got on a train and left the country for a month! Goddammit, Hays, you *know* better than that."

"I know," he said. He hung his head. "I know it. Damnit!"

We had been riding for about an hour. I got out my watch and looked at it. It was about half past nine. "Let's kick these ponies up and make a few miles."

We put the horses into a slow gallop, the packhorse staying right up and not having to be led. It was a good road, straight and flat, but then it didn't have much to curve around. As we rode we now and again met a farmer in a buckboard or a man and woman in a buggy. You could tell they were Indian, but they were dressed just as proper as anyone you'd want to see. I didn't understand this reservation business, and one of these days I was going to have to ask somebody about it. I couldn't figure if the reservation was intended to keep the Indians in or the whites out or both.

It was strange seeing an occasional teepee, though these now were made out of canvas rather than buffalo or deer skins. Usually they were set in the middle of a big patch of drying and dead corn stalks.

Now and again we'd see a cabin, the lower half made out of logs or rough-sawed timber and the roof out of canvas. Most of them had a corral outside with a few horses standing around with their heads down. Like the teepees the cabins looked weather-beaten and lonesome. But you knew somebody was home on account of the thin trail of smoke rising from the chimmney pipe up into the cold air.

There were some cattle scattered here and there, but they didn't appear to be of any particular breed. They were kind of poor-looking. I figured that, in a harsh country such as central Oklahoma, they sold off most of their stock except mamma cows and bulls before the winter.

Most of the country was poor-looking, but now and again you'd see a big two-story clapboard house painted white set well back from the road. Most of them had two or three well-kept barns or outbuildings with several corrals, and usually some fields of winter wheat or oats along with stubbled fields of harvested wheat or corn.

Hays said, as we pulled the horses down to give them a blow, "This here country is dead."

"Now it is," I said. "But I got a feeling it does fancy well at other times of the year."

He pointed to the telegraph poles that ran alongside the road. "How come we didn't take the train?"

"Because there ain't one to Anadarko. At least that's what the agent in Fort Worth told me. I know what you're thinking, but there are places where the telegraph runs that the trains don't go. Remember, we're on a reservation. Everything ain't going to be exactly as you expect."

"What the hell is a reservation anyway?"

"I'm the wrong one to ask that question."

"Hard to believe we was in Blessing just a few days ago."

"Let's push these horses up some more. I'm already hungry again. I'd like to get into that town and get some lunch."

"From the sound of the name of the place all we likely to be able to get is pemmican."

I just give him a sour look. Hays wasn't physically able to go more than half an hour without saying something smart-alecky.

About an hour and a half later we topped a little rise and saw a pretty little town about a mile off, nestled down in a little shallow valley. We rode straight on toward it. It was about the size of Blessing, and could have been Blessing had Blessing had a bunch of teepees scattered around outside of town and if most of the horses on its streets were pintos and paints.

Hays said, "Boy, them Injuns like them colored-up horses, don't they?"

"If it was what you were used to you'd like them fine yourself."

We were looking for the sawmill, and it wasn't hard to find. It was by far the biggest structure in town. We were still a half mile out of town when I spotted it down to the south and a little behind the buildings on the main street. I pointed it out to Hays. "Let's look for our man there."

As we rode closer I could see clouds of steam rising from the place. Obviously Charlie Stevens had converted from a mill race that would only rough-hew logs to a steam engine that would run a blade fast enough to cut fine lumber.

And as we got closer we could hear the sound of the place. It sounded like the biggest hornet's nest in the world, giving off a variety of high-pitched whines that made you just want to grit your teeth. I had no earthly idea how men worked inside such a racket for any stretch of time.

We went past the main street and rode around the line of buildings at the top of the town. I could see a big pile of logs up at the back of the sawmill. And beyond them was the biggest pile of sawdust I'd ever seen. Back in Matagorda County it would have made a fair-sized hill. The sawmill itself was made out of corrugated tin and was nearly two stories high. I could see the line of the river that Howard had mentioned to me running close to the mill. I figured the mill race was long since gone, but then we got closer and I saw that it was still in operation, though now it appeared to be used to turn big fans that blew into an open side of the mill. They were disconnected now, but I figured they were used in the summer to cool the place off. The sun beating down on that corrugated tin in the summer could probably make it hot enough to heat soup without a fire.

Hays leaned toward me. "What a racket!"

"Yeah." If Charlie Stevens was in there we were going to have to go someplace else to talk.

We pulled up at what appeared to be the office. I dismounted, once again leaving Hays to watch the gold. I went inside a little room that had one desk and a little wood-burning stove. An Indian-looking fellow was at the desk. He looked up. He said, "Howdy."

I told him howdy. There was a big window in the back of the office that gave off into the mill. It appeared to me that they were running three band saws, all cutting at the same time. There appeared to be about four boilers. I could see men shoveling sawdust into the fireboxes of each one. That, I thought, was a smart idea. Make your own fuel. The only thing I wondered was where they got the logs. I figured they had them hauled in from somewhere because there damn sure wasn't enough trees around the area to support such an operation.

I said to the man at the desk, "I'm looking for Charlie Stevens."

"Mister Charlie gone to his house. Went to eat." He pointed to a clock at the wall. "Noontime." He looked young and smart, but I'd given up on figuring Indians.

"Where's he live?"

The clerk pointed south with a pencil. "Down that way, just a little beyond the edge of town. Big white house. But Mister Charlie making his meal right now."

"All right, how long has he been gone? Long enough to eat? This is important. I've come a long way to see Mister Stevens."

"Mister Charlie gone half hour. Not long enough to eat. Then Mister Charlie make a little nap. Mister Charlie getting old."

"I know how old Mister Stevens is. Does he still work here?"

The Indian pulled his head back like I was a fool to be avoided. "Work here? This Mister Charlie's mill. Mister Charlie don't let nobody else run his business. We all work for Mister Charlie."

"Is this an Indian town?"

He gave me a blank look. "What you mean, Indian town? This Anadarko."

"Is there a place where me and my partner can get a bite to eat while we wait for Mister Stevens to eat his lunch and take his nap."

"Sure." He swept his pencil. "You go back up to the end of town and ride down Main Street, plenty places to eat. Maybe three, four."

I hesitated. "Uh, are white men welcome?"

He looked at me for a few, long seconds and said, "I don' know, brother. You don' look white to me. You tryin' to make some people think you ain't an Injun?"

Then he smiled slightly. "Go anyplace. They don't care so long as you got money. I got to tell this one to Mister Charlie."

I went back outside feeling like a damn fool. As I was mounting up I told Ray what the situation was. He said, "Aw, goddammit, Justa, that just means we got to lug these saddlebags into another damn cafe and sit there eatin' with one eye on the floor and the other on the plate. Hell, ain't they someplace safe we can store this dynamite?"

"Maybe there's a bank. Hell, you're right. I'm as sick of this damn gold as you are."

We rode back the way we'd come and circled the line of buildings on our side of town, and then started down the main street looking on both sides for a bank. At the second intersection we saw an imposing brick building on the corner with a sign that said FIRST UNITED STATES CHEROKEE BANK. I said, "Let's try in here. You wait with the horses and the saddlebags until I go in and see if they'll take it."

I went inside. It appeared to me that most of the customers were Indian and most of the clerks and such that ran the bank were white. I went up to one of the windows and told the young man there that I wanted to see one of the bank officers, preferably the president. He stood there in a high-starched collar wearing a foulard tie on an Indian reservation and gave me a good looking-over, obviously on the premise that I was probably a bank robber. I was pretty trail-worn, or rather pretty train-worn, so I could understand his suspicions. I just didn't have time for them. I said, "Look, go tell the head man that a friend of Charlie Stevens is out here and I need to discuss something with him in private. Now be quick about it."

Well, the name of Charlie Stevens did the trick, as I had expected it would. The bank president came out, and I introduced myself and said I had a little problem. We went back to his office and I told him about the gold. He tried not to show any expression, but he couldn't keep a tone out of his voice when he said, "You have come all the way from south Texas with twenty-five thousand dollars in *gold* in your saddlebags? My gawd!"

He was an obliging fellow, and said he'd be more than glad to put the gold on deposit for us. I went outside, and me and Hays lugged in the saddlebags and went directly into the president's office. He closed the door after calling a couple of clerks in to handle the counting and sorting. He said, "No use telling everybody in town about this. We don't have many bad apples around here, but you never can tell who might be drifting through town."

When the counting was done he gave me a deposit slip and said he was actually glad to have it on hand. "The natives around here prefer gold for some reason."

It kind of stopped him when I said, "Sir, I wish you wouldn't do anything but hold it for a little while. A few hours."

"You mean you want to keep it as it is?" He gave me a kind of funny look. He half smiled. "I can assure you that money is money. Are you Cherokee?"

Hell, I was getting tired of that damn question. Here he was taking me for some Indian that didn't trust greenbacks and preferred gold. I said, a little stiffly, "No, it has nothing to do with me. It has to do with Charlie Stevens, my father's old partner. I'm only acting under orders." As I said it I gave Howard another damn good cussing in my mind for saddling me with the damned gold. "If you'll be kind enough to leave it in its present form, somebody will be here to tell you what to do with it."

He said, not near so friendly, "We close at three."

Going out, Hays said, "That's some high-hat bastard."

I said, "Hell, Hays, he figured he was getting an unexpected deposit of twenty-five thousand dollars. That's a big deposit to a bank like that. Then he finds out I only want to put it there for safekeeping. Man was disappointed, he wasn't high-hatting."

"Hell, he's gonna git it anyway, ain't he? Turn it over to this Stevens fellow. This town don't look like it's got more'n one bank to me."

We mounted up. I said, "Let's get something to eat and then go see Charlie Stevens. God, it feels good not to have that damn gold to worry about."

"I heard that," Ray said. "And you can say it again. I never knowed money could be such a bother!"

"It gets heavy," I said.

We ate at a little cafe that looked to be about the best of the bunch. It had already gone one o'clock, so we had the place pretty well to ourselves. I had my mouth all set for a steak and a few beers, but they didn't have steak and they didn't have beer, so we made do with some beef stew and corn fritters.

Hays said, "Don't they sell liquor in this town? Is this an all-Injun town an' they ain't got no spirits?"

"I saw a couple of saloons. Both ends of town. Maybe Mister Stevens can put us straight on the matter."

"I can't remember when I was so anxious to meet up with a genn'lman as I am with this Mister Stevens."

"Not as much as me."

"I take it as soon as we see him and you do your business we can light a shuck fer home."

"Just as fast as it's done."

Charlie Stevens himself answered the door. He lived in a large, nicely built, two-story white house right at the edge of town. He had a nice yard that still had a little bit of green in it, and I'd caught sight of a little winter vegetable garden out back as we rode up. I'd left Hays outside the white picket fence, and climbed the steps to the porch and knocked on the door. I didn't figure Hays needed to know why we'd packed that gold all the way from Blessing, and if it got to eating on him so much, I'd just make up some lie. But right now, it was business between Howard and this Charlie Stevens.

A friendly-looking gray-haired man came to my knock, opening the big wooden front door but leaving the screen door between us. He was in his shirtsleeves, only his right sleeve didn't have an arm in it. He said, "Yes?" looking me over through the screen.

I'd done what I could to knock some of the dust off my clothes, but I still didn't look all that fair. I said, "Charlie Stevens?" trying not to look at his missing limb.

He nodded and I could see, the way the sun was slanting in under the porch roof, that his hair was more white than gray. But he was still a vigorous-looking wiry man for his age. It give me a pang to think Howard could have looked as good except for the death of Alice, our mother, and the bullet through his chest. He said, "Yeah, I'm old Charlie Stevens. Least that's the way they refer to me around here. Now who might you be? Something familiar about you, though I can't place it right now."

"My name is Justa Williams. I'm the oldest son of Howard Williams. He sent me up to deliver something to you."

He stared at me for a long moment and then opened the door. I saw him glance past me at Ray Hays. But he said, "Then I expect you'd better come in. What about your companion out there?"

I was in the hallway of the house now. It was dim in contrast to the bright sunshine outside. I said, "He's all right for now. He's one of my hired hands."

Mister Stevens said, "Still no reason to leave him sitting a horse out in the cold."

I was uncomfortable and really didn't know why. "I don't reckon our business will take all that long."

He was leading me into the innards of the house. He said, looking back at me, "That so? You've come a long ways if you've come from where I think you have. Long trip, short visit, huh?"

"I'm just a messenger boy, Mister Stevens."

CHEROKEE

We were in a large comfortable living room by then. It seemed to kind of jut out from the house because it had windows, big windows, on three sides and was just flooded with sunlight. Mister Stevens sank into a big, overstuffed morris chair that looked like the mate to the one in my own parlor. He waved his hand. "Take a chair, take a chair. Sit anywhere you want to."

I thanked him, and sat down in a straight-backed chair with padding on the bottom but none on the wooden back or arms. There was a piano over in the corner and the room, though well lived in, was obviously furnished by someone of means and taste. I set my hat down on the floor beside me.

Mister Stevens pointed over at the hat. He said, "They don't do that around here. In fact, come to think of it, they don't do it much of anywheres except Texas."

I didn't know what he was talking about. "What's that, sir?"

He pointed again. "Set their hats down on the crown. They set 'em brim down around here."

I half smiled. "Then all the luck will run out. Besides that, it saves the shape of the brim. But Texans tell folks about the luck. Makes a better story."

He was looking at me carefully. He had lively blue eyes and a kind of naturally inquisitive look to his face. Maybe it was the wrinkles in his forehead that made him look like he was about to ask a question. He said, "So you're Howard's oldest boy."

"Yessir," I said. His sleeve was pinned with a safety pin.

"You favor him. Some. But I can see a lot of your mother in you."

I was surprised. I said, "You knew my mother?"

He gave me a quick look and then smiled, a big smile. "Oh, yes. I knew your mother. Yes indeed." He looked over toward a sideboard where some decanters that I reckoned to be different kind of liquors were sitting. He said, "Would you like something to drink?"

161

"Nosir," I said. He didn't seem at all conscious about the stump of his arm.

"I never knew Howard Williams to pass up a drink of whiskey. Has the acorn fallen far from the tree?"

"Nosir, I just had some lunch. We were waiting for you to eat and get in your nap." The truth of the matter was I wasn't certain of what was going to get said in the next few minutes, and if the occasion was to turn ugly or unpleasant I didn't want to be sitting there with a drink of the man's whiskey in my hand. Of course I didn't see how it could turn unpleasant. I was bringing him money, and Charlie Stevens didn't look like the kind that held a grudge or could even be provoked into being unpleasant. Still, a man never knew and it was best to be certain. After all, it had been Howard that had caused the man to lose the biggest part of his right arm. But I had never seen a man maimed like him who seemed to take no notice of it. He used his left hand just as readily as if he'd been using it all his life. I wondered how he fared with his everyday habits and chores, like lighting a cigar or cutting his meat or saddling a horse.

He said, "You must have stopped by the mill."

"Yessir. Then we went by the bank and saw the president, Mister . . ." I looked at the ceiling trying to think of the man's name. "Mister . . . uh."

Mister Stevens said, "Felton Holmes. Comes from Missouri. Been down here a long time. He give you what help you needed?"

I had been studying on how to tell him about the $25,000 in gold. I figured about the only way was just to up and tell him. But he'd aroused my curiosity so much by saying he'd known my mother that I couldn't get my mind off that. I wondered when. I knew it couldn't have been when he'd come to Matagorda County to get his money, or whatever it was that Howard had said he'd come for, the time he'd lost his arm as a result of Buttercup's shot. It couldn't have been then because Howard hadn't even married Alice. Didn't even know her so far as I knew. But then Howard had said he and Charlie Stevens were both from Georgia and my mother had been from there. Maybe he'd known her as a girl. Maybe that was the trouble. Maybe they'd both been courting Alice and my father had won out.

But then that didn't make any sense because Howard had said he'd met her when he'd driven a herd of cattle to Georgia, and that had been toward the end of the Civil War. Hell, it was all a mess and all so damned long ago that it was none of my business, and anyway, Hays was sitting out in the cold and probably getting madder and madder by the minute. I said, "Yeah, Mister Holmes gave me all the help I needed. Took some gold off my hands I was sorely tired of packing around."

"Gold?"

"Your gold. Howard sent me to bring it to you. Damnedest fool thing you ever heard of. Insisted the money had to be in gold and wanted me to horseback it cross-country clean up here because that was the way he'd gotten it and he wanted it returned the same way."

Mister Stevens laughed a little and shook his head. "Is he back on that? That little loan? Hell, I don't even remember how much it was. I bet I've had ten, fifteen letters from him through the years and he always mentions that money." He shook his head. "Howard has his own way of thinking, I reckon."

I got out the deposit slip. "Well, it's in your bank. I figure all I got to do is sign my name on this paper here and write in yours and that ought to do it. Or we can go by the bank and get it straight." I got up and handed him the deposit slip.

He looked at it for a minute. Then he said, "Twenty-five thousand dollars! Hell, Howard is really trying to buy off his conscience. You packed this much gold cross-country from south Texas?" He looked up at me.

I shook my head. "Naw, I cheated. We trailed for the better part of three days, but then I said the hell with it and we took the train. I've got a fair-sized ranch to run and I just can't spend this kind of time, not even to please my own daddy. It was a damn fool idea anyway. And then he wouldn't let me bring the best gun hand on the place, my youngest brother, Ben. Wouldn't have it, wouldn't let me tell him."

He looked at me. "I know who Ben is."

Then it struck me. He'd said he'd been getting letters from Howard. That meant that Howard knew where the man was. Then why in hell didn't he just come out and tell me instead of suggesting I might have to look all over Oklahoma for him? By God, I decided Howard was going to have a few things to answer for when I got home. If I did.

I was still standing by Mister Stevens's chair. He handed me back the deposit slip. "I don't want this money."

I just shrugged and went and sat back down. "I was just told to bring it to you. What you do with it after that is your business. On our way out of town I'll stop in at the bank and have it put in your account. I reckon you got an account there? If you don't I'll open you one."

He frowned slightly. "Mister Williams, I don't think you understand it. This matter between me and Howard is not about money."

"Mister Stevens, Howard is getting old. I guess if he's been writing you you know he took a bullet through the breast some years back. That and the death of our mother have taken their toll. Howard is in bad health and sometimes he don't think so straight. But he wants this matter off his conscience before his time comes. He said it in those exact words. So I'd like to be able to go back and tell him that you took the money, that the debt is square. He's got it in his head he stole the money."

Mister Stevens was looking at me intently. He said, "I think I'm beginning to understand why Howard sent you. He wants me to tell you something that he's either afraid or too ashamed to tell you."

I straightened a little in my chair. "Mister Stevens, with all respect, my daddy is the bravest man I've ever known.

If something needs doing or telling he doesn't lay it off on someone else."

Mister Stevens nodded. "Yes, Howard Williams is a brave man. But I could see how he could not face you on this. And I can understand why he wouldn't let you bring Ben or even tell him about it."

"What the hell has this got to do with some money Howard has got in his head he got off you one way or the other?"

Charlie Stevens said, "Oh, Howard Williams stole from me, all right, but it wasn't money."

"Then what was it?" I said. I was starting to get a little irritated. Seemed like we'd been talking in circles, beginning with Howard.

Mister Stevens was looking at me with that intent look on his face. "You really don't know, do you?"

"Hell, no!" I said, frowning. "What'd he steal."

He said slowly, "My wife. And your mother. And Ben's mother."

CHAPTER 9

I sat back in the chair, staring at Charlie Stevens, trying to get a wrap on what he'd just said. Finally I said,
"What the hell are you talking about? You talking about
my mother, Alice?" For the life of me I couldn't, all of a
sudden, remember her maiden name or I would have added
that on.

But Charlie Stevens was shaking his head. "I'm not talking about the lady you always thought was your mother.
You were better than a year old when Howard married
her. No, I'm talking about *my* wife. Or the woman who
was going to be my wife as soon as a preacher passed
through. It was like that in those days. A man and woman
would live together as man and wife until a preacher rode
through and made it official. Lot of people had to do it that
way. Of course we could have had an Indian ceremony but
she was only half Cherokee."

My head was whirling. I didn't know what to think, much
less what to say. I finally said, "I don't believe it. Howard
would have told me, he'd of told me a long time ago."

Stevens said, "When? While the lady you thought was
your mother was still alive? She took you to raise just
like you was her own. And then Ben. You reckon Howard
would have cut her up like that? Then after she'd passed on,
you reckon he could have told you then? Reckon he could
have said not to grieve for your mother because she really

166

wasn't your mother at all? When you reckon he should have told you?"

I looked at him, not saying anything.

He said, "Ever wonder how come you and Ben was so different from Norris?"

I said, wondering, "You know about Norris?"

"Justa, I know about your whole family. I know when you took over the running of the ranch. I know how good Ben is with horses and guns. I know how hotheaded he is. I know how smart you are, how you can use your head when most men draw a gun. I told you Howard has been writing me over the years, telling me about you two boys, asking my forgiveness for both my wife and this . . ." He touched the stump of his right arm. "I don't blame him for this. It wasn't his doing, and if it hadn't of been for him I'd of died. At that time I didn't much care. But now I'm glad I didn't. I guess the reason he sent you was so I could get a look at you. And also tell you about your mother."

I said, looking at the floor, "I don't know what to think."

He got up. "Well, while you take in what I've just told you, and I reckon it's a load, why don't I go out and bring your friend in. We had a good norther blow in and I don't reckon it's going to get any warmer."

I looked up quickly. "I don't want him to hear any of this. Right now I want it to be private between you and me."

"I'll take him through the other hall to the kitchen. I've got a cook back there can get him some coffee or a drink or whatever he wants." He started out of the room and then stopped. He pointed with his left hand at the sideboard. "You might want to pour yourself a drink."

After he was gone I got up, slowly, and went over to the sideboard and figured out which one of the decanters was whiskey, got a tumbler, and poured myself out a generous measure. I took it back to my chair, got out a cigarillo and lit it, and then sat there smoking and drinking. I couldn't believe what Stevens had told me except that it all made sense, even the silly way Howard had sent me to Oklahoma, even making me lug that gold to atone for his grave deed, even sending me to the only man who could and would tell me the truth. I finished my drink and got up and got another, my mind still whirling. When I went back to my chair Stevens had come quietly into the room and seated himself across from me. He watched me work on the second drink. Then he leaned forward and said gently, "Her name was Lucy. She was nineteen years old when your father took her from me after almost two months in my company. I knew the first time he laid eyes on her he wanted her, and your daddy was always a man who went after what he wanted either by fair means or foul. I can't blame him. She was the most beautiful thing I'd ever seen. Her father was French, a gambler and sometimes trader in whiskey. He was a rounder and no mistake, but he was a handsome devil and had a great sense of humor. Her mother was full-blooded Cherokee and the Cherokee women have always been known for their beauty. Her mother was an exceptional beauty."

I said, "Well, how . . . I mean . . ."

"You mean how did he take her?"

"Yeah."

"She went with him. He didn't steal her against her will if that is what you're thinking. But you didn't know your father at that age. He was something, was Howard Williams. Tall, tall as you, built a lot like you, and had a way about him that was a natural with the ladies. See, I was just a man going to run a sawmill, but Howard talked to her about a vast ranch in Texas, thousands of cattle, a palatial mansion. Of course it was just talk. I knew it couldn't have changed that much since I'd given up on it and come back here. But Howard and I had been boyhood friends from Georgia. We shared everything, horses, food, guns, money. I guess he thought that extended to my wife. I tried to tell her what it was going to be like but she didn't want to hear. I tried to tell her the thousands of cattle were there, all right, but that they were as wild as so many black bears. I said the mansion was going to be a dugout in the middle of the prairie. She didn't listen. Howard had this big dream of supplying cattle to the South, getting rich. It happened, I know, but not like he told Lucy." He got up and poured himself a drink one-handed.

He said, "When I knew she was going I loaned Howard five hundred dollars in hopes it would make life easier on Lucy." He came back to his chair and sat down and sipped at his drink. It looked to be the color of brandy. "About a year later I went down to Texas to see if I could persuade her to come back." He touched his stump again. "That's when I got this. It was an accident, a misunderstanding by one of Howard's men who thought I was threatening Howard."

"Buttercup," I said.

"What?"

"Tom Butterfield. He's still with Howard. Cooks for us, worst luck. We got to calling him Buttercup as kids. Least he cooks for us when he ain't drunk."

"Yes," Stevens said. "That was the name. He helped your daddy nurse me."

"What about, uh, Lucy?"

"Your mother?" He took a drink of his brandy. "I didn't see her. Howard said she was pregnant. With you, I would reckon. It times out about right. In fact she may have had you when I was there. What year were you born?"

I said, "1864."

He nodded. "That would have been just about right."

I shook my head. "Mister Stevens, you'll have to forgive me if I just set here and think about all this. I reckon you can imagine I've got a hell of a lot of questions, but right now my head is just going right and left and up and down."

"I would reckon. Why don't you go back in the kitchen and have a cup of coffee with your friend? I think the cook located him a piece of pie. I would imagine all this kind of come at you from your blind side and has got you off in a storm. Whyn't you go think about something else for a time." He got up. "I reckon I ought to run down to the sawmill and make sure things are still operating. You gentlemen make yourself at home. Need anything,

Margaret, that's the cook, will find it for you." He started toward the hall that led to the front door, and then stopped and turned back to me. "Ain't only you been took kind of sudden." His voice softened. "Seeing you has brought back a world of memories I thought I gotten swept under the carpet in my mind a long time ago. But now . . ." He shook his head. "I can just see Lucy in your face."

"You ever answer any of Howard's letters?"

"Just once. No, make that twice. The first was many years ago when he wrote saying he wanted to send me some money to pay back what he'd borrowed. Some little time had passed and he wrote to ask after my health and my business matters and to ask what I figured he owned me on the five hundred, figuring interest. I wrote him back to say to forget the money, that was the least of it. Of course I kept hearing from him, always with news, writing just like we were still partners. Then, of course, he wrote about Lucy when she died." He looked down at the floor. "Of course by then I'd already remarried, but it was still a very painful letter to get. I wrote him thanking him for letting me know. That was all my end of the correspondence. Of course he's sent money up here to this bank before and I've had it sent back. I don't know if you count that as correspondence."

I said slowly, "So he sent me up here with money he knowed in advance you was going to turn down."

"That wasn't the reason he sent you, Justa."

"Then why encumber me with such a load of gold?"

"Maybe to make you think it was important. Besides, that's the most money he's ever sent. I think the last time he wired money up here, some ten, twelve years ago, it was ten thousand if I remember a-right. Maybe it was to impress me. Maybe he was saying, 'Look, here's Lucy's son, look how I'm taking a chance with him putting him on the road with this dangerous money. Now you've got to take it.' Who the hell knows what he thought. Let me tell you, Howard Williams's mind might be going, but you'll be hard-pressed to ever run up against another one could think like him. Your daddy was an original. I've never met his equal since. But that doesn't mean I'm ever going to forgive him."

He went out, and I got up and went seeking the kitchen in the big house. After a few wrong turns I found it at the back and side of the house. It was a large cheerful room with plenty of sunlight. I found Hays established at the big round kitchen table with the remains of an apple pie still in the pan in front of him along with a plate and a fork and a cup of coffee. There was a Negro woman at the sink, pumping out a stream of water into a bucket. She looked around as I came in and said, "Yassuh, what kin I be a-gettin' you, suh?"

She was a comely older lady in a kind of a gray uniform-looking dress. I said I'd just have a cup of coffee if it wouldn't be too much trouble. I pulled up a chair and sat down and Hays said, "Boss, you better have a piece of this pie. I swear you never eat no better pie in all yore life."

The maid, or cook, or whatever she was gave a soft laugh. "That gennelman shore likes his pie. Would you be a-lettin' me cut you just a bit?"

I nodded and said I wouldn't mind. She said, "You want that with a little wedge o' this yeah cheese we got?"

I was kind of doubtful. I'd never heard of putting cheese on pie, but Hays said, "Boss, you got to try it! I swear it's the best idee you ever heard of."

I said, "Shut up, Hays. I wouldn't listen to you about food. I've seen you put gravy on cake, for God's sake."

He said, "Yeah, an' it was good too."

Margaret came over and cut me a piece of pie and put a wedge of cheese on top, and then stuck it in the oven for a few minutes. When she set it back in front of me, along with a cup of coffee, the pie was warm and the cheese was kind of soft and runny. She said, carrying her bucket in one hand, "I be gonna warsh them back stairs. You gennelmens wants anythin' else just sing out."

I tried the pie and cheese. It was different, but it was pretty good. Hays was watching while I chewed. He said,

"There! Now ain't that good? Ain't that the damnedest thing you ever tasted?"

"No. Damnedest thing I ever tasted was when you busted a jar of syrup in amongst the beef jerky the time we were moving some cattle out to the island. But that wasn't on purpose. At least I don't think it was."

"How you and that Charlie Stevens feller gettin' along?"

I just nodded, still eating the pie and drinking coffee.

Hays said, "You get that gold handed over to him? I mean, it's off our hands, we're shut of it, right?"

"Hays, you are worse than having a pet raccoon around the house. You have got to have your nose in everything."

"Say, did you notice that Mister Stevens is missing a arm?"

I gave him an amazed look. "Well, yes, after about half an hour of talking to him I kind of took note of that fact."

He ignored what I'd said. "I don't reckon as how I'd ever shook hands with a man missing his right arm. I mean, I was out there, settin' my horse, an' he come out an' hailed me to come up on the porch. So I got off my old pony an' went up the steps and stuck out my right hand and then, right then an' there, I seen he didn't have one. A right hand. So it was kind of awkward, but I got out of it."

"What fool thing did you do?"

He looked proud of himself. "Right quick, so quick I bet he never noticed it, I brung my right hand back and stuck out my left. An' we shook like that, like it was the most natcheral thang in the world."

I just shook my head. "Hays, you beat all. I mean, you flat beat all."

I finished my pie and got up. I said, "Let's go out front and loosen the girths on the horses. Give them a little blow."

He said anxiously, "We ain't going to be here all that long, are we?"

"I don't know," I said. "I still got some business with Mister Stevens to get handled."

CHEROKEE

We went out and tended to the horses, and then went up on the big wide porch with the verandah roof and sat in the white-painted wicker furniture. The chairs and the little settee were almost a match to what we had on the front porch of the headquarters house back home. I sat down and lit a cigarillo, looked out over the bleak Oklahoma landscape, and did a good little bit of thinking. Ray Hays tried to interrupt at first, but then he saw I didn't want to talk and he fell silent himself. After a while he went out to his horse and came back with a half-full bottle of whiskey. He had a drink and then passed it to me. I took a pull and handed it back. After a while I looked at my watch. It was nearing four o'clock. I had some more questions for Mister Stevens, but they could wait until the next day. As soon as those were answered me and Hays could start back for Blessing. I had a whole bunch I wanted to talk over with Howard, and I didn't reckon he was going to find it all that pleasant. Now I could understand his need for secrecy about the matter, keeping it hidden from Ben and Norris. If I'd been him I'd of kept it hidden too. Except I'd of kept it hidden from me, especially me.

I was just on the point of telling Hays we'd better go to hunting for a hotel for the night when I saw a buggy coming from the sawmill. In another half a minute I could see it was Charlie Stevens driving, using the reins one-handed. He managed to turn the corner of his house and give us a little salute at the same time. I figured his barn was around back and he was going to put his horse away.

Hays said, "Boy, he is mighty handy with just that one arm, ain't he? And ain't he spry in his manner. You say he's an old friend of your daddy? He must be a sight younger. They can't be the same age."

I was still staring off, thinking about first one thing and then another. I just said, "I don't know."

"Listen, Boss, if we gonna try and make it back to Chickasha by tonight we ought to get on the road here pretty quick."

I looked over at him. "What do you want to be in Chickasha for tonight? They ain't got no whorehouses there."

He grimaced. "That ain't what I mean. But that's whar the depot is. I thought we'd be gettin' on the train and headin' home. I'd like to see some country I recognize pretty soon. Hell, I can't tell north from south up here."

"I don't figure to leave until tomorrow morning, maybe even later than that. This matter is a little more complicated than that."

"Hell, Boss, we brung the gold. I thought that was our job."

"Hays, you draw the same wages here as you do laying around the ranch in Matagorda County. Just lay around here and don't ask so damn many fool questions. We'll go when I say go and not before. Now hand me that bottle and hush up."

The afternoon sun was beginning to wane, and with it the little warmth that it had brought. I'd left my jacket inside, and it was getting too cool to sit out in my shirtsleeves, even if it was a heavy cotton shirt. Just as I was getting up from my wicker chair Charlie Stevens came to the front door. He said, "You boys better come on in. It's going to get a little nippy out there for porch sittin'."

We went on in, going down the hall to the big, cheerful parlor. Mister Stevens went up to the sideboard and got himself a glass of brandy, and invited us to help ourselves. Hays and I took whiskey, and Hays plopped himself down in a chair like he was going to homestead the place. I figured me and Mister Stevens could make some small talk before I felt obliged to run Hays off so that I could discuss the questions that were churning through my mind. I said, "That's some sawmill you got there, Mister Stevens. It appeared you had three steam engines turning a like number of blades."

He nodded. "We put out a lot of board feet."

"I noticed a lot of logs piled up at the back of your place. But I don't see many logging trees around here."

He smiled. "No, this place is just about logged out. When I first set up here there was pine for miles and miles. But the cattlemen wanted the land for pasture, and I could take what they cut down and turn it into planks for houses and barns and fences and whatnot. Worked out pretty good. But that's all done now. We get our pine logs about twenty miles to the northeast. We got a little narrow-gauge railroad that runs up to the logging camp and fetches back the logs."

"I don't quite get how business is done around here. Are we still on the Cherokee reservation?"

"Oh, yes. In fact all of my business is done with the Cherokee Nation. Right now I'm the only mill supplying sawn lumber to the tribe. At least the only white man. There are some mills run by Cherokees, mostly men I've taught, but they're not a concession like mine is. You have to have the approval of the Tribal Council to run a business on the reservation. That is, unless you're a sutler. Or an agent for the Bureau of Indian Affairs."

"Tell me, just what the hell is a reservation? Is it to keep the whites out or the Indians in? I don't get it."

He shrugged. "Well, at first, especially with the hostiles, like the Apache and the Comanches, the idea was to pen them up so they couldn't raid and pillage over the countryside. So a reservation was to keep them in. Not that it did much good. They were usually placed on land where there was no game and the Indians had no way of feeding themselves except for what they could get from the sutler. These men were usually crooks and scoundrels who got the concessions to feed the Indians from the Bureau of Indian Affairs. But what they did was mostly starve the hostiles into open rebellion. They'd buy poor cattle for three or four dollars a head, claim to have bought, say, a hundred head, but they'd only buy twenty, maybe thirty. Then they'd turn around and bill the government for a hundred head at twenty dollars a head. But the bad thing was the few poor cattle they'd buy couldn't feed the poor people they were intended to feed, so some of the hostiles broke off the reservation and give the reservation idea a bad name."

"What about the Cherokees?"

Charlie Stevens smiled. "Well, they hardly fit the same mold as the Apaches or the Comanches. They've been farmers most of their existence, hunters and farmers. Oh, they can fight when they have to, but they'd rather talk the matter over."

Hays said, "They always been up here in Oklahoma?"

Mister Stevens shook his head. "No. In about 1820 the United States government decided to move the Cherokees out of their native land, Georgia, where they'd lived for centuries. The War of 1812 was not too long over and people wanted to settle the southern Gulf Coast states. So the Indians had to go. Back then Oklahoma looked like the most worthless piece of real estate around, so they marched them up here on what has since come to be called the Trail of Tears and established a reservation. I'd have to say that the reservation here is intended to keep the white man out, though it hasn't done a very good job of it even though the Cherokee is the most civilized and advanced of any tribes I know of. But after the land rush there has been great infringement on their rights and on their property. Frankly, I fear for the future. They are a unique and valuable people. I would hate to see them trespassed on again."

To my ears it sounded a little bit like a lecture, and I couldn't help wondering if he was saying it for my benefit. Now I was beginning to understand why people would occasionally ask me if I was Indian-blooded. The reason they were asking that was that a quarter of my blood was Cherokee. It made me feel funny to realize it. And I kind of figured that Charlie Stevens had said what he had to make me feel proud of that quarter of myself.

I looked over at Hays. I said, "Ray, I've got a little confidential business I need to discuss with Mister Stevens. Why don't you fill up your glass and wait on me out in the kitchen? I'd appreciate it. I ought not to be too long."

He got up quickly. "I don't need no more whiskey, but I wouldn't mind seein' if that lady ain't got a bit more of that apple pie and cheese. I never hear'd of such."

CHEROKEE

Charlie Stevens got up to show him the way back to the kitchen. While he was gone I got up and replenished my tumbler with some more of Charlie's good whiskey. I was back in my seat before he came in. He stopped at the sideboard and asked if I wanted a cigar. I told him I'd just stick to the cigarillos I was comfortable with. He made a business out of getting his cigar lit and then sat back down. We were about four or five feet apart.

Truth be known, I didn't know what I was feeling. A couple of hours past I'd been told that the woman I'd always thought was my mother wasn't my mother. But just the saying of the words couldn't all of a sudden make my feelings change. To me Alice was still my mother whether she was the one that birthed me or not. From the time I was aware, she'd been there as my mother, and I'd always called her that and thought of her as that, and this, this Lucy was just a faceless somebody I couldn't connect with myself. If my feelings were aroused about anything or toward anybody, it was Howard. It made me mad as hell him letting me live a lie, and him living a lie all these years. Here I'd thought my mother was some genteel Southern lady from Georgia when, all the time, she'd been a half-breed off the reservation in Oklahoma. No wonder me and Lew Vara were so close. Hell, we practically had the same bloodlines.

I said to Mister Stevens, "I'd like to get the straight of it if you know it. Do you know all the facts?"

He sort of shrugged. "Well, I'll tell you as much as I know. I don't know all of it, maybe, by the lights of what you want to know."

"When did Howard marry my mother?"

"He never did."

"I'm talking about my mother Alice."

"Oh," he said. He looked away for a second, thinking. "I'm trying to recollect. I know he wrote me about it. Said he wanted me to know he was still looking after Lucy if news of his marriage reached me and might cause me to have any worries on that score."

"That was damn big of him."

He smiled slightly. "Well, yes, but that was Howard. He was having his own way, but he wanted you to understand that he was looking out for the rest of the hired hands at the same time."

"Well he had to have married Alice sometime between when I was born and when Norris came along, because I can guarantee you Norris ain't got no Indian blood in him. Talk about somebody favoring. He favors my mother . . . Alice."

Charlie nodded. "Yes, it was sometime in there. He'd made it big selling cattle to the Confederacy along toward the end of the war. They'd already eat every cow from Mississippi to Virginia, so those Longhorns your daddy drove up found a ready market. And he got gold for them too." He thought again. "I would reckon you were running close to one year old. I remember in the letter he wrote that he was telling his high-born Southern society wife that your mother had died, but that I wasn't to believe it. She was going to raise you as her own, and Lucy was being taken care of and not to worry."

"Wait a minute," I said. "Where the hell was . . ."

"Your mother?" he said. "Your birth mother?"

"Where the hell was Lucy while all this was going on? Howard comes waltzing in with a wife. What does he do, move her out and my mother in and take me away from Lucy and . . . I mean, what the hell happened?"

I was getting hot about it. I wasn't getting hot at Charlie Stevens. I was just getting confused, and that made me angry. And the more I thought of the whole damn situation the madder I got.

Charlie said, "Well, I wasn't there. But I guess Howard didn't figure he was gonna rise too high in the world with a half-breed for a wife, especially when he could have one from a high-born family in Georgia. And yes, I reckon she come with a dowry. And right then I reckon Howard could use the money. You got to understand, Justa, that your daddy was a pistol. He was young and full of piss and vinegar and ambition. Mostly ambition."

"Fine. Fine for Howard. But what did he do with the woman he stole from you? Your wife."

A little look of sadness passed over his face. "Well, he built her a cabin a ways from his main house. Two or three miles. I'm sure he done for her as proper as possible. I doubt she wanted for anything that was in Howard's power to give her."

"Well, what the hell was I doing all that time? And what did my mother, Alice, think about it? Hell, she had to have known."

"Well, like I said, your mother Alice took you to her breast just as if you were one of her own. I don't mean to her breast like for milk. I imagine you was weaned by then. And besides, your mother Alice wouldn't of had no milk."

"And this woman who borned me, Lucy, didn't she kick up a fuss about having her baby taken away from her?"

Charlie sighed and looked even sadder. "Son, I wasn't there so I don't know the particulars. But your daddy was a forceful man and Lucy was still awful young. I imagine he made her see that was the way it had to be. She'd lived with me, been taken off by Howard, lived with him, had a son by him. . . . Well, you got to remember she really wasn't brought up to expect much out of life. I imagine she was grateful for what come her way."

I said, "Hell!" I got up and walked over to the sideboard and poured myself out another drink. "Well, I reckon I'm beginning to see why Howard, as you say, was either too afraid or too ashamed to tell me all about the matter. Still, I wish he hadn't loaded me up with all that gold."

Charlie chuckled quietly. "Maybe he thought I'd take it."

I looked around at him from the sideboard. "Why don't you?"

He sipped at his drink. "I don't need it. I got more money now than I know what to do with."

"Take it anyway."

He just shook his head.

"Why not?"

He sighed. "Because that would allow Howard Williams to take me off his conscience. It would mean that I had forgiven him." He turned his head so he could look square in my face. "And I ain't ever going to do that."

"Hell, he's an old man. He's just trying to clean up an old debt before it comes time to go out of business. I know what he done to you was wrong, but it was a long time ago."

I felt a little strange taking Howard's side and trying to complete the errand he'd sent me on, especially as angry at him as I was. But I was thinking that it might do Charlie more good than Howard if he was to forget the old grudge. I'd seen men bowed by the weight of grudges, and this Charlie Stevens appeared to be a mighty fine man. I didn't like to see him carrying that load that was as much trouble to him as the gold had been to me.

I said, "Charlie, I was gonna say this is none of my business, but I guess it is. We both been harmed by this matter. I ain't going to pretend that my hurt is anything to compare with yours. But I reckon I'll have to end up forgiving Howard. I'm going to do it for my own sake more than his. What about you? What word can I take back to him?"

He said slowly, like a man who wants to get the words exactly right, "I can forgive Howard for my arm. And I can even forgive him for stealing Lucy from me. If he'd of gone on and treated her like a wife, married her as I was going to do, treated her like a lady, then I could have forgiven him. I loved Lucy and I wanted what was the best for her, even if it meant Howard got her instead of me." He stopped and took a sip of his drink, and then stared off as if he was seeing ghosts from the past. "But the one thing I can never forgive Howard Williams for is the shabby way he treated Lucy. He didn't marry her. Hell, he did worse than that. He treated her like someone he was ashamed of. He found him a fine lady and hid Lucy away in a cabin that he would sneak off to visit like a plantation owner going to visit one of his bitch slaves. He treated her like shabby goods, he treated her like a half-breed. He treated her like a worthless Indian." He looked up at me. "And he expects me to forgive him for that?" His voice was trembling. "I will never, under any circumstances, forgive Howard Williams for the way he treated the woman I loved. And I hope his conscience burns him the rest of his life like a red-hot poker. I hope he burns in Hell on earth."

CHAPTER 10

There wasn't much I could say to him about that. There wasn't much I could disagree with in what he said. Hell, I figured I would have felt the same way. I went back to my chair and sat down, and for a little while neither one of us said anything. The blood had rushed to Charlie Stevens's face with the emotion of his last remarks. Now his color was slowly returning to its normal light tan. I let some time pass and then I said, "You told me you remarried, Charlie."

He nodded. He was his cheerful, benign self again. "Oh, yes, and I made a very fortunate find." He smiled like someone remembering a fond memory. "I married a young lady the Tribal Council had brought out here to teach the Cherokee youngsters their ABC's. She was from Virginia. She looked upon it as a great adventure, coming out here to the Wild West to teach Indian children. Her name was Jane, Mary Jane Sheridan before I married her." He picked up the long-dead cigar he'd been smoking out of the ashtray on the table by his chair and went through the motions of getting it relit. When it was drawing he said, "We had fourteen happy years together."

"What happened?"

He shook out the match he was still holding. "The cholera took her. Oddly enough, she died about the same time that I had a letter from Howard telling me that your mother Alice had passed over."

I noticed he was careful of my feelings, calling Alice my mother even though he knew damn good and well she wasn't.

"You have any children?"

He looked sad. "Just the one. A daughter. She didn't live very long."

"I'm sorry."

He shrugged. "Many a man has said this country is too rough for horses and women. And children."

"Yeah," I said, wondering if he was talking about me and Ben and Norris. We'd been children once, back when all this was happening. It was a little too far back for me to have any recollection, but I had to reckon I'd been a child at some point, though I'd never much felt like it.

We were both quiet for a few moments. Then I kind of heaved a breath and said, "I'd appreciate it if you'd tell me the rest of it."

He fiddled with his cigar. "There's not much more to tell. Howard wrote me when Ben was born. Of course Lucy died in childbirth." He looked away for just a second. Then he said, "To tell you the truth, when I read it in Howard's letter, I was relieved. I envied Howard, him getting another son from her, but I was glad that she was out of it, through with playing second fiddle, through with being hidden away like damaged baggage."

I said, "I'd of been four."

Charlie glanced at me. "I expect so. Though I doubt if you'd of knowed much about how they got babies."

I nodded. "I've got some dim memory of it. One day there was a tiny baby in the house. How'd they take care of it? My mother Alice . . ."

"I reckon they'd of got a wet nurse in. With as many Mexican women around, one wouldn't have been hard to find."

I sighed and shook my head. "Was a hell of a lot going on I didn't know a damn thing about." I took a quick pull on my drink. "And you figure Alice just took the baby in and acted like it was her own?"

Charlie said gently, "What else could she do? Don't you suppose she knew about Lucy? You can't hide that sort of thing in a little closed place like your daddy's ranch."

"And she just put up with it?"

Charlie said, "She was already raising one son by Lucy. You. Where was she supposed to draw the line? From what little I've been able to gather about her, she was an extraordinary woman."

"Then why wasn't Ben by her? She had Norris. What happened after that? Did Howard get tired of her?"

Charlie said, "I don't know."

I said viciously, "What'd he do, alternate 'em? Like breeding cows? 'All right, Lucy, it's your turn now,' or, 'Alice, get in the stall.' Shit!"

"Makes you angry. I don't blame you."

"You don't know anything about Norris?"

Charlie shook his head. "No, I really don't. Your daddy has been sparing with the ink. I suppose he thought I only wanted to know about the sons he had by Lucy. What's Norris like? What does he think about?"

I gave a thin smile. "Norris. He thinks about Norris."

"You're not close with him?"

"It's funny coming here. It hasn't been pleasant to find out, but it at least explains how I've felt about Norris. I never quite felt the same way toward him as I have Ben. Ain't anything I can explain. It was just that he was so different. And not just in looks. Looks are the least of it. We just don't seem to pull in tandem. He looks at matters completely different than me and Ben. More than once I've had to remind myself that he was my brother when I've been on the point of taking his head off or punching him in the mouth. Now I know the reason why."

"He's still your brother."

"Half brother," I said.

"He's Alice's son. You still consider her your mother."

I looked off, seeing through the walls, seeing a long way off. "I think I would have liked the chance to get to know Lu . . . , my mother Lucy. And there was time. She was alive four years while I was on this earth. I might have knowed her just a little, but that's a sight more than what I got now."

Charlie shrugged. "Was neither one of us there. We ain't in a good position to judge."

"I wonder why Alice didn't have any more children after Norris? Hell, there was a good ten or eleven years in there for her to try. Surely she could have done better than Norris on a second try."

Charlie half smiled. "That ain't the kind of talk you're going to want to remember tomorrow. Justa, you been stung. From what your daddy has wrote me about you you are a man who likes to hold the reins. Now you're finding out somebody else was directing the wagon. You don't like it. Right now you're angry. You know better than to talk when you're angry."

"Yeah, I do," I said. I finished my drink and stood up. "I reckon I better go collect Ray Hays. We got to find us a hotel for the night. And I got to find out about southbound trains out of Chickasha. I didn't expect to find you so easy."

Charlie got up. "Why, what do you want a hotel for? I got four big bedrooms upstairs ain't doing nothing but gathering dust. And my man Washington has been smoking a ham for the last week. Washington come down from Virginia as a young man with Jane. If there's anybody knows how to sweet-smoke a ham it is a Negra from Virginia."

I said something about not wanting to put him out, but the truth was I wanted to stay. I felt a kind of kinship with Charlie, though there was no reason to. By rights he should have hated the sight of me, reminding him, as I must have, of his lost Lucy. But he'd been uncommonly hospitable and uncommonly charitable in doing Howard's dirty work for him. I said, "I figured the quicker I was out of your sight the better you'd like it."

He shook his head. "That's a hell of a thing to think. I know you don't regard yourself as Lucy's son and I don't blame you. But I do. I see some of her in you, and it makes me feel good to know there's a little of her still here on the earth."

I got out my watch. It was after six o'clock. I couldn't imagine where the time had gone. I said, "Well, we need to see to our horses. And I would like to get cleaned up a little." I glanced down at my clothes. "I hadn't figured on doing no visiting at anybody's house."

Charlie said, "Why don't you take a bath? We got hot and cold running water. Got a bathtub right off the kitchen."

"You got *hot* running water?"

He laughed. "You don't reckon I'd let all that steam go to waste over at the mill. Long time ago I had a pipe run over here for Jane's sake. Now I've even got partial to it."

I ran my hand over my face. "I would certainly admire getting cleaned up. We got time before supper?"

"We eat supper around here when we're ready, not by any clock."

I went in the kitchen and found Hays in close conversation with Margaret, the cook and maid of all work. There was a tall, white-haired colored man washing his hands at the sink. I figured it was Washington. He turned around and nodded and bid me a good evening. I gave him the same, and then told Ray we'd be spending the night with Charlie Stevens and that we'd better see to the horses.

Washington said, "I done ar'ready seed to that, suh. With ya' permission."

That kind of surprised me. I said, "When did that get decided?"

He said, "Mistuh Charlie thought wadn't no sense lettin' them fine animals stand out in de cold. So ah brung 'em in the barn and tuck off they saddles and undressed they moufs and give 'em a good rubdown 'n den give 'em some grain."

I said, "Well, I'm much obliged. If you'll show me where they are, we need to get our saddlebags. I want to get me a bath and a shave and put on some clean clothes."

He was drying his hands on a towel. He nodded with

his head. "De be back there on de back poach. I kin fetch 'em."

I said, "We'll get them. You just show us where the bath is and where we're gonna sleep, I'll be much obliged."

He said, "Sho! You jest let ol' Washington git you a bath runnin'. You ain't used to it, they's mo' things 'n valves to turn than you ever seed. I'll git the water runnin' an' then show ya'll where ya'll gonna bed down. Plenty room."

He had a Southern accent you could have put in a syrup bucket.

An hour later me and Hays walked into the living room, where Charlie Stevens was sitting, much improved by soap and water and a change of clothes. While we were going through our ablutions Hays had shown more than a passing interest in what Charlie and I had been talking about. He'd said, "Was he pretty well taken up about the gold?"

"Not so you'd notice," I'd said.

That had fetched a startled look from him. He'd said, "Twenny-five *thousand* in gold an' he didn't do a buck-and-wing?"

"Not so you'd notice."

"Now this is yore daddy's bidness, ain't it?"

"You could say that."

"They go pretty fur back?"

"You could say that."

Finally he'd seen the futility of his questions and had given up. But he had asked me when we'd be going back. I'd told him I wasn't certain. "I might want to stick around for a time. Place feels kind of homey to me."

"Homey?" He'd given me a good stare. "Maybe you ain't noticed, but they ain't nothin' but a buncha damn Injins 'round here."

I'd said, "The word is Indian. Don't forget it. They're Cherokee Indians. Understand?"

That had fetched another look. "Well, all right, but when did you take up the war hatchet?"

"Hays . . ."

"All right, all right. Indians. See, I can say it."

Charlie poured us out a drink all around and we sat down. He said that dinner was ready anytime we were. Hays sat, shaved and washed, in clean clothes, looking around the room glowing in the lamplight. He patted himself on the chest and said, "Yessir, that bath and cleanup hit the spot. I feel nearly human."

I said, "Just keep your mouth shut and nobody will know."

We ate in the dining room at a big table that could have seated eight or ten people. The three of us just sat at one end with Mister Stevens at the head. Washington, in a white starched coat, waited table. I said something to Charlie Stevens about not going to so much trouble on our account. "We're just a couple of tramps that fell off a train. Hate to infringe on your hospitality."

He shook his head. "We do this every evening, even if I'm by myself. This is the way it was when my wife was alive, and Washington won't have it any other way. Washington is a proud man, and if he didn't have this to do he'd have to quit, ain't that right, Washington."

Washington was standing back, alert to see what someone needed on their plate. He said, "That sho' de troof, Mistuh Charlie."

It made me think of Buttercup and his insistence on cooking. The only difference was that Washington knew how to wait table.

I said, "Washington, if you ever get out of a job I'd put you on steady just to sweet-smoke hams. I believe this is the best ham I ever ate."

And it was. Folks in our part of the country generally just fried ham. So far as that went, it being cattle country, we didn't make all that good a usage out of any meat except beef.

We ate until I thought I was going to bust, eating the ham and candied yams and winter turnips and creamed potatoes and the best bread, outside of Nora's mother's, that I'd ever tasted.

Charlie said, "If it was summer we could have ice cream.

CHEROKEE

I got an ice plant down at the mill."

Washington brought in some blackberry pie and some cheese along with the coffee. Hays insisted on going on until he made a fool out of himself, or got sick, by tackling the pie and cheese. I just settled for coffee and a cigarillo.

Charlie said, "Justa, why don't ya'll settle down here for a few days? You just got off a hard trip, why rush back? Give Margaret somebody else to cook for besides me and my little dried-up appetite. Be doing me a favor. She fusses all the time about me keeping up with what she cooks."

I said, "Charlie, that's a mighty kind offer. Tell you what I wouldn't mind doing. I wouldn't mind learning something about the sawmill business. Nearest sawmill to Blessing is thirty miles away. I ain't sure but what we ought to have one right there in town. Never thought about it before I saw yours."

"How close is your nearest timber? Pine. Has to be pine. And I mean a lot of it."

Hays said, looking at me, "Nearest big stand of pine is forty, maybe fifty miles away. Nearly to Houston, ain't it, Boss?"

I said, "We could ship the lumber in like Mister Stevens does."

But Charlie was shaking his head. "No future in that. If you're already shipping lumber thirty miles, what's the point of shipping logs fifty miles? Just to make lumber?"

I said, "You do it."

"Aaah," he said. "But it doesn't cost me anything. This is a U.S. Government Cherokee Indian reservation, and the U.S. Government Department of Indian Affairs built that railroad."

I said, a little troubled, "But you sell the lumber to the Indians, to the Cherokees."

"No, I don't," he said. "The Tribal Council sells the lumber to the tribe at whatever price they want. And they base that on what a man's needs are. I just cut the lumber for the Tribal Council. Don't charge them a cent. In return I get to sell what they don't use to whoever I want."

189

"What if they use it all?"

"They don't and they wouldn't, and even if they did I'd just put on another shift and cut more. I been making lumber longer than they been used to nailing it up. I reckon I ought to be able to stay ahead."

I said, "Well, I guess we won't go into the lumber business."

Charlie said, "I bet I can ship you lumber from up here and beat the price you're paying right now."

I said, "Well, that would be a nice trick." But I was pleased at the idea of a continuing relationship with Charlie Stevens, even if it was just business.

He said, getting up, "Let's go on in the parlor, as Jane always called it, and let me look up the shipping charges and get out paper and pencil and see what can be done. I can make rail connections about five miles from here if I've got enough to ship."

We got settled in the living room with some drinks —me and Hays having whiskey and Charlie taking brandy—and set in discussing the lumber business. After that we just had a good talk, not about anything in particular, but just letting the conversation wander as it would. Charlie had been around and done considerably more than just sawing lumber, and he was interesting to talk to.

The time passed, and I noticed that Hays was starting to nod off. It was either too much whiskey or too much hard traveling. I said, "I think I got a hired hand here is looking for a place to sleep." I got out my watch. It wasn't quite nine o'clock.

Charlie raised his voice. "Washington!" he called.

When the Negro came Charlie just indicated Hays, who'd woke up some. Hays said, "What?"

I said, "Go on up to bed, Ray. I'm going to sit up and talk a while longer."

Washington said to Hays, "Come along wid me. I show you de way to yo' bed."

Hays went out yawning. I didn't figure he was going to have much trouble getting to sleep. I smiled and said,

"Don't let him fool you. He ain't much in civilized society, but he's a steady hand to have by you if it comes to trouble."

Charlie said, "That's worth a lot of table manners, ain't it?" He put his hand over his mouth and then laughed. "Jane never did get that out of me. Saying ain't."

"I know what you mean. I'm married to a schoolteacher. Or she was. Now she's got her hands full with just the one."

"You got a boy?"

"Yeah." I grimaced. "Named after me. We call him J.D." I looked away. "But at least he'll be certain about who his mother is."

Charlie said, "I said *I* couldn't forgive Howard. I don't mean to be an example to you. They were confusing times. I can see that now. Washington has to cut my meat for me, but it didn't stop me from getting a wife like Jane. But I think if I'd been embittered about losing my arm I could never have won Jane. I'm saying don't turn bitter against Howard for the way he handled matters. If you do it will hurt you more than him."

"Charlie, I ain't feeling so bitter as much as surprised, surprised Howard would carry this around with him all these years and surprised he'd want me to know now."

"You know Howard was always a gambler."

"Yes," I said. "But a plunger more than a thinker. The kind that trusts to his luck."

"Fate," Charlie said. "Not luck. Howard always believed in fate. That's probably why he sent you up here. Hell, he knew I wasn't going to take that money. But he had to have a reason. He couldn't just say I want you to go up and see an old partner of mine in Oklahoma."

"You're saying, then, that Howard left it to chance whether you told me or not?"

"That's my view," Charlie said. "It was bothering him but he didn't want to make the decision. So he left it up to me. I chose to tell you because I figured you ought to know."

"He had plenty of chances before."

Charlie said, "A man's opinion and attitude changes as he gets older. He looks at matters differently. I can know that and you will too, someday. Though, from what I can judge, you seem to be a man who deals with the situation as it is rather than what he wishes it was. The word for that is being a realist. Maybe you got that from your birth mother. Maybe that's why she was willing to stay in that cabin and see Howard occasionally rather than be in the big house as the mistress."

I just glanced over at him. "Well, at least I know a good deal more about myself. I reckon that makes the trip worthwhile."

"What are you going to say to Howard?"

I shook my head. "I don't know." Then on a thought I half smiled. "Maybe I won't tell him anything. Maybe I'll just say you wouldn't take the gold and we just come on home. Maybe he ain't the only one can hold back. I can see him right now squirming around and trying to find out if maybe we didn't talk about *anything* else."

Charlie was smiling. "Yes, that would work on Howard. It might force him to tell you himself. I don't think he could stand it. Just say that I didn't have much at all to say about those years."

I looked over at him. "And you don't know much about my mother Alice? You don't know if she didn't or couldn't have any more children after Norris?"

He shook his head. "That I'm in the dark about. Some women figure they owe the man a son. Once that's done they figure their work of that sort is over. That's a prevalent attitude among ladies of society. But I just don't know. That is something you'll have to ask Howard."

"I may not feel like asking Howard the time of day. Right now I ain't sure he'd know."

Next morning Charlie and I were sitting out on his front porch about ten o'clock, having a cup of coffee. The sun was out and, while it wasn't warm, it was pleasant and bright. Hays had gone downtown, claiming that riding in stock cars was taking a terrible toll on his wardrobe. Charlie and I had been down giving me a close-up look at a working sawmill. There had been a good deal more to it than I'd expected, and near enough noise to last me the rest of my life. Now we were just sitting, watching the town and surrounds, and talking about first one thing, then another.

About that time a boy came running up and handed Charlie what appeared to be a telegram. He looked it over and then handed it to me. He said, "That's for you."

It was addressed to me, care of Charlie Stevens, Anadarko, Oklahoma. I opened it up. It was a short message and a simple one. It said:

BAD TROUBLE STOP COME QUICK STOP

It was signed BEN. I showed it to Charlie. I said, "I've got to go find Hays and get moving. We've got to get over to Chickasha and get a stock car and get the first train out. That's from Ben and that means it's serious." I could feel my heart taking little jumps. "It means it's more than he can handle. And that means it's considerable."

Charlie said, "Maybe it's just outside of his range. Maybe it's something only you can handle."

I shook my head and pointed a finger at the word "trouble." I said, "That means exactly what it says. And it don't mean the new haying machine is broke down or that Howard has had a heart attack. If it was something like the last he'd say exactly that. It means we got trouble. Either a fight or some new fever is sweeping through the cattle or he's shot someone. Anyway, I got to get moving."

Charlie consulted his watch. He was wearing a coat with a vest, and he carried his big gold watch in his vest pocket. I always carried mine in my jeans pocket, where sometimes it galled me. Charlie said, "It's five after ten, and a three-hour ride to Chickasha if you ride your horses to the knees. So you've missed the one o'clock through there. Next train

southbound stops at five-fifteen." He snapped his watch
shut. He said, "You go look for your friend and I'll go
send a telegram to the TP&O in Chickasha to have you a
stock car ready for that train. It'll get you to Fort Worth.
How you want me to route you after that?"

"Through San Antonio if it can be done. That's the only
way down to Blessing. But I might ought to look at those
connections myself. See how tight they are. Just get us to
Fort Worth."

"Right."

He took off one way and I went the other to hunt up
Hays.

I was full of a feeling of hurry even though I couldn't
go any faster than the train could get out of Chickasha and
head itself for Fort Worth. But it was all part of the feeling
of dread I'd had ever since Howard had forced me off on
his errand. Of course I could see now that the trip had been
as much for my benefit as his, but even knowing that now,
I couldn't shake the feeling I should never have left. I could
only hope, as I fretted and worried away the time, that the
trouble didn't have anything to do with Nora or J.D. I felt
pretty sure that it didn't, else Ben would have made some
mention of it in his telegram. And the fact that it was from
Ben was an indicator to me that it was more than likely
rough trouble, gun trouble, shooting trouble. Otherwise, if
it were family or business trouble, it would have been more
likely for Norris to have sent the wire. I had to figure it
didn't have anything to do with Howard, or if it did, that
he was still conscious enough to give Ben, or Norris, the
directions as to how to send the telegram since he was the
only one who knew where I was.

We ate lunch about eleven-thirty. I'd wanted to start
without it, but Charlie had quite sensibly pointed out that
we were going to spend the same amount of time eating
in a cafe in Chickasha as we were at his house and we
might as well have a good lunch than a bad one in the
middle of the afternoon. Margaret fixed us some fried pork
chops and some mashed potatoes with pork gravy and some

black-eyed peas. She came out while we were eating to tell us she'd fixed us up a big bunch of ham sandwiches and fried chicken and it was in a sack in the kitchen and not to forget it.

Washington said, "Sack ain't in de kitchen. Woman don't know nuthin'. 'At sack o' vittles is in yo' saddlebags whaeah it's 'spose to be. An' them hosses has got they saddles on an' they bridles in they moufs. Ain't pulled yo' girths 'cause at's a man's own bidness how tight he pulls his girt on his own hoss. But they be ready oth'wise. Saddle blankets is smoothed down. An' they be eatin' grain right now."

I shook my head. "Washington, they ever don't treat you to your liking around here, you know where you can find a home."

It was all I could do to hold myself still to have one final drink with Charlie Stevens. Ray had bolted his down and then gone on outside to see to the horses and bring them around to the front. I said, "Well, Charlie, I don't quite know what to say. Needless to point out this has been a mighty interesting visit. Takes a good bit to throw me off, but this done it."

He said, "Don't be too hard on Howard, whatever you decide to do."

I looked at him directly. "Why not?"

He shrugged. "In the end all you got are your folks and your friends. There's no profit in hurting either one of them."

"What if they've hurt you?"

"Two hurts don't make a heal. Let it scar over."

We walked out on the front porch. I said, "You sure you don't want that money?"

He laughed. "Not no, but hell, no."

"Well, I don't have time to tend to it right now. Tell your friend the banker he can go ahead and use the gold."

"He'll appreciate that. Some of these unenlightened savages around here, for some reason, still don't have a great deal of faith in the Great White Father in Washington. They like their money to clink in their pockets."

"Just tell him I'll draft on it from home. Anyway, I've appreciated all you've told me, Charlie. Wish you'd come for a visit."

"I don't know," he said. "Last time it cost me an arm." But his eyes were twinkling as he said it.

"I'll get you back whole," I said.

Hays was coming around the corner with the horses. I started down the steps. I said, "Well, I better get to kicking."

Charlie said, "Justa . . ."

I stopped and looked back. "What?"

He said, "What are you going to do about Ben? And Norris?"

I thought about it for a minute, and then I heaved a sigh. "That sonofabitch Howard laid that off on me too, didn't he?"

"Looks like it."

"Would you tell them?"

He shrugged. "It's my good fortune I don't have to worry about it."

"Goddammit," I said. "Goddammit to hell." I shook my head. "Well, it's something to think about."

Charlie said, "You can make a good argument either way."

"Yeah," I said. I walked over to my horse, took the reins from Hays, and swung aboard. I raised my hand to Charlie. "Come see us. Maybe you can sell some lumber."

He said, "Write or wire me about the trouble. I'm anxious for you."

We turned the horses and rode around the town and started up the road for Anadarko. It was not quite one o'clock and we had plenty of time, but I found myself pushing the horses up into a slow gallop. Hays said, "What was ya'll talkin' 'bout so seriously there on the porch?"

"Kinfolks," I said. "Let's get a move on."

We made it to Chickasha with time to spare. In fact, on account of Charlie wiring ahead about the stock car, we ended up with about an hour to spare after we got the horses loaded. I spent a little of that time wiring Ben that I'd got his telegram and that we were on our way. I couldn't give him an exact time because the schedule was very difficult to figure out. Me and the Cherokee ticket agent went over what timetables he had, but all I knew for sure was that we'd get into Fort Worth the next morning about nine o'clock. After that it looked like we'd have to go to Austin, and then change trains to get to San Antonio, and then change again to make it to Blessing. The best I could figure, we'd be a good fifty or sixty hours on the rails and waiting. But I felt sure we could do better than that. I'd never taken it, but I felt sure there had to be a direct train out of Fort Worth to San Antonio.

We killed a little time by going down to the Cigar Store and buying a couple of bottles of whiskey for the trip. Before we went in I told Hays to watch himself as he'd be the only white man in the place. He said, "What about you?"

I didn't answer him, and we went on in. There were a bunch of men sitting around at tables drinking and a few eating. There was no bar, but a kind of counter like you'd see at a mercantile store. A pleasant-looking young man with long, black hair and a Roman nose waited on us. He put two bottles of a good brand of whiskey in a flour sack and asked if there was anything else. The whiskey was a little higher-priced than I was used to paying, but I figured it was bootleg. I told him that was all we needed, and he said, "Don't let that firewater get you in trouble, brother."

I said, "White man's medicine. Bad for Injun."

He laughed.

Going out, Hays said, "How come everybody goes 'round calling one another 'brother'? They think they're all kin? Hell, that damned Injin even called you brother."

I said, "Didn't I warn you about that Injin' business?"

"All right, all right. But how come they call you brother? You ain't no more Cherokee than I am. Even if you do look like one."

"Hays, just start worrying when they call *you* brother."

We went on back to the depot and sat down to wait. After what seemed an eternity I faintly heard the far-off wail of a train whistle. The ticket agent said, through the bars of his window, "That'd be your train. Once he gets in and gets hooked on to what rolling stock is going, he'll be out of here. I'd be in my car with my horses was I you."

We finally got rolling about dusk. After we were a ways down the road and used to the motion of the car, Hays and I made a good supper out of watered whiskey and fried chicken and that good bread Margaret made. Hays said, "That woman can cook. Damn shame she's a Nigra. Got a mighty appealin' figure."

"She might feel it's a damn shame for you you're white."

He looked up at me. "Now that is some remark. You don't reckon she'd rather be white?"

"Why?" I said.

He just shook his head. "Boy howdy, Boss, you get some strange ideas in yore head from time to time. We gonna save them ham samwitches fer breakfast?"

"If we want any we better. Likely come dawn we'll be rolling along in the big middle of nowhere."

I had two days to think about all I'd learned from Charlie and to roll it around in my head. I thought of myself and Lucy and Alice and Ben and Norris. I thought of Howard. I thought about all of us. I kept running the events through my mind the best way I could, trying to figure if Howard had had a whole lot of selection or if he could have done a better job with a bad situation. I didn't begrudge him his appetites, either for the beauty of Lucy (I'd had that from Charlie) or for the genteelness of Alice. I could understand him wanting both. I just kept trying to figure out if he couldn't have made a better job of it.

I gave a lot of thought to Norris. He was the only one of us three, me and him and Ben, who'd had a proper momma and daddy right there that he could see and know. Ben and I had just *thought* we did, and that wasn't the same thing. Norris had always acted like he was the anointed one and maybe it was that knowledge, even if he didn't realize it, that knowledge that he felt somewhere down deep, that give him such a smug, superior attitude. His mother was playing queen of the castle while mine and Ben's was shucked away in a shack somewhere waiting until Howard got the urge to visit her. And try and try as I could, I couldn't squeeze a single memory out of my past of anyone who could faintly resemble her, even though Charlie had said I'd been with her nearly all the time for the first two years, and then a lot of the time up until I was three or four. I could remember being left with a woman who wasn't like Alice, but I couldn't put a face on her.

So I thought and thought for two days. On the morning of the third day, when we finally stepped out of that stock car in Blessing, I was no closer to knowing what I thought than I had been when I started. Nothing had been resolved in my mind, and that included what I was going to say to Howard or what I was going to tell Ben or Norris.

First, there was some trouble that had to be tended to, and I didn't even know what kind of trouble it was.

CHAPTER 11

Ben was there to meet us. I'd finally gotten our schedule straightened out as we got closer to home, and I'd wired him from San Antonio what time we'd be arriving.

We got down from the stock car, stiff and sore from getting jolted around for all that time, and walked up the platform while the railroad hired hands unloaded our horses, and there was Ben standing by the depot. I'd been gone nearly a week, and it was good to get out of the cold wind and the heavy jacket and get home. Except it wasn't good to come home to trouble.

Ben stepped out from the depot. It was going on for ten o'clock of a fine, mild fall day. I said, "What the hell has happened, Ben?"

He was smoking a cigarillo, and he threw it away and said, "It's Norris. He's been shot."

"Bad?"

"I never heard of anybody getting shot was good. No, it's his arm. His right arm. Shay Jordan come up in his office and shot him." He jerked his thumb toward town. "He's over at Doc Adams's. It's bad enough the doctor wants to keep him handy."

"When did it happen?"

"About three hours before I sent you that telegram. They sent word out to the ranch. Lew Vara did. And I come as fast as I could, and wired you soon as I seen what happened and found out who done it."

I eyed his face. "What have you done in the meantime?"

He nodded. "I was expecting that one. I done exactly what you told me to do, nothing. I figured this was going to take some serious thinking, so I wired you and sat back to see. Waited for you. I have not seen Shay Jordan since it happened and I ain't gone looking for him."

We were walking as we talked. We came to the town end of the depot and stepped down off the platform right by Ben's horse. I said to Hays, "Ray, go get the horses. Ben and I are going to walk down to Doctor Adams's office. Come on down there."

Hays said, "Howdy, Ben."

Ben said, "Howdy, Ray. Horse herd is fine."

With Ben leading his horse we started for the doctor's office, which was right in the middle of the town, almost next to our hotel. Ben said, "The doctor's watching him. His arm's broken, but if there ain't no infection Norris ought to be all right."

It made me think of Charlie Stevens. It was ironic in that way and ironic in another. Doctor Adams was way above the average small-town Texas doctor. He'd been trained in one of those big Eastern medical colleges, the kind that turned out the very latest in an up-to-date doctor. Normally a town like Blessing could never have attracted such a doctor, who'd normally have been practicing in one of the big Northern or Eastern cities where he could make the money his training deserved. But Norris had argued that it was worth our while to get such a doctor and let our company pay him the difference between what he might have made in Chicago, say, and Blessing. Norris's original thinking had been for Howard's welfare, but he'd also pointed out that it wouldn't hurt the rest of us none to have such a doctor around when bullets started flying. And he'd said that it was just another way of keeping our less fortunate neighbors from being overly jealous of us, providing them with the kind of doctoring they could never afford. In the end he'd convinced me and, though Doctor Adams cost us five to six thousand dollars a year, I considered it money well spent. It was maybe paying off now for Norris.

And if Charlie Stevens had had such a doctor he might not have lost his arm.

We crossed the dusty street and stepped up on the boardwalk. I said, "Without giving me a whole bunch of details, what's Lew Vara doing about it?"

Ben said, "I reckon you better hear that from Lew himself. It's kind of complicated."

I nodded. I wasn't feeling much at that moment, wasn't even trying to think much of anything. I wanted to know all of what had happened and how Norris was before I turned anything loose inside.

Ben said, "I been holding in just like you told me." He glanced at me. "But if Norris goes to getting worse I ain't promising a damn thing. If ever a sonofabitch needed shooting it's Shay Jordan. And I'm gonna do it. No sonofabitch like Shay Jordan shoots *my* brother and walks around talking about it for very long."

I just give him a look. I wondered if he'd be just half as mad if he knew the truth about Norris.

We got to Doctor Adams's office, and Ben opened the door and we went in. His office had once been a store, and still had the plate-glass windows in the front. Now it had been partitioned off so that he had a kind of small waiting room up front, with all the important stuff in the back. There were a few chairs and a little desk where the lady that sorted out the doctor's patients usually sat, but now there was nobody home. Ben stepped to the door that led to the back and called out in a hoarse whisper, "Doctor Adams? Doctor Adams?"

Over his shoulder I could see Gregory Adams come out of one of the little rooms he had back there and step into the hall. He saw Ben and came toward us. Doctor Adams was a short, sandy-haired man not much older than I was, with one of those Yankee accents where the words sounded like they had edges on them. He came walking down the hall putting his finger to his lips for us to keep still. He was wearing a long white linen coat that came nearly to his knees. I'd always figured doctors wore those to keep the blood off their good clothes.

He come up to us. He said, "I've got Norris heavily dosed on laudanum. He's sleeping right now, getting some relief from the pain."

I said, feeling a little stir of anger, "Can I see him?"

Doctor Adams said, "You can take a quick look, but nothing more."

We followed Doctor Adams down the hall to a door that was about half open. He pushed it further open so we could see into the room. Norris was laying on his back with his right arm suspended from the ceiling with some kind of arrangement of cords and pulleys. His arm appeared to be resting on a little board, but I couldn't tell on account of it was covered with bandaging. His light hair was outlined against the pillow and he looked mighty weak and wan. I just stared at him for a moment, and in that moment he wasn't my half-brother, he was the same brother he'd always been. He was smug and he was hardheaded and he was selfish and superior-acting, but he was my brother.

Ben started to say something, but Doctor Adams put his finger to his lips and led us up to the waiting room. When we got there he said to me, "He's lucky. The bullet didn't catch the bone square or it would have shattered it. It's broken, and I had to dig out some bone splinters, but the bullet went on through, thank heavens, and I think it's going to heal all right."

I said, "What about infection?"

"What about it?"

"Is he going to get any?"

Doctor Adams just shook his head. "How in hell should I know? Medical science is doing everything it can to learn about infection. Right now we don't know any more than you do. Also, he's lost a lot of blood. Rest is what he needs right now. Rest and food."

Ben said, "Will it weaken his arm, them chips out of his bone?"

Doctor Adams said, "Yes. Why? Is he planning on leaving the business world and taking up a new profession of herding cattle?"

Ben said, "Well, no, but . . ."

Doctor Adams said, "He'll be more than strong enough to use a pencil. Now you two get out of here. I've got a child with a fever back there. You can come back this afternoon if he's awake."

We started to leave, but he called after us at the door. "Look, I don't mean to sound so brusque. The next twenty-four hours ought to tell the tale on the infection. You worrying about it is not going to help a thing."

Ben said, "If it does get infected, will you have to do what I think—"

I cut him off by shoving him out the door. I said, "Goddammit, Ben, don't even think about such things. Just keep your mouth shut."

But I couldn't get the thought out of my mind, and I reckoned it was because of seeing Charlie Stevens and thinking about justice being visited on Howard, with Norris losing his arm. I knew it was nothing but coincidence and that the one didn't have anything to do with the other; still, it was a thought I had trouble keeping out of my mind.

We walked down the boardwalk toward Lew Vara's office. I said to Ben, "Look, you hunt up Hays and the two of you go on back to the ranch. Go by and tell Nora that I'm home, but that I'm going to spend the night in town."

Ben said, "Hell, Justa, he's my brother too. I want to wait around and see. Hays can tell Nora and Howard you're back."

I hesitated. He had every right. But then I had to say, "No, Ben. I don't know what's going on and I don't know the Jordans, don't know what they might get up to. Somebody from the family needs to be out watching the ranch— just in case. And I've got to see Lew Vara and get myself oriented about this whole matter. Before we start doing anything I want to get the straight of it."

"I can tell you that," Ben said. "That motherfuckin' Shay Jordan walked into Norris's office and shot him."

"I understand that, but what were the circumstances? You don't just walk in and shoot a man with no provocation."

"Some people do," Ben said. "Trash like the Jordans. I know Shay Jordan shot Norris. That's good enough for me."

"But you know Norris. He's always got to play gun-fighter. Ben, if he provoked that kid into it, that's another thing entirely. Now I want you to go on back to the ranch. If there's any news I'll send word to you as fast as I can. If there's any change in Norris's condition I'll get word to you. I'll be home tomorrow and you can come back in then."

We had come to stand in front of Lew Vara's office. Hays was just coming up the street, riding his horse and leading the two others. I told him to hitch my horse and then go on to the ranch with Ben. He said, "What's the trouble?"

I said, "Ben will tell you all about it on the ride home. Now ya'll get going."

I watched Ben mount up on his own horse, and then they went trotting off down the main street, Hays leading the packhorse that hadn't gotten to do a whole lot of packing. I opened the door to Lew's office. He was sitting at his desk in the middle of the room, and I caught him with his head back in the beginning of a yawn. I said, "Things a little slow?"

He said, "Sit down, boy. Tell me about your travels. Been up to Injun country, huh? Get scalped?"

I sat down in a chair across from Lew and got out a cigarillo and lit it. Lew pulled open a drawer in his desk and took out a bottle of whiskey and two tumblers. He poured us out drinks while I got my smoke lit and drawing. We picked up the drinks, said "Luck" as befits the toast, and then knocked them back. I said, "I appreciate you back-trailing me when we left."

"You have any trouble?"

I shrugged. "Not so's you'd notice. Didn't go cross-country like I was supposed to. We took the train in Bastrop."

"Yeah," Lew said. He was watching me, waiting.

I jerked my chin toward the door that led to the cells in the back. "Shay Jordan back there?"

Lew shook his head. "No."

"Then he's got to be dead or on the run, and Ben didn't say anything about either one of them possibilities."

Lew put his hands on the desk, his fingers intertwined. "Justa, there ain't a damn thing I can do. They called me from the bank right after it happened. Sent a boy over. I got there before the doctor did. Norris was on the floor and there was a gun right beside him. His desk drawer was open on the right side. On what I could see I didn't have any reason to arrest Shay. I went out and talked to him, and he claimed that Norris had pulled a gun on him and he'd shot in self-defense."

"What did Norris have to say?"

Lew shook his head. "I ain't really had a good chance to talk to Norris. The doctor said he was in shock. I know he was in pain. But from what little I could get from him, the drawer had fallen out when he fell from the gunshot. I guess the gun could have fallen on the floor then. But I don't know how the drawer got put back in the desk."

"Shay done it," I said. "Or whoever was up in that office, clearing space around Norris. Not realizing the drawer was important."

Lew shrugged. "All I know is they ain't a damn thing I can do until Norris can talk. He's been feverish and a little out of his head the last couple of days. Doc says he ain't gonna make a hell of a lot of sense until his fever breaks."

"Lew, you don't no more believe that Norris pulled a gun on Shay than I do."

"I know that," he said. "But what's the good of arresting him? It would still come down to a swearing match between the two as to what happened. A jury might be more inclined to believe Norris, but they might not believe him enough. And Justa, you know that Norris is always on the prod, scared folks won't think he can handle himself like his two brothers. It's going to get him killed someday. But no, I don't think this was the time. I think he might have provoked Jordan with his mouth, but not with a gun. But everybody doesn't know him like you and I do." He paused and glanced at the wall before he went on. "I hate to say this, especially with him laying over there in Doc's infirmary hurtin', but they's some folks think Norris has got some mighty high ideas about himself. Some folks wouldn't mind seeing him split his britches. You take this to court and a jury, and I ain't sayin' for sure, might be more persuaded to look at it from Shay Jordan's viewpoint. Remember, he'll come swaggerin' into that courtroom like a small rancher fightin' for his life against the giant Half-Moon ranch."

"Lew, that ain't the way of it and you know it. The Half-Moon ranch has gone out of its way to be fair with—"

He put up a hand. "You're preachin' to the converted. I didn't say it was fair. I didn't even say it was right or made any sense. Envy ain't got no sense. That very sonofabitch that's calling you *Mister* Williams on the street is probably wishing your horse would fall over with you. You and your family have been more than fair, Justa. But you're rich. And rich draws envy and hate just like whiskey draws a drunk, I don't care how fair you are. Some folks' idea of you being fair would be you give them all your money and leave the country. So don't look for no big tide of sympathy for Norris."

"I see," I said. I sat quietly for a few moments, thinking.

Lew said, "What'd you want me to do, lie to you? I've been talking as the law. I haven't talked as your friend."

"Norris loses his arm, or anything worse, and I'll wipe that family out." I didn't say it fierce or angry or vicious or loud. I just stated it as a simple fact. It didn't matter about the different mothers anymore. Even if we hadn't shared a drop of common blood, we'd been raised as brothers and that was all that it took.

Lew said, "I wonder why that doesn't surprise me, you saying that."

"Well, you are the law. I thought I'd let you know. I figure you got to take an attitude on the matter."

He shook his head. "As far as I'm concerned this is a private matter that they started."

"I'd still prefer the law to handle it, but if you say there ain't nothing the law can do, then I understand."

Lew spread his hands. He said again, "I can lock him up, Justa. But a court is gonna turn him loose. You know that and so do I. I reckon you've seen Norris?"

"He was sleeping. I'm going back over this afternoon. Maybe he'll be able to say something."

Lew said, "That fever takes you, it can get a power of a hold." He stood up and said, "Let's go down to Crook's and eat some chili and drink a few beers. You look like you just got off a cattle car, got hay all over you."

We went on down to Crook's combination cafe and bar, and got a table and had some chili with beans and flour tortillas on the side along with some mugs of beer. I was good and hungry. Me and Hays had been on the train when breakfast had come around, and the train had been moving and we were out of supplies, so we'd made do with conversation for grub, and conversation with Hays wasn't very filling. Lew asked me about the trip to Oklahoma, and I described it without telling him the reason I'd gone to see Charlie Stevens, other than to look into the sawmill business.

Lew said, "That what the twenty-five thousand dollars in gold was for?"

"Yeah," I said. "You know them redskins, don't trust the white man's dollar."

He knew, of course, the places I'd been in Oklahoma, and was surprised to find they'd grown as much as they had in the ten years since he'd been there. He said, "Just shows what can happen to an area when you take the undesirable element out."

I said, "I was just about to call that to your attention."

After lunch I went to the hotel and had a bath. We kept a room there just for the use of the family, and I kept several sets of clean clothes stored in it. I shaved and cleaned my teeth, and felt considerably better when I stepped out onto the street. I went first down to the bank and talked, one at a time, to all the people that worked there. A young clerk named Ben Johnson had been the first to react to the sound of the gunshot. He'd met Shay Jordan on the stairs, hurrying toward the bottom, with the gun still smoking in his hand. Johnson had asked him what had happened, but he said Jordan hadn't said a word, just brushed past him and gone out of the bank. Johnson had said he'd gone to Norris's office and found Norris bleeding on the floor, laying on his right side. I asked him if he'd noticed a drawer. He said, "Yessir, Mister Williams, it was the drawer out of Mister Norris's desk. It was layin' on his leg. I shoved it back in the desk to kind of clear the scene up. Was a bunch of people had come running up right behind me."

"Where was Norris's gun?"

"There was a gun over in the corner. I guess you'd say it was Mister Norris's gun."

"You tell the sheriff about putting the drawer back in the desk?"

He shook his head. "Nosir. Never come across my mind."

"But you saw it clean out of the desk? Not just pulled halfway open?"

"It was layin' on Mister Norris. Heavy old drawer. Then they was all that blood. And I could see Mister Norris was hurt good and proper. I wasn't studyin' about no desk drawer. Wasn't no drawer shot him, was that goddam Shay Jordan."

When I got done with all of them it was going on for half past two. I went by the sheriff's office and gathered up Lew to go over with me to see Norris. I told Lew on the way over what the bank clerk had said. I said, "That don't sound like Norris was opening a drawer to get at a pistol. I don't know what happened, but that ain't the way a man gets a gun out of a drawer."

Lew said, "I ain't disputing that, Justa. Goddammit, I'd hang Shay Jordan right now if I could get a judge to give the order. Ain't but two people know what happened in that office, and you are probably going to have two different versions."

We got to the infirmary and went inside. The lady who ran the desk was back in her place, and there was a lady patient sitting there with a goiter hanging over the collar of her dress. I was just about to ask for Doctor Adams when he came in from the back. He saw me and Lew and motioned us to come back. He said, "He's awake, but his fever is still high. And he's awful weak. He can't keep food down, just vomits it right back up. Which is making it more difficult to get his strength up. You can see him for a minute, but don't expect too much."

We went into the room where Norris was laying in the bed. The place smelled like a sickroom. I'd been told the smell was carbolic acid, something they used to keep sickrooms clean, but I'd smelled carbolic acid outside of a sickroom and it didn't smell nothing like a sickroom.

Norris turned his head slightly as we came quietly through the door. He said, his voice kind of hoarse, his face taking on an anxious cast, "Justa, I never provoked him. You told us before you left not to cause any trouble. I swear I didn't."

I went up to the bed and put my hand on his left shoulder. "I know you didn't, Norris. Don't worry about it. If you can, try and tell me what happened."

Doctor Adams said, "In as few words as possible."

Norris seemed to be out of breath. He said, "He came in, unasked. He began making remarks about, about our, our family. I . . ."

He had to stop and breathe for a second. When he went on he seemed a little calmer. "He said he'd heard you were out of town. He said that was lucky for you because he was looking for you. I'd . . . I'd . . ."

Doctor Adams said, "Take it easy, Norris." He looked around at us. "I'm afraid that's enough."

But Norris was shaking his head. He said weakly, "Justa, all I did was stand up to, to or . . . order him out of my office. He pulled his gun and shot me. Justa, he meant to kill me."

I said, "What about the drawer? The desk drawer? The drawer your gun was in?"

He frowned, trying to think. "I don't know. I grabbed at something. I . . . I . . ." He started having trouble breathing again.

I said, "What's the matter with his lungs, Gregory?"

The doctor was turning Lew toward the door. He said, "There's nothing wrong with his lungs. He's just too weak to talk. It gets him out of breath. Now get out of here. Come back in the morning."

I said, "You need somebody to sit up with him?"

Gregory said, "That's what I get paid for. What use would you be, sitting up with him?"

Lew and I left the infirmary and walked back over to his office. We sat down and Lew poured us out a drink. I gave him time to have a good part of the whiskey and then said, "Well?"

He said, "Goddammit, Justa, I am not going to tell you again. It don't make no difference. There's that gun laying there on the floor. There's your brother with a hole in his arm. There's Shay saying he didn't pull first, that Norris did. What the hell you want me to do?"

"Lew, did I ask you to do anything? Hadn't you already made it clear how you see it?"

"Hell, you just got through asking me."

"I was asking you, just out of curiosity, what you thought happened. I think Norris stood up, Shay shot him, and Norris reached out to grab something to slow his fall, grabbed hold of the handle of that drawer, pulled it out when he fell, and then the gun spilled out. I figure Shay saw that and nearly split his britches grinning because it was a lucky break he'd of never been able to think up.

I doubt Norris even remembers what happened. I know the few times I've been shot I've been stunned for a few seconds and couldn't have told you if it was night or day, much less if I was pulling on a desk drawer or not."

Lew thought a minute. He shrugged. "Makes as much sense as anything. Norris ain't overly smart when it comes to guns and gun situations, but I can't see him being fool enough to try for a gun out of a drawer when a man's standing in front of him who's got a revolver an inch away from his hand."

I said as evenly as I could, "Lew, kind of watch what you say about Norris right now."

He gave me a startled look. "I didn't say anything you ain't said, except it wasn't as bad."

"But Norris is my brother."

Lew put his hands on top of his head and grimaced. "Fine. Norris is a gunman, he's good with a gun. I know you feel bad about him right now and so do I. I consider I'm friends with the whole family. I was just trying to look at it as it was or might have been. I didn't mean nothing against Norris. Hell, I was just agreeing with you and giving the reasons why. What you thought how it happened."

"Forget it. I'm a little upset." I got out a cigarillo and lit it. "Pour us out another drink and forget I said anything."

"Actually I was paying Norris a compliment. I was saying I didn't think he was fool enough, no matter how eaten up he is with this being-tough business, to try and get a gun out of a drawer when a man is standing right there who can shoot him before he can even open the drawer, much less get at a gun."

I sighed. "Goddammit, you are starting to sound like Ray Hays. Now pour us a drink."

He didn't exactly smile, but it was close enough to it for most purposes. "Well, now, I don't know as I want you drinking my whiskey if you go to making accusations like that."

"Pour the damn whiskey, Lew. Hell, I think I'll move to Oklahoma. I seem to get along better with the Indians than I do with folks around here."

"You look like one. You look more like one than I do and I'm part Cherokee. I go up there to the reservation they call me brother. They probably call you white-eyes."

I threw back half the whiskey in my tumbler. I said, "No, they call me brother also."

I had supper that night at the hotel. I could have gone to Nora's parents, the Parkers, and had one of my mother-in-law's meals, but that would have meant I'd of had to have talked and I didn't want to do that. After supper I walked around town, being careful to not go in anyplace where I had friends. I looked into the hotel stable to see if my big rawboned gelding was doing all right. He'd done more train riding in one week than a lot of folks got to do in a lifetime. He was fine, and gave me a nicker to let me know.

After that I went back to the hotel and went to bed. I had a considerable amount to think about, but I tried to keep my mind off it. A great deal depended on how Norris was the next day. But in a way, it didn't matter. You don't shoot somebody at close range in an office with the intent of just doing them a little harm. If Norris got out light it wouldn'd be for lack of trying on Shay Jordan's part.

Next morning I took my time shaving and putting on some fresh clothes. Then I went to the dining room and had a long breakfast. I didn't want to rush right over to the infirmary, half because of what I was scared I'd find, and half to give Norris time to get better. Lew came in as I was finishing my last cup of coffee. We visited about nothing in particular, and then I got up to go and see Norris. Lew asked if I wanted him to come with me. I shook my head. "No. But I'll probably be looking for you later on." He said he'd be around.

Doctor Adams was in the waiting room looking at some papers when I came in. It was a little past nine. He looked up and smiled. He said, "Got some good news. His fever broke last night."

I said, a little uncomfortably, "Does that mean—"

"His arm? Yes, I would definitely say so. I'm not saying all danger of infection is past, but there's none of that red streaking up and down his arm that would say there was definitely a bad infection. Obviously there was infection, but it localized. It didn't spread. I'm going to give you cautious encouragement. Also, he's not so sick anymore. He held his breakfast down this morning. I'd say it's just a matter of time."

"I can see him?"

"For a few minutes. But goddammit, don't get him excited. And I mean that, Justa."

I went in Norris's room. I could see immediately he was feeling considerably better. There was even some color in his face. He gave me a small smile as he turned his head and saw who it was. He said, "I'll be glad to get out of this bed. How was the trip to Oklahoma?"

"Fine," I said. "We'll talk about that later. Right now I want the straight of what happened in your office."

He lay his head back on the pillow and stared up at the ceiling for a moment. He said, "I'm still a little weak."

"Take your time."

"I just have the impression his intention was to scare me. I think he thought I'd be the one to scare, that he couldn't scare you or Ben. I remember thinking that, that that was his intentions. I remember it made me mad as hell. I don't recall a great deal of what he said because it all happened so fast. I stood up and reached in my vest pocket to get my watch. I was going to tell him he had exactly ten seconds to get out of my office. Next thing I know he'd shot me, and it was very confusing after that. Justa, they know they can't win a lawsuit. This is just bullying tactics. They think if they interfere with us enough, become enough of a nuisance, we'll give them a few thousand acres so they'll let us be. Well, I won't stand for it."

I had to half smile. This was the old Norris. Here he'd narrowly missed dying, or at best losing his arm, and now he was concerned about business matters. I told him not to worry about that. I patted him on the shoulder and put my hat on. I'd taken it off when I'd come in the sickroom. Folks did that, though I'd never understood why. It didn't help the patient none near as I could figure out. I said to Norris that I had to be going, but that Ben would come into town and see about him. I patted him on the shoulder and started for the door. Norris said, "What are you going to do, Justa?"

"Go see my wife and son. Get some rest. Tell Howard and Ben that you turned the corner."

"You leave Shay Jordan to me. I've handled bullies before."

"You don't worry about none of that right now. Just see about getting well. Every day you are in this bed is costing us money."

I left the infirmary with the relief flooding through my body, able now to let myself acknowledge just how worried I'd been. But even though I was thankful and grateful, I was no less full of purpose. I went straight to Lew's office and, without preamble, told him what I wanted. "Lew, I want a favor out of you. If you won't or can't do it, on account of you being sheriff, I'll understand it. I'll get somebody else. But I just feel it will carry the weight I want it to coming from you."

He said, "How's Norris?"

I told him. He said, "Whew! I am mighty glad to hear that. Now, what is it you're wanting me to do?"

I looked at my watch. It was ten o'clock straight up. I said, "I want you to ride out to the Jordans'. I can't go myself or send Ben for fear they'd shoot us off our horses. The same applies to anyone else I might send. I got a feeling they are forted up out there waiting to see what we do. I want you to ride out there as the sheriff and tell them I am ready to settle this matter. Tell them I want to see Shay Jordan at the northwest end of that drift fence that seems to bother them so bad. Tell them I want to see him at ten o'clock tomorrow morning. Tell him it can be guns or not. That's up to him. Tell him I'm coming alone. Tell him I'm going to break his arm. One way or the other. And tell him if he doesn't show up I'll shoot any Jordan I see, on sight, over the age of sixteen years old that is male. Will you do that for me, Lew? I'd like to get home and see Nora."

He yawned. "I figured it would be something like this. But don't you want to rest up a little more from your trip? Take some time to play with the baby?"

"Be time enough for that later on. Will you carry that message out there for me?"

He nodded, still yawning. He finally said, when he could get his mouth shut so he could open it, "I'll go this afternoon. If Shay ain't there, I'll tell Rex Jordan or whoever is there. If Shay has cut and run, I'll get word to you so you don't make the trip in vain."

"I got to get. I got to tell Ben that Norris is all right, and sit on him to keep him from doing anything about the matter."

I pushed the sorrel hard, and got home just at lunchtime. Nora was all a-flutter to see me, and gave me a long kiss and a short scolding for not letting her know I'd be home in time for lunch and so I'd just have to take what they could throw together at the last minute. As it was, I wasn't thinking so much about lunch, but I ate some beef stew and some new bread, baked that morning, and then took on about the baby and got brought up to date on all he'd been doing while I'd been gone. And while I was hungry enough to eat, and glad to see my son and interested in his antics, I had my eye on Nora and my thoughts elsewhere from being a father.

But the maid finally went off, got J.D. down for his nap, and then took herself off for her cabin behind the house, and I had Nora to myself. She said, "Now Justa, not in the middle of the day! Not with the baby in the next room! Justa, folks just don't carry on like that. Justa, we're old married folks."

But I got her hemmed up in our bedroom and that was that.

Later I rolled over and got dressed and, while I was pulling on my boots, she asked where I was going. I'd already told her about Norris being better, but since she'd never realized how bad he'd been hurt, she had no way of knowing what a big relief it was for all of us. I told her I had to scout up Ben and Howard and give them the news.

She said, "And everything went all right in Oklahoma? We've been so rushed since you come in the door, and then rushing me in here, shame on you, that I haven't had a chance to ask you about it."

I said I would tell her all about it later, and then I went out and saddled up a horse and rode for the big house. It was a beautiful fall day for our country, mild and sunshiny. I rode through my cattle, glad to see them again. I didn't spot Ben anywhere on the range, and I figured he might be at the house with Howard.

But Howard was sitting out on the big porch in his rocking chair when I rode up. I dismounted, dropped my reins to the ground, and went on up the steps and dropped into a wicker chair. Howard was rocking gently. I noticed he had a whiskey in his hand that looked slightly darker than it was supposed to. But what the hell, he had one son in the infirmary and one just back from an enlightening trip to Oklahoma. I figured he deserved it. I was not, however, of a complete mind as to what I was going to say to him. I said, "Well, Dad, it looks like matters got a little out of hand around here while I was gone."

He said, "Son, I can't tell you what a relief it is to have you home. Ben and Norris just ain't the same without yore steadyin' hand on the reins."

"Well, it looks like matters are going to be all right." I told him about Norris and what the doctor had said. "It appears he's out of danger and should be home in a day or two. Though it will be a sight more time than that before he has the use of that arm."

Howard said, "Heaven be praised." He looked at me. "To tell you the truth, they never let on it was that bad.

Ben just said he got winged. He never give me none of the particulars."

"Well, that was smart of Ben."

We sat silent for a moment. I was gazing out at the ranch and the range I'd missed so much. Mainly I was waiting for Howard to start asking me questions. Finally he said, "You got the telegram all right?"

"Yeah," I said. "Got it the second day after I got to Anadarko. I was at Charlie Stevens's house when it come." I glanced over at him. "Mighty precise directions for someone who didn't know exactly where he lived."

Howard said, "I just went on the last place I knowed about." He cleared his throat. "You made mighty good time getting there."

"Yes," I said. I crossed my legs and took off my hat and put it on my knee.

Howard said, "Couldn't of taken you more than five days to get there."

"Four," I said. "You got any water in that whiskey?"

He was chewing tobacco, and he leaned over and spit off the porch. He said, "That's making mighty good time. I'd of thought it would have taken you the best part of ten days goin' horseback."

"Maybe they moved it," I said.

He looked over at me. "Moved what?"

"Oklahoma. Seemed like a lot was different than what you told me."

He didn't say anything for a moment. I just let him sit there and stew. Then he said, "So you seen Charlie Stevens?"

"Yeah," I said. "Spent the night in his house, me and Hays."

Howard hesitated. "You get there all right with the money? The gold?"

"Yeah. We had a little trouble, but we got it worked out."

"Well, you got up there and back so fast I was kind of surprised."

I lit a cigarillo, scratching the match on the sole of my boot. "I thought you just wanted the gold carried up to Oklahoma. I didn't know you was worried about the time."

He hesitated again. "What'd Charlie say about the gold?"

"Didn't say."

"But he taken it?"

"It's right there in the bank in Anadarko."

"What'd he think? He send any messages?"

I shook my head slowly. "Not that I know of. You mean to you?"

He was starting to look uncomfortable. By his lights I should have been either full of questions or raising hell with him. But I was acting like I'd just got back from a cattle-buying trip. He spit again. He said, hesitating even longer, "He didn't talk much about the old days? Days when we was partners and then split up?"

"Yeah. He mentioned some of that. What you didn't tell me, though, was that you carried on a considerable correspondence with him. How come you never mentioned that? He said he even wrote you back a few times."

He cleared his throat and took a drink of his whiskey. "Well, I never could be sure if my letters found their mark."

"Even though he answered you back?"

He said, looking away from me, "There was considerable time passed between them exchanges. So he taken the money? Taken it in full payment of all debts?"

"I don't know what you're talking about, Howard. What debts? I thought you told me you stole some money from him. Or felt like you had. That's just one debt. And he said he give you the money gladly. What are you talking about?"

I didn't know why I was carrying Howard along like I was. I didn't have no good reason. I didn't feel bitter toward him about the way he'd treated my birth mother, or angry because he'd let us three boys go all those years without the truth. Hell, I might have acted the same in his place. Lucy was my birth mother only because Charlie Stevens had said she was and I believed him. But I couldn't feel nothing for a woman I'd never known, and had only just heard about. Maybe all I was doing with my silence and pretended ignorance was giving Howard back some of his own.

He said, "Well . . . I ain't really talkin' about nothing. I'm just surprised to find that Charlie didn't have more to say. There's his arm, or the lack of it, for instance."

"You didn't shoot him. He doesn't blame you for it."

He spit out his cud, and took a long pull of his whiskey and finished the glass. "Well, it might be said I was the cause of it."

"Why? Charlie said he wasn't down here threatening you. He said he hadn't come for any money. Was there some other reason he come?"

He turned around and gave me a keen look. For a good half a minute he didn't say anything. Then he said, "No, I reckon not. If he didn't say there was another reason, then I guess there wasn't." He looked away, staring far out. "It was a long time ago. I guess he wants to forget too."

"Forget what?"

He heaved a sigh. "Oh, nothing. I just thought he'd have more to tell you than it sounds like he did. I guess it's for the best."

"What I'll never understand was what the big secret about the whole business was. You not wanting me to take Ben with me, nor to even tell him or Norris what I was up to. I ain't figured that one out yet."

He held his glass out to me. "You wouldn't favor me with another one of these, would you?"

"How many is that today?"

"Just the one. Well, maybe the second. But you been gone and that's been a worry. And now Norris layin' up there in the infirmary with a ball through his right arm."

"Just like Charlie," I said.

His face flinched a little. "Yes, I thought on that. I thought maybe my sins were catching up to me."

"What sins?"

He looked at me. "Why, Charlie gettin' shot here on this place."

I gave him a slight smile. He could read what he wanted to in it. But I got up and took his glass, went in the house and poured him half a tumbler of whiskey, and then topped it off with water like it was supposed to be. The color was considerably lighter than the drink he'd been holding when I'd come up on the porch. I took it to him, but I didn't sit down. I put my hat on. I said, "Well, I guess I better get going. I need to find Ben and tell him about Norris. I promised he could go back in town as soon as I was home."

Howard said, "Charlie seem to be doing all right financially?"

"Oh, yeah," I said. "Got about the biggest sawmill I've ever seen. I may buy a big lot of lumber from him and set up a lumber yard in Blessing."

Howard said, "Seems a long way to send for lumber."

I started down the steps toward my horse. About halfway down I stopped and turned. "Charlie mentioned in one of his letters about Alice, your wife Alice."

"You mean your mother?" He was looking at me with narrowed eyes.

"Yes. You know who I'm talking about. Charlie said you wrote and told him that she had a terrible hard time with Norris, giving birth to Norris."

The trouble that had been in his face for a moment cleared. "Oh, she did. It was an awful trial for her. She said she never wanted to go through nothin' like that again. Poor thing was never of very strong stock an' the birth took a lot out of her."

I said, going down to my horse, "That must have been mighty hard on you."

He looked puzzled. "Hard on me? Whatever in the world are you talking about?"

"Oh, a young buck like you was then, cut off from his wife. She was scairt to get with child again. And delicate as she was, it might have killed her birthing another baby.

Kind of left you doing without, didn't it?"

I stepped up on my horse. His color had deepened appreciably. He said awkwardly, "That ain't no way for you to be speaking about the memory of your mother. The woman was a saint."

"I reckon to put up with you she'd of had to be," I said. "But I reckon she give in to your wants finally, though."

He was in deep water and stepping carefully from rock to rock. "What are you talking about?"

"Well, she'd of had to have. Ben got born, didn't he?"

He stared at me, not saying anything, just sitting there with his drink in his hand. Now he knew that I knew. And he also knew that I had put him in a position where he couldn't talk about it, couldn't give his side of it. I didn't want to hear his side of it. If he'd of wanted to tell it, he'd had plenty of years to do it in.

Just before I rode away I said, "Funny thing, Howard. I was up there on that Cherokee reservation and folks kept taking me for an Indian. How come that, I wonder?"

I didn't give him time to answer, just turned my horse and rode off to look for Ben.

CHAPTER 12

I found Ben out looking over the horse herd. He was having his *vaqueros* run the herd past him single file so he could get a look at the more than seven hundred horses. Hays was on the other side of the slim stream of horseflesh. I waited until the last horse had passed, and then rode up beside Ben and gave him the good news about Norris. He didn't say anything for a moment, just took off his hat and wiped his forehead with the sleeve of his shirt. He put his hat back on and shook his head and said, "Whew! Goddam, that's good to hear. Even if he is as hard to get along with as an old maid steeped in vinegar. I been having a hard time studying on these horses, I been thinking about him so steady. Him and Shay Jordan. I'd about decided to shoot Jordan to pieces a little at a time. Now I'll just shoot him clean."

"No," I said. "You're not. You're not going to have anything to do with it."

He turned around and looked at me. "You ain't letting him get away with that, are you?"

I grimaced. "Don't talk like a calf. Of course not. I'll handle it."

He flared up. "You? How come you? Norris is just as much my brother as he is yours. And that Shay Jordan is nearer my age. By God, Justa, you are not going to stop me on this. An' you better make up your mind to it."

I said carefully, so there'd be no misunderstanding, "The very noise you are making is the reason I'm going to handle it. I don't want to start a blood feud in this country, and you haven't got any more sense than to say the hell with it and go right ahead. I'm going to handle it because I know when to stop. You don't. If it comes to shooting that will be up to Shay, but I'm not going to draw a gun first. I'm going to pay him back in kind. I'm going to break his arm. Now whether I do it with a bullet or over my knee is of no consequence to me. But that will be the end of it."

Ben said, "Huh! That's what you think. Listen, I been asking around. His uncle, Luther? That sonofabitch is meaner than hell. And he's just out of prison in Matamoros. You think that bastard is going to be willing to say that's an end to it?"

I said, as grimly as I could, "Ben, it is all planned and it don't involve you." I told him how I'd arranged for Lew Vara to carry the word out to the Jordans, and how I was going to meet Shay in the morning at ten o'clock and that I would be alone. "We are going to meet at the northwest corner of that drift fence and settle the matter. Now you wanted to go into town today and see Norris. All right, you and Hays can take off. You've got plenty of daylight left and I'm sure Norris would welcome some company. Ask Adams if you can take him in some whiskey."

He looked at me for a long time, maybe half a minute. "You're going to ride out to that drift fence by your lonesome?"

"Yes."

"Just expecting Shay to show up."

"I told Lew to tell him that if he didn't show up I'd shoot every Jordan I saw on sight. Lew will probably tell him I just intend to beat the hell out of him. He'll show up. He can't take the risk and not do it. Lew will convince him."

"Oh, I ain't got a doubt that Shay will show up. Him and half his family."

"That's wide-open prairie. You can see for miles. If more than him is coming, I'll have plenty of time to make other plans. Now you and Hays get on into town. Get drunk, have a good time. I'll see you tomorrow. I may have something I want to talk to you about."

He just looked at me and shook his head. "And to think I always looked up to you because I thought you was so smart."

I ignored the remark and asked him if he'd seen Harley, our foreman. Hays had ridden over close and kept his mouth shut while Ben and I were having the argument about Shay Jordan. Now Hays said, pointing, "Boss, I think he's down thar on the south range. They got a pretty good herd gathered there and are cutting out the shippers."

I said to Ben, "How's Harley coming along with the cut?"

He was still sulking a bit. But he said, "I reckon he's just about finished. Didn't you notice the amount of cattle they got held up near the headquarters range?"

"Ben, I ain't been able to ask Norris. Do you know if he got the stock cars arranged with the railroad before he got shot?"

He shook his head. "I don't know."

"Then you better look into that when you get into town. Make that the first thing you do. You got any idea how many cattle Harley finally thinks he'll be able to get?"

"He told me somewheres between a thousand and 'leven hunnert. Closer to 'leven hunnert."

"Then you better see to those cars. We either ship 'em or feed 'em, and I'd a hell of a lot rather ship 'em. Does anybody know what the market is doing?"

Hays said, "I hear'd it's still up."

I said, "Well, I'm going to find Harley. I want to start moving cattle toward the rail spur day after tomorrow."

I was starting to turn my horse away when Ben said, "We might have more important matters to attend to."

I was far enough around so I had to turn to look back at him. "Like what?"

He said, "Your funeral. You ride out there depending on the honor of the Jordans."

I didn't say anything, just touched my spurs to the horse's belly and set out to look for Harley. I wanted to be able to give Norris the good news that I was getting him some money to invest. That'd be the best medicine I could put in his hands.

I spent a quiet evening with Nora that night. After supper she was surprised to see me bring my whiskey into the parlor and settle down with her. She said, "You're not going up to the big house for your usual confab?"

I shook my head. She was over on the settee darning one of my shirts. I did not believe it was possible for Nora, without company in the house, to sit down on the settee without her hands being busy with some kind of sewing or knitting or crocheting. At least I'd never seen her that way. I said, "Naw, hell, I haven't seen you in a week. Thought we'd do some catching up."

"But you're a week behind on the ranch and the latest men-talk. And whiskey-drinking. What have you told Howard? About what Charlie Stevens told you?"

"To begin with, I ain't told you all of it yourself."

"Stop saying 'ain't.' "

"Howard took his time letting me in on some information. I reckon I'll do the same."

"What haven't you told me?"

"What I haven't told you."

"That's no answer."

I poured myself a drink and got comfortable in my big overstuffed morris chair, which was just like the one Charlie Stevens had. I said, "It's all the answer you're going to get. I take it J.D. has calmed down on the teething business. He ain't squalled near as much as he was before I left."

"Doctor Adams was out on his weekly visit to Howard. He came by and left me off some paregoric to rub on his gums. It does do the trick."

I was very comfortable. My mind was a long ways away from the next day. We talked until about ten o'clock, not about much, but just the sort of quiet conversation men and their wives can make. I said, "It will be good to get things back to normal again."

"What's normal for you, Justa? I've known you six or seven years. I mean known you close, and the nearest thing to normal for you is mostly trouble. What are you going to do about the Jordans?"

I yawned. "Well, one thing I'm not going to do is worry about them. That's what we pay a lawyer for."

"No, I mean about the young one, the one that shot Norris."

I looked at her. I'd learned it was much better to look at her straight if you felt a lie coming on. "What about him?"

She stopped darning. "Justa Williams, if you think that I believe you're going to let someone shoot your brother and not take some sort of action, then you've got another thing coming. Or else you believe I can be fooled mighty easy. Now tell me the truth. What are you up to?"

"Goddammit, Nora—"

"I have asked you and asked you not to swear in the house."

"Yes, and we screw, but you won't let me say it."

She raised her hands and let them fall back in her lap. "I never thought I'd hear the day you'd talk like that to your own wife. Who do you think I am, one of the floozies in Wilson Young's house of prostitution?"

I said, trying to keep from laughing at her pretended indignation, "How do you know Wilson has got a whore-house?"

"Because he told me on his last visit. And now that you've succeeded in getting the 'little wife' off the subject of the Jordans, are you pleased with yourself?"

I went over and knelt down by her and put my head on her breast. "I know something that would please me more."

I left my house at about nine-thirty the next morning, riding the big sorrel gelding. I'd decided he was about as steady as any animal I had around the place. It was a cool morning, but I'd eschewed a jacket, settling instead for a heavy shirt. I didn't expect guns to enter into it, but I still wanted to be as unencumbered as possible. I figured Shay for a bully, not a fool. I figured he'd know he couldn't match me in a shooting contest. Trying to frighten Norris was one thing, coming at me was another, and I reckoned he'd asked around and had been told.

I passed the headquarters house and saw Howard sitting out on the front porch taking the morning sun. He'd probably been up since four. He said it was hard to sleep when you got old. He said he didn't know if that was because you didn't need as much sleep, or you just didn't want to waste what time you had left on laying there with your eyes closed, which you'd be doing soon enough anyway. I gave him a wave, but he wasn't looking my way, and I was a good hundred yards off and his old eyes might not have been able to make me out at such a distance.

The end of the drift fence was, because of the direction it ran, nearly as close to town as it was to the ranch. It was at the far western edge of our deeded property, though we grazed cattle beyond it, but not so as to interfere with anybody else's grazing rights.

I rode slowly through the tall yellowing grass. As soon as we got the herd shaped up for shipping, we'd begin haying it with the big McCormick reaper every cowhand on the place hated with a vengeance. If you couldn't do it on a horse a cowboy didn't want any part of it, and we generally lost one or two good men every year during haying season just because they couldn't put up with it.

I was taking my time. There was no rush. For a minute or two I let my mind stray to Ben and Norris, wondering what I was going to tell them about the truth that had been withheld from us for so long. But there was no rush to decide. Norris was hurt, and what I knew really didn't matter that much. Certainly it didn't change anything.

Off to my left I could see the fence at a distance. Rather I could see the tops of the fence posts straggling along over the prairie; I certainly couldn't see the wire. I turned my horse slightly to the north a little more so as to hit the end of the fence when I arrived at it. I was in a part of the prairie that was a little more rolling than flat, and I couldn't see any sign of Shay Jordan. That didn't mean he wasn't coming; it just meant he might be hidden down in a meadow or behind a little hummock.

I kept riding, and then I saw him. I traced the line of the fence with my eye and saw that he was already at the end of it, about two hundred yards away. I put light spurs to the gelding and loped him until only about thirty paces separated me and Shay. Then I pulled the sorrel down into a walk and headed straight toward where Shay was sitting his horse. As I approached I shifted my eyes back and forth over the near terrain. It was just high-grass prairie with no trees or anyplace else to hide. It looked empty. I figured Lew had succeeded in convincing the boy that the only way to end the trouble was to show up and take his medicine.

With about ten yards between us I pulled up my horse. I didn't waste any time on pleasantries. I said, "You shot my brother. I'm here to settle the matter."

He might have been a fairly handsome young man except for the sneering, insolent look on his face. He said, "He pulled a gun on me."

"No he didn't. And you know he didn't and I know he didn't."

"What, was you thar?"

"Don't get smart with me, boy. You and I both know how that gun got on the floor. Maybe it matters to the law, but it don't matter to me. Now, how you want to settle this?"

"You whupped my pa. Th'owed down on him with a pistol and whupped him. I was jest evenin' the score."

"I used a gun to make your pa get off his horse. He was making threats and I was going to settle it. It was a fair fight. If he told you different he's a liar. Now you Jordans don't seem to be willing to let this land dispute be settled in court. I reckon, then, we'll get it settled here and now.

I'm gonna break your goddam arm just like you broke my brother's. I can do it with a bullet, though I got to warn you I ain't that good of a shot and I might miss and hit you in the chest. Or I can do it with a fence post. It's your choice. But I can guarantee you that you are leaving here today with a broke arm."

"Like hell I will," he said. He let his hand come up near the butt of his gun. His horse took a nervous pace or two toward me. I was watching his horse; the animal was jittery, not well-trained. One gunshot and he'd probably go to bucking.

I said, "Boy, you better give this some thought. You are setting yourself up to be looking at the inside of a pine box. Get off that horse and take a licking. And this is my last warning."

Even as I said the words I became aware of something to my right. I shifted my eyes. Just off to my right side a man was coming up in the grass to one knee. He was no more than ten yards away. He had a gun in his hand. I started to draw, and I heard gunshots from behind me. The man, a man I'd never seen before but who looked vaguely familiar, stood up, and then dropped his gun and fell over. I heard someone from behind me yell, "Justa!"

And then the gelding suddenly reared up, and I felt something *thunk* into the pommel of the saddle, and then a burning on my leg and I had my revolver out and was leaning down and to the right, keeping a tight hold on the gelding, keeping him reared up, and firing under his neck at Shay Jordan. I thumbed and fired as rapidly as I could because it was difficult to aim with the gelding dancing around like he was. I thought the first shot hit Shay, but on the second I saw him go backwards, throwing his revolver in the air. I got off one more shot as he was going over the end of his horse.

Then the gelding was settling back to all fours. I sat there for a second, the sound of the gunfire still ringing in my ears and the smell of the gunpowder all through the air. There was a man standing to my right with his hands in the air.

It wasn't the man I'd seen aiming at me. This man was Rex Jordan.

After a moment I holstered my revolver and stepped off the gelding. He was trembling a little. I looked at my saddle. The slug from a bullet was embedded in the pommel. I looked down at my leg. My pants were torn midway down the inside of my thigh. A little blood was trickling out. I couldn't, for the life of me, figure why the gelding had reared up. But if he hadn't, Shay's bullet might have found me instead of my saddle. I'd probably never know what had spooked the gelding. It could have been a snake, it could have been an insect, or it could have been Providence. I didn't figure I'd ever find out. All I knew was that I'd been lucky as hell.

I looked over to my far right. Ben and Ray Hays and Lew Vara were coming toward me, though Lew was veering off more toward where Rex Jordan was standing with his hands in the air.

They came up and stopped. I looked at them for a second, and then I walked over to where Shay was laying on his back in the tall grass. He was dead. He'd taken one bullet in the chest and one in the face. I figured he'd gotten the last as he was going off his horse. The third shot had caught him in the right arm. I didn't know if it had broken the bone or not. I turned around and walked over to where Lew was holding Rex Jordan under guard. The man I'd seen go down was laying on his side a few yards away. He looked like he'd been shot to pieces. I said, "Who's that?"

Lew said, "That's Luther, Luther Jordan."

I turned to Rex Jordan. "Well, ya'll wouldn't have it any other way except the hard way. This is the result."

Rex had his head down. "I was not here to shoot you," he said. "I never drawed a gun. I come to try and settle this matter with words."

Lew said, "That don't mean you ain't going to jail. You and your brother and your son set up a bushwhack. I was here and I seen it."

I said to Lew, "Let it go, Lew. He's lost enough."

Lew said, "Yeah, but does he know it?"

Jordan was still staring at the ground. "Yes, I know it. I don't want no more trouble."

I looked around. "You'll need help getting your dead home. I'll ride back to my headquarters and have a buckboard sent."

Lew said, "Justa, I ought to put him in jail."

I said, "Did he ever draw his revolver? Did he ever fire?"

Lew shook his head. "No, but maybe that was because he never got a chance to. When Luther come up out of that grass we cut down on him before Rex could do anything. Who knows what he might have done if we hadn't been here, if you'd been alone."

I looked at Ben, who hadn't said anything. I said, "I was wrong."

He give me a little smug look like he knew it, had known it the day before, and was always going to know it and never let me forget. "Yeah," he said.

Hays said, scratching under his shirt, "W'al, if this ain't worth a bonus I don't know what is, and I don't mean the shootin'. We had to tie the horses near two mile from here an' then *walk* all the way to here. An' had to start early so's to git here ahead of these bushwhackers. Had to lay in the goldarn weeds for better'n a hour waitin' fer these sonsabitches to show up! Bugs bitin' me an' snakes crawlin' around an' I don't know what all. Lordy!"

I bought Jordan out to give him a way out of the country. We didn't need the extra deeded acreage, but it was a way to end the matter and end the lawsuit and get his kind out from underfoot. It was an easy enough purchase since our bank held the loan on the ranch he'd bought, so I just gave him back his down payment and five hundred dollars on top of that to smooth his path out of the country. It was all handled through the bank, so I never saw the man again.

The wound in my leg was caused by a little brad that had been popped out of my saddle by the force of Shay's bullet. It had actually had enough force to bury itself about a quarter of an inch under my skin. I'd had Nora dig it out so she could see what it was and see that it wasn't no bullet. But she'd still been suspicious. She'd said, "I have never heard of a piece of hardware coming out of a saddle with enough power to go into a man's leg. There is something fishy going on here, Justa Williams."

I'd said, "There you go. Always doubting me. Now I'm responsible for how they make saddles and what can happen when you rope a two-thousand-pound steer going full tilt and the rope hits the saddle horn. That's right, I'm trying to put something over on you. Actually, Nora, I was in a gunfight and this here brad you'd just dug out was what he was using for bullets."

She'd given me a look. "Now you are trying to act the fool. I swear, Justa, if I could ever get a straight answer out of you I'd probably drop over."

A few days after Norris got home I got hold of Ben, and he and I walked a ways out into the pasture from the headquarters house. We stopped at a place where the sound of the bay could come softly to us, and lit cigarillos. As simply as I could I told him everything I knew and everything I'd learned from Charlie Stevens and Howard. When I was through he just stood there for a moment staring off. Then he turned around and started back towards the house. I was not at all sure how he was going to take it. I said, "Well, what do you think?"

He shrugged. "It's kind of sudden. I don't know what to think. I'm going to have to study on it."

"That's the way I was."

"Explains a lot, though, don't it? I mean about how different me and you are from Norris."

"Yeah."

We kept walking. About halfway back he stopped. He looked at me. "But it really don't make a hell of a lot of difference, does it?"

"Not to me."

"It ain't like we was kids. We're grown men. And both of them mothers is gone. And Howard will be gone soon enough. Then it will just be the three of us. Have you told Norris?"

I hesitated a moment. I wanted to tell Ben how I felt, and I wanted to tell him in such a way that he'd understand it and maybe feel the same way. I said, "The truth be told, when I found out up in Oklahoma that Norris was my half brother I was kind of glad. There was so much difference between us. I didn't want us to be full-blood. But then . . ." I hesitated again.

Ben said, "Then you saw him in that sickbed."

I looked at him and nodded. "Yeah. Then he could never be anything but my full brother."

Ben smiled slightly. "I reckon you don't think we ought to tell him anything about this."

"I don't see the point. You know Norris has always felt like he wasn't as much a part of us as he should be. If he knew this, I think it would hurt him bad."

Ben said, "Then let's don't tell him. Like I say, what difference does it make? He's gonna act like a horse's ass anyway. What about Howard? You ever going to break down and let him know you know?"

I shook my head. "What for? He'll probably come around you trying to act sly to see if I've told you."

Ben laughed. "I know you don't think I can look innocent, but I can."

I punched him on the shoulder and we started back for the house. Just before we got to the steps Ben said, "One damn thing that pisses me off. You know when you left you give me permission to buy twenty-five thousand dollars worth of new blood for the horse herd? Well, you told Norris to transfer some money into the horse herd account on account of it was empty. Well, the sonofabitch got hisself shot before he could do it. An' that auction is due up damn quick and he's laid up in bed."

I stopped and reached in my hip pocket and got out my wallet. I found the deposit slip on the First U.S. Cherokee National Bank for the $25,000 and handed it to him. I said, "I'll endorse that and you take it down to the bank in Blessing and draft on that Cherokee bank for the money. You don't need Norris for that."

He looked at the slip for a second and then he smiled. "Hell, why not. We got Cherokee blood, we might as well have some of that Cherokee money."

"Present from your momma," I said.

We went on into the house to drink some whiskey and give Norris and Howard a hard time. Just before we went through the door Ben said, "Damn palefaces, drink Injun's whiskey. Maybe Injun take scalps."

I said, "Damn right, brother."

Classic Westerns from

GILES TIPPETTE

*Justa Williams is a bold young Texan who doesn't
usually set out looking for trouble...but somehow he
always seems to find it.*

__JAILBREAK 0-515-10595-3/$3.95

Justa gets a telegram saying there are squatters camped on the Half-Moon
ranch, near the Mexican border. Justa's brother, Norris, gets in a whole
heap of trouble when he decides to investigate.

__HARD ROCK 0-515-10731-X/$3.99

Justa Williams and his brothers have worked too hard to lose what's taken
a lifetime to build. Now the future of the ranch may depend on a bankrupt
granger who's offering his herd of six hundred cattle at rock-bottom price.
To Justa, a deal this good is a deal too risky. . . .

__SIXKILLER 0-515-10846-4/$4.50

Springtime on the Half-Moon ranch has never been so hard. On top of
running the biggest spread in Matagorda County, Justa is about to become
a daddy. Which means he's got a lot more to fight for when Sam Sixkiller
comes to town.

__GUNPOINT 0-515-10952-5/$4.50

No man tells Justa Williams what to do with his money-at gunpoint or
otherwise. . .until crooked cattleman J.C. Flood hits upon a scheme to bleed
the Half-Moon Ranch dry-and Justa's prize cattle and quarterhorses start
dying . . . .
